THE WARRIOR QUEEN

'Now, prepare to feel the kiss of your tormentor. You enjoyed the pain of the lash last night; your cries of orgasm were proof enough of that. Now, let us see how you respond to the sting of the tawse!' He cradled the leather implement lovingly as his eyes feasted on the sight of the hapless girl's delightful bottom. She moved herself as best she could, bending her back and stiffening her jutting buttocks in readiness for her punishment. He stroked the rough leather of the tawse gently across her bottom. He would take her soon, but for now she must be satisfied with her punishment.

THE WARRIOR QUEEN

Kendal Grahame

This book is a work of fiction.
In real life, make sure you practise safe sex.

First published in 1998 by
Nexus
Thames Wharf Studios
Rainville Road
London W6 9HT

Typeset by TW Typesetting, Plymouth, Devon

Printed and bound by
Cox & Wyman Ltd, Reading, Berks

ISBN 0 352 33294 8

One

Suetonius Paulinus stood quietly on the small rise just ahead of his encampment. He surveyed the scene before him with mounting satisfaction and pride. Across the narrow channel, thick clouds of smoke rose from the blackened embers like grey pillars in the still air. The sacred island of Mona had been levelled to resemble the scarred, volcanic wastelands of the northernmost regions of his homeland. Not a single oak remained. The groves had been destroyed, and the druids that had worshipped within their shelter had vanished into the interminable mist, taking their evil practices with them.

The scent of the burning wood invaded his nostrils. It was a pleasant aroma, which served to complement his feeling of well-being. A gull screeched overhead, shattering the peace momentarily. Suetonius eyed the offending creature dispassionately as it swooped into the distance, then turned to walk back to the camp.

A weary soldier saluted him as he passed through the hastily erected wooden gates. The man's uniform was tattered and dirty. Normally, Suetonius would have reprimanded the individual soundly for his impertinence in appearing before a senior officer in such a ragged condition, but the battle had been hard, and his men were exhausted. Tonight they would rest, and tomorrow they would feast on the animals looted from the hapless Celts before preparing to march south.

He too felt tired. Tired of battle, tired of the endless trudging along the newly constructed roads which scarred the lush landscape of Britain and tired of the damp cold atmosphere of the place. The air seemed to bite into his very soul. It cut through his armour and heavy robes like a thousand spears. He hated this place, and longed for the warmth and dryness of his homeland.

But his duty was to the Emperor. It was Nero himself who had ordered the subjugation of the Celts. They were to be given no quarter, no mercy. The revolt in the West was to be put down with utmost speed. Suetonius had followed his orders meticulously, only to learn that the Iceni tribes of the East had risen and were, even now, marching towards Londinium. He cursed them under his breath as he approached his tent and drew back the flap. He took one more look at the dismal sky above him and wondered if he would ever see the sun again.

Stepping into the relative warmth of the tent, he drew off his cloak and cast it on to the floor. The girl was still there, of course, shackled by her wrists to a stake with her back turned to him. She glanced over her shoulder and whimpered softly as he approached her. His face broke into a cruel smile as he surveyed her vulnerability. She hung there, as naked as a wild animal, with her toes barely touching the ground. Her soft white flesh bore the evidence of the previous night's excesses. Marks of the whip decorated the alabaster-white skin of her long, smooth back and plump buttocks. Suetonius remembered with much satisfaction her cries of pain and pleasure as he had administered her punishment. He reached out with his hand and let his fingertips touch her soft bottom.

The girl took a sharp gasp of air and shuddered with unconcealed trepidation and excitement.

Suetonius ran his fingers between the pert globes and then moved them down to touch her at the tops of her thighs. She moaned quietly and closed her eyes. She was wet, very wet. He grinned. For all her protestations, she had been a willing participant while he'd enjoyed his carnal pleasures. He eased all four fingers into her soaking pussy and she moaned again, loudly this time. He twisted his hand inside her and her breathing became stilted. He bent his head forward and gently bit her shoulder while, at the same time, easing his thumb into her tight anus. He felt his cock rising rapidly under his heavy skirt. She pushed her bottom out as far as her position would allow and gasped as his thumb entered her completely.

'Oh, my lord,' she breathed, her voice quaking with lust, 'before you take me again, please, I must eat.'

For once, Suetonius felt a stab of compassion for this delicate creature. After all, she had served him well on the previous night. Her expert ministrations and her total subservience had delighted him and he had slept heavily after their final encounter. He had woken fully refreshed and the battle had been quickly won, thanks to the sharpness of his mind.

He eased his fingers from her fleshy grip and slapped her playfully on the bottom. There was food on the table, enough to satisfy the hunger of a dozen whores. He took up a goblet of wine and put it to her lips. She gulped the cool liquid gratefully. A little of the wine seeped from the corners of her mouth and ran over her chin to drip on to her large breasts. Suetonius bent his head forward and licked the sweet taste from her skin then suckled one of her thick erect nipples. He stroked the crease of her bottom again

3

and then reluctantly moved back to the table and took up a leg of roasted pig.

The girl's eyes watched him avidly and she ran her tongue across her lips. He put the flesh to her mouth and she bit into it ravenously. She shook her head like a wolf tearing at its prey as she ripped the meat from the bone and swallowed it. Her whole body shook as she took more and more of the welcome sustenance into her mouth. He smirked to himself. Perhaps he had neglected her over the past two days, at least in this way.

She began to chew the meat and her movements became less intense. Her eyes regarded him thankfully. He threw the remains of her meal on to the floor then, once more, allowed her to drink from his goblet. He would eat soon, but first he would satisfy other needs.

He set the wine back on the table and then stared into her eyes. The girl caught the cruelty within his expression and her pupils became dilated with fear and anticipation.

'You're a wicked woman,' he sneered.

'My lord?' The girl was trembling visibly, which pleased him greatly.

'You have taken my food and my wine, and yet you have given nothing in return.'

'But I gave you so much before the battle,' the girl protested. 'Your every demand, every wish. There was nothing that you asked of me that I didn't allow!'

'Allow?' Suetonius angrily snatched up a tawse that was lying on a nearby stool. 'A whore such as you does not allow anything! I took what I wanted, and I will take more as I please!' He thwacked the tawse loudly on the palm of his hand. The girl jumped and a small tear trickled from the corner of her eye. He watched the salty fluid slip down the softness of her cheek and felt his erection stiffening once again.

4

'Oh, no, my lord,' the girl begged, 'please do not beat me again! My flesh still stings from the last time you punished me.'

Suetonius moved the cloth of his skirt to one side and allowed his cock to jut from within its folds. The girl's eyes widened as she regarded the thick long shaft and bulbous head and she ran her tongue across her lips again. This time, her hunger was for neither food nor wine.

'Turn your head, whore!' he commanded. She obeyed immediately and pressed her forehead against the wooden stake. He knelt behind her and examined her backside closely. 'Your arse is well marked,' he said quietly. 'A few more strokes will complete the picture admirably.' He put his thumbs to her pert globes and parted the cheeks of her bottom, then kissed her lightly on the cleft, just above her anus. He leered hungrily at the smooth inviting curves of her bottom and noted with much satisfaction that the juices of her arousal were beginning to trickle down the insides of her thighs.

'My lord,' the girl said meekly, 'if you must thrash me, then please assure me that you will soothe my pain afterwards.'

He bit hard into her fleshy backside, causing her to yelp. 'I have already told you that I will do with you as I please,' he snarled. He drew himself up to a standing position behind his trembling victim. 'Do not make any further demands of me, woman, or it will be all the worse for you.'

'Yes, my lord.' The young girl's voice was almost indiscernible.

'What?' he demanded loudly.

'I said, yes, my lord,' she repeated with more force.

'Good. Now, prepare to feel the kiss of your tormentor. You enjoyed the pain of the lash last night; your cries of orgasm were proof enough of that. Now, let us see how you respond to the sting of the tawse!' He cradled the leather implement lovingly as his eyes feasted on the sight of the hapless girl's delightful bottom. She moved herself as best she could, bending her back and stiffening her jutting buttocks in readiness for her punishment. Her position merely served to accentuate the pert roundness of her wonderful arse to Suetonius's hungry eyes. He stroked the rough leather of the tawse gently across her bottom. The girl pushed her backside out further in response. He gazed lustfully at his prize. He could see the dark puckered sphincter and the wet bushy lips of her cunt. His cock throbbed. He would soon plough it once more into her succulent sheath, but for now she must be satisfied with her punishment.

He stroked the hard leather over her bottom again and then slipped it between her thighs and carefully rubbed it against her pussy. He turned it so that both sides were soaked with her juices, then brought it to his face. He breathed in deeply and took in her strong womanly scent. His stiffness grew even fiercer with the desire to plunge into her. He raised the tawse high above his head. He heard the girl take a deep breath. Holding his position, he waited patiently. Eventually she gasped as the air left her lungs. He immediately brought the strap down viciously on her white flesh. The crack of leather against skin rang sharply in his ears. The girl squealed and jumped inches into the air as she tugged on the bonds that secured her wrists to the stake. She fell against the unyielding wooden pole, her entire body trembling. He waited patiently until she settled herself down. After a moment, she nervously pushed her bottom out again in readiness for the next blow.

Suetonius gazed at her behind as a red welt began to form on her white skin. He touched the stinging flesh with the end of the damp leather and she whimpered softly. He raised the tawse again above his head and brought it down fiercely on her other buttock. She jumped again, but didn't cry out. He delivered another blow neatly across both cheeks and she began to sob. Her small frame was shaking and the insides of her thighs were soaked and glistening with her juices. Just one more, he thought to himself.

She looked over her shoulder at him as he raised the tawse for the last time. He looked directly into her eyes. Her expression was one of pure lust. He smiled cruelly and dropped the thong to the ground.

'Oh, no, my lord!' she begged. 'Please, please, one more kiss from the beast. Just one more!'

'Why should I?' he teased. 'Surely you have suffered punishment enough?'

'Please, my lord,' she pleaded loudly. 'Beat me just one more time. Whip my poor bottom with all the strength you possess!'

Suetonius grinned and bent down to retrieve the tawse. The girl smiled slightly and turned her face from him. She drew her legs close together and forced out her buttocks as far as was possible within the constraints of her position. He raised the weapon high. There was a long pause. The girl's breathing became sharp and laboured. She began to allow her body to relax slightly. Suddenly and without sucking in a deep breath, which would have warned her, he brought the strap down hard across both buttocks. The flatness of the leather whacked against her stinging flesh with a sound that sang in his ears. The girl threw back her head and screamed as her orgasm took hold of her lithe body. She ground her crotch against the roughness of the wooden stake and tugged violently at her bonds, as if attempting to wrench herself free to satisfy her cravings with her own fingers.

Suetonius allowed the tawse to fall to the floor and watched happily as she gradually slowed her movements until she hung limply once more. She was sobbing loudly, and her tears were those of total joy. He knelt behind her and gazed adoringly once more at her lovely bottom. The perfect globes were glowing and he could feel the heat of her stinging flesh against his face. He bent his head and kissed each buttock lightly. The scent of her arousal was even stronger than before. He longed to impale her with his hard tool, but he decided that he would adhere to her request and soothe her pain.

He pushed out his tongue and licked her right buttock gently. At first she jumped, then relaxed as he worked his tongue wetly over her hot skin. He traced the shape of her bottom with the tip before moving to the other glowing cheek and licking wetly over the tortured flesh. She groaned and began to sway her bottom from side to side in response to the gentleness of his ministrations.

He put the tip of his tongue to the top of the cleft between her buttocks and then slowly moved it down, drawing it now and then into his mouth to soak it with saliva in order to make the delightful journey easier. He paused just above her anus. She pushed her bottom against his face. It was clear what she wanted. He moved his tongue down and licked her tight little sphincter until it was as wet as her pussy. The girl mewed contentedly. He drew her buttocks apart with his fingers and arched his tongue to harden it. He pushed forward and felt his tongue slip up inside her tight little hole. He heard her moan a cry of pure enjoyment. He moved his head backwards and

8

forwards, fucking her bottom with his tongue. She groaned again and he moved faster as he endeavoured to delve as deeply as possible into her forbidden treasure.

He put his hand between her legs and his fingertips quickly found the engorged lips of her pussy. He tugged at the wet flesh, probing and searching until he blindly found the erect bud of her clitoris. He pressed his fingers hard against her and rubbed her rapidly while still pushing his tongue in and out of her arse. She came within moments, a shattering climax that caused her to jerk violently and forced him to fall back on his haunches. He watched in fascination as she once again ground her crotch against the splintered wood of the stake. She was clearly oblivious to its roughness or any pain that she might be enduring as she sated her lust on the inanimate staff.

Gradually her movements subsided until she again hung limply from her bonds. He decided that it was time. He would impale her sweet body now. The demanding ache between his legs had become too much to bear. He stood and moved slowly towards her. The girl glanced over her shoulder and looked down at his bared genitals. Her eyes widened and a smile began to play across her lovely face. He gripped his raging erection by the root and aimed it at the open succulence of her pussy. The girl bent her back again and parted her legs slightly. She was fully aware of his intentions and was evidently more than ready. He put the huge plum-sized head to the soft inviting sex-lips. He sensed an ache building within his loins. Suddenly, without warning, he knew that he was coming. He cursed loudly and gripped his erection tightly under the thick ridge. His cock throbbed heavily. His cream was fighting to be released from within his body and he squeezed himself tightly in the vain hope that he could stop the inevitable. It was too late. The sight and taste of the young girl's bottom had been too much. He relaxed his grip and the semen gushed out, jetting across her glowing buttocks. He rubbed himself rapidly and roared with both anger and pleasure as more and more of his cream throbbed from within his body to soak her bottom. He pumped himself furiously with a practised hand until at last he was sated and there was no more to give.

He stepped back and rested one hand on the table, allowing his cock to droop heavily between his thighs. His knees trembled and, for a moment, he thought that his legs would give way. The urgency of desire passed and his anger with himself abated.

He looked at the girl's backside, the pert globes streaked with the evidence of his release. He walked over to her and stroked her soft, hot bottom. Gently, he massaged his cream into her flesh. She purred happily. It was having the required soothing effect.

The sounds of horns blasting outside his tent woke Suetonius from a deeply satisfying sleep. He opened his eyes slowly. The candle had almost burned itself out. He must have slept for hours. He struggled out of his cot and drew his heavy cloak about his shivering body. Not for the first time, he cursed the Emperor for sending him to this cold and dank place. He glanced across at the girl, whose lithe form was still hanging where he had left her, with her body resting heavily against the stake.

He shuffled over to her and put his hand under her chin to raise her head. She murmured incoherently but remained soundly asleep. He let her head fall to her chest and her temple knocked against the hard

10

shaft. He waited for a moment but she didn't stir. He looked at her bottom, its shape and texture enhanced by the flickering candlelight. The welts were beginning to turn darker to form bruises. He patted the firm pertness of her buttocks lightly, then drew his cloak tightly round his body and headed out of the tent to discover the cause of the racket.

The light of dawn was attempting to force its way through the thick veil of clouds that seemed to hang perpetually in the grey sky. Through the gloom, he saw a small group of approaching horsemen and immediately recognised the standard proudly held above the leading rider. He moved quickly forward to greet the newcomers.

'Catus!' he cried happily. 'Catus Decianus! What brings you to this forsaken place, my friend?'

The tall Roman slipped from his mount and the two men hugged each other warmly. 'Suetonius!' said the newcomer as he soundly slapped his friend on the back. 'You old devil! It is good to see you looking so well.'

'No thanks to this accursed climate. How goes it with you in the east?'

Catus's expression soured. 'Not good, old friend, not good. But first, before I tell you of my troubles, a bottle of wine and some good hot food would not go amiss.'

Suetonius slapped his friend on the shoulders and signalled to his men to bring them food. The remaining soldiers who had arrived with Catus dismounted and ambled off in search of similar sustenance. Suetonius led his friend into his tent. As they entered, Catus laughed loudly when he saw the girl in her prone position. The raucous sound awoke the slumbering form and she raised her head and looked over her shoulder. She regarded the two men through glazed eyes.

'I see that you have not changed, Suetonius,' he said. He walked over to examine the girl as one might inspect a newly purchased horse. He put his hand under her chin and raised her head. He looked appreciatively at her lovely features. 'This one is quite delightful,' he mused.

Suetonius shrugged. 'A Celtic whore, nothing more,' he said as he lit a couple more candles from the dying stub of the first. 'Accommodating enough.'

Catus bent and looked closely at the girl's bottom. 'So I see, friend, so I see.' He slipped his fingers between her thighs. 'She is dry, my friend. You must be losing your touch.'

'She was wet enough last night, and will be again.'

'She has fine breasts,' Catus continued as he reached round her body and weighed each one in turn in the palm of his hand, 'and a good mouth. She has delightfully thick sucking lips.'

Suetonius laughed loudly at this as he handed his friend a goblet of wine. Catus drained the vessel in one and thrust it back. 'A refill, my friend, if you please. I have barely lifted my arse from the back of that filthy horse for the past three days. And, speaking of arses, the whore has a fine firm pair of white globes. Have you rammed that big pego of yours into that dark little hole yet?'

'You know that is more your pleasure than mine,' replied Suetonius as he handed another brimming goblet to his friend, only to see it drained in similar fashion to the first.

Catus tossed the goblet on to the floor and walked back to stand behind the hapless girl. He ran his rough hand across her bottom, then eased a finger between her buttocks. 'She is tight,' he said, 'very tight. Perhaps she is a virgin, at least there.'

The girl was appearing to take the two soldiers'

verbal abuse placidly. She stared at the wall of the tent, her face betraying little emotion as her backside was fondled and probed. Catus eventually tired of humiliating her and walked over to join his friend, who was now relaxing on the couch. He poured himself yet another goblet of wine and rested back on the soft cushions.

'It is a hard ride from Lindum, and I have an even harder ride ahead of me,' he said.

'But I thought all was well in the Fens. I thought that you and the king of the Iceni tribe were allies or, at least, had developed an understanding.'

'Prasutagus, the king, is dead. Under the terms of the will, his kingdom becomes the property of the Emperor.'

'I am aware of the law. It is the same for all the kings of the Britons.'

'Indeed. But, in this case, there is one who does not like the law.'

'So kill him. Where is the problem?'

'It is not so easy, my friend. For a start, it is a woman, the good king's widow. Secondly, she is surrounded by a horde of vicious soldiers, both men and women.'

'You mean you are telling me that you can't defeat a rabble of men and women? You, the most revered of Rome's generals?'

'There are many of them, and they are well disciplined. And you know full well of the Celtic belief in life after death. The druids have taught them that their souls merely pass into another body. How can you defeat a people when they are totally unafraid of death? But there is more. This woman, the Queen of the Iceni. She is called Boudicca. She is revered by her people, almost to the point of worship. No one can get near her.'

'So you've never seen her?'

'Oh yes, I've seen her. Just once, in battle. She stood atop a fearsome chariot, which she drove as though possessed by demons. Anyone who stood in her way regretted it, I can tell you. She is taller than most men are, with long fire-red hair that falls to her waist. Her face is that of a goddess and, even though she was dressed in her armour, I could see that she had massive breasts.'

Suetonius laughed. 'My dear Catus,' he said, handing yet another vessel of wine to his friend, 'even in the heat of battle, with some fiery harridan bearing down on you in a great chariot, you still find time to appreciate her breasts!'

Catus laughed. 'A woman like that would be a challenge to any man.' He signalled across at the tethered girl. 'You would not be able to do something like that to one such as Boudicca.'

Suetonius shook his head. 'You are wrong, my friend. All women enjoy being subjugated to the whims of their men. That is what makes them different from us. That is why it is the men who are the warriors.'

'Boudicca is a warrior. I have seen her disarm four of the finest Roman soldiers in one movement. Even the length of that fine cock of yours would not be enough to overcome her.'

'Perhaps I should meet this Queen of the Iceni.'

'You will have your chance.'

'What do you mean?'

Catus took a long sip of his wine. 'I have been ordered to return to Rome. You are to march to Verulamium to take on the Iceni forces.'

Suetonius thought for a moment. 'But why?' he asked eventually. 'Your army is more than a match for the Celts, surely?'

14

Catus drew a long breath. 'You saw the guard that accompanied me when I arrived? Twelve men. That is all that remains of my army.'

The girl had been released from her bonds at Catus' request. She sat naked, opposite the two men on the straw-covered ground. Her legs were shamelessly spread wide apart while she happily devoured the last morsels of her meal. Catus sipped on his drink and watched her thoughtfully. He allowed his gaze to wander over her luscious body, her large, firm breasts, her smooth, flat stomach and the inviting openness of her juicy pussy. He stared brazenly between her legs whilst she nonchalantly wiped her mouth on the back of her hand. Suetonius smiled proudly as he saw his friend lick his lips.

'This is a fine specimen that I have acquired, don't you think?' he said.

'I agree, my friend,' replied Catus as he reached over and raised the girl's head so that he could look directly into her eyes. 'The Celts are a wild, untamed race, and their women are the hardest to force into submission.'

'This one fought like a vixen, until I tamed her with my pego.' Suetonius moved to kneel beside the woman and slid his hand between her outstretched thighs. She looked into his eyes and the vestige of a smile appeared on her face. Her expression held a mixture of lust and respectful adoration. He slipped his fingers into her wet bushy warmth. The girl drew a deep breath and closed her eyes momentarily as she savoured the sensation of his tender caress.

'There is nothing this one likes more than to be shackled and thrashed,' he continued, 'then to be fucked within an inch of her life, as hard as possible.'

Catus shuffled over and sat on her other side. He

slipped one arm about her slim waist and fondled her large breasts with his other hand. He pinched one of her thick nipples into instant erection. 'Are you willing to share this prize with me, my friend?' he asked. He pinched her other nipple and the girl lay back against some cushions.

'Of course, Catus. Do with her what you will.'

'Why don't we both have her, right now? We can give her the hard fucking for which she craves and, who knows, perhaps I can take her final virginity?'

'I didn't doubt it for a minute,' laughed Suetonius. 'No woman's arsehole is safe, when Catus Decianus is around!'

The girl must have understood the obscenity of their words, but she seemed unconcerned. Suetonius rose to his feet and walked over to the tent-flap. He peered out into the gloom of the early morning and ordered his guard to allow no one to enter, then turned back into the tent. He grinned as he saw that Catus was already lapping greedily at the young girl's willing pussy.

Suetonius threw off his cloak. The girl's eyes widened as she surveyed his manly nakedness. Although still flaccid, his cock hung heavily from his bushy groin. It stiffened rapidly as he moved towards her until it was jutting forward as firmly as the shaft of a spear. He knelt at her side with the thick bulbous end inches from her pouting mouth. She reached out with her hand and gripped the heavily veined stalk and tugged him towards her. She opened her mouth widely and enveloped his knob, her wet lips closing just under the thick ridge. He sensed her tongue licking the tip and probing the large slit. It throbbed heavily and sent a jet of the juices of his arousal to the back of her throat. She swallowed hard and then rubbed his long shaft rhythmically, until he throbbed again. He pulled away from her quickly. He wasn't going to be denied his pleasure a second time.

Catus raised himself to his knees. His face was soaked with the woman's wetness. He wrenched off his tunic and skirt as though his life depended on it. The girl looked between his legs and smiled. Catus leapt on her like a madman and rammed his hard prick into her to the hilt, in one swift movement. She gasped loudly. She threw her head back and her eyes widened as Catus fucked her like an animal. He thrust in and out of her at an alarming rate while, at the same time, pawing her heaving breasts and gnawing passionately at her shoulder and neck. She raised her legs high and wide as he thundered into her, as though urging him to delve ever deeper.

Suetonius was content for a moment to sit and watch while Catus continued to pound in and out of the girl's suppliant body without pausing, even for a moment. He felt a pang of envy as he looked on, marvelling at his friend's staying power. He would surely have come by now if he had fucked a girl so violently for so long. Eventually, he moved to kneel close to her and she took his stiff cock once more into her soft mouth. She sucked him voraciously as her small frame shook with the intensity of the assault on her body. She was clearly loving every sweet moment.

Presently, Catus relaxed and pulled from within her. His cock gleamed with her wetness. 'Come, Suetonius, let me see her accommodate your monstrous prong while I fuck her sweet mouth.'

Suetonius didn't need telling twice. He moved quickly to kneel between the girl's widely spread legs. He gripped his cock tightly by the root and watched proudly as it swelled to even greater proportions. The girl looked on, her face a picture of delight. He gazed at the welcoming hole between her legs. The outer lips

17

had become splayed apart like the petals of a flower soaked with the dew of the morning. She raised her legs high and tugged her lips further apart with her fingertips, in blatant invitation. He looked at Catus, who was staring enviously at his erection. He moved forward until the tip of his cock touched the hot wetness of her cunt. He had fucked her before, of course, but this was different. Having his good friend watch his every movement made it all the more erotic.

He slipped a couple of inches inside her. She groaned loudly. Two or three more inches slid into the succulence of her sheath. She muttered words that were unknown to him, under her breath, and closed her eyes. He drew back until her tight pussy-lips gripped his stalk under the thick ridge. Catus shook her roughly by the arm. 'Watch, vixen,' he ordered. 'Watch as he impales your young body with that monstrous pole. You will never see its like again!'

The girl opened her eyes and raised her head to stare between her thighs. Suddenly, Suetonius plunged the full, massive length into her with all the force he could muster. She cried out in pain and joy as the head hammered against her cervix. He raised himself, then lunged into her again. Her response was identical to the first time. 'Oh, yes, my lord!' she cried. 'Fuck me. Fuck my cunt as hard as you can!'

It was the first time that she had spoken that morning. Suetonius responded by quickening his pace. He thrust his full length in and out of her again and again. His belly slapped loudly against her thighs in time with her moans of pleasure. He saw Catus move his groin close to her face. She immediately took hold of his stiff cock and put it into her mouth. Her groans became muffled as she sucked the hard flesh and moved her head backward and forward. Catus responded by gripping both of her breasts tightly. He kneaded the fleshy mounds roughly and pinched the thick nipples. The girl squealed when he nipped them a little too hard, but his cock remained fully engulfed within her luscious mouth.

Suetonius found himself fascinated by the sight of his friend having his cock sucked so expertly by the same woman that he was pleasuring. It was an encounter that he had never experienced before, and he determined that he would enjoy such delights again. He also knew that they had only just started to satisfy the writhing creature that lay between their thrusting bodies.

The girl had made much noise, but she had yet to climax. Suetonius decided that he must make her come, not just for her pleasure but more for his own hedonistic satisfaction. He pulled his long, thick cock from within her tight pussy and shuffled his body back a little, then bent his head and put his lips to the succulent flesh. He lapped hungrily around her engorged lips and sucked them into his mouth, nipping them between his teeth. He heard her now familiar muffled groan and knew that she was enjoying the experience. He sucked harder at the soft flesh and ran the tip of his tongue between the lips, probing and searching for her clitoris.

He found the hard bud quickly. He relaxed his mouth and let her thick flesh slip from between his lips, then concentrated his attentions on her ultimate centre of pleasure. He flicked the tip of his tongue rapidly over it and then pressed against it firmly with his mouth. The pressure seemed to excite her even more than the fluttering of his tongue, so he moved his mouth around her soft cushion of sex-flesh. He alternately sucked and probed deep inside her then nipped her clitoris gently between his teeth. She began to wriggle her hips against him, and he could hear her breathing becoming more and more stilted as she sucked his friend's stiff cock.

She still wouldn't come. His jaw and tongue were beginning to ache. He moved away from her and watched her minister to Catus for a while. She turned herself over and moved between his friend's legs without allowing his shaft to slip from her mouth for a second. She was now on her knees and her pert, round bottom was presented to Suetonius in the most blatant fashion. He lowered himself on to his stomach and pressed his face to the sensuous globes and licked them gently. She tasted of fresh sweat. He ran his tongue slowly between them until the tip touched the tiny puckered sphincter. He eased his tongue inside her and moved it backward and forward a couple of times, but his jaw began to ache again and he slowly withdrew. He moved his tongue down and lapped around the lips of her juicy cunt, then moved to kneel down, ready to once again impale her with his stiffness.

He moved forward slowly as he gripped his stiff prick tightly by the root. The head swelled as it touched the girl's suppliant sex-lips. He eased it inside her and pushed forward to the hilt, without pausing for a moment. His tortured flesh throbbed heavily. He knew that he was in danger of coming himself, if he wasn't careful and he didn't want that – not yet. He desperately wanted to see Catus experience his orgasm before it happened to him. He wanted to be in the right mood to enjoy the sight of his friend's cream soaking this young girl's face.

He moved his thick rod in and out of her at a gentle pace. Occasionally he would pause whenever the tingling sensation at the base of his cock warned him that release was imminent. Despite this, however, it soon became too much for him and he withdrew from her, content to watch for a while.

Catus was now lying on his back with his legs held high. He was gripping his ankles tightly as the girl lapped around his balls while gently pumping his stiff cock with one of her hands. Suetonius looked closely. He could see that she had now started to lick his anus.

'By the Emperor's teeth, she's a wicked one!' hissed Catus.

His words reminded Suetonius of recent events, when the girl had been shackled to the stake, and it gave him an idea. He knelt by her side and smoothed the palm of his hand over her creamy buttocks. Then he raised his hand high and brought it down swiftly to slap her pert flesh soundly. The girl yelped loudly, then pressed her face harder against Catus, so that Suetonius was unable to see what she was doing. The look on Catus' face told him everything, however.

'She's sticking it up my arse' his friend moaned. 'She's actually tongue-fucking my arse!'

Suetonius felt a pang of seething jealousy. She hadn't done that to him. He decided to punish her severely. He raised his hand again and brought it down on her bottom as hard as he could. The stinging slap left a red imprint of his hand on her white flesh. He delivered another blow, then another, each more severe than the one before. A final, stinging smack gave her the orgasm that he'd been longing to witness. She raised her head and stiffened her body, then moaned loudly. It was a long, low moan that developed into a squeal of delight as her release took control of her senses in every way. She rolled over on to her back and clawed at her pussy as though in agony. Her fingertips rubbed her little bud violently and she came again with another loud cry. Then she rolled over on to her side and curled up into an embryonic pose, mewing softly to herself.

21

The two men watched the proceedings with mounting fascination. There were a few quiet moments while the girl recovered, then Suetonius lay on his back and beckoned her to mount him. He held his stiff cock upright and she moved to his side. She gazed at the proffered organ and smiled. 'It is truly magnificent, my lord,' she purred.

'Never mind that,' he snapped. 'Get astride me and sink it into your hot little cunt!' She obeyed immediately. She squatted across his body and lowered herself gingerly on to him. His stiff erection slid effortlessly into her until their groins met. She bent forward and made as if to kiss him on the mouth, but he pushed her face away roughly. Kiss a Celt on the mouth? The very idea!

'Ah, such a tempting prize!' said Catus. Suetonius looked over the girl's shoulder as she allowed her lower body to slowly rise and fall on his groin. Catus was staring lustfully at her backside as she steadily fucked herself on the hard flesh that was trapped inside her. He reached over and stroked her bottom, then Suetonius felt him ease a finger inside her anus. The sensation of having another man's finger so close to his own erection was somewhat odd, but he had the distinct feeling that it was as nothing to what he was likely to feel shortly.

The finger became two, and then three. 'She is already well lubricated with her own juices,' muttered Catus. He squatted across Suetonius' legs and gripped the girl's thighs; he held her still with just the head of the thick cock enveloped inside her well-oiled pussy. Suetonius decided to close his eyes. Moments later, he felt the pressure of his friend's penis against the head of his own as it slid slowly into the girl's bottom. She moaned a little with the discomfort, then relaxed as Catus entered her completely. Suetonius pushed his abdomen upwards so that the full length of his massive cock slipped deep inside her hot cunt and she groaned with delight.

'Oh, my lord, I feel so full,' she whispered, 'I have never been taken in this way before.' Suetonius began to pump upwards steadily and Catus matched his rhythm perfectly. The two men thrust into her alternately so that, as one hard cock withdrew from her, the other filled her other sheath. The sensation of his friend's stiff erection rubbing steadily against his own, with only a thin membrane of tissue between the two stiff stalks, was driving Suetonius to the point of no return. Catus began to quicken his movements. Suetonius held still, content to allow the strange stimulation of his raging erection to take him over the edge.

Suddenly, with a force unknown to him before, he came. His cock seemed to stretch enormously and the cream erupted into the depths of the girl's cunt with a violence that tore at his very soul. He roared, then gasped for breath as his thick shaft pumped more and more fluid into her. Catus cried out and Suetonius sensed that he could feel his friend's stiffness throbbing against his own. With a final madness, the two men hammered in and out of the girl sandwiched between them, until they were completely sated and their movements slowed to a stop.

Catus eased himself from her and fell back on the cushions. The girl raised herself slowly and allowed the big cock to flop noisily on to Suetonius' belly. No words were spoken; there was nothing that could be said.

The sounds of the soldiers' revelry were fast turning into the noises of total bacchanalia. The magnificent feast had quickly been devoured and the men were enjoying the copious amounts of wine looted from the druids as well as the wildly enthusiastic attentions of the Celtic women. Suetonius and Catus watched with amusement as the sea of nakedness writhed and humped before their eyes.

Suetonius drew his cloak around his body. His cock ached and hung limply between his legs. There had been many, too many. He knew that his penis would not rise again that day. Besides, he had to rest in order to prepare for the long march ahead of them. The short day was nearing its end and the murky, misty gloom was fast turning into twilight. He knew that he must sleep alone, and wake refreshed in the morning.

Catus on the other hand, was still sporting a fine erection, which was being orally serviced by a nubile maiden with long near-white hair and a slim, sylph-like body. He seemed blissfully unaware of her, however. He was clearly quite content to watch the orgy rather than to pay her any attention, apart from to nonchalantly move his finger in and out of her pussy as she knelt beside him.

Suetonius watched them for a few moments and then felt a slight twitch within his flaccid tool. He turned his head away and looked into the distance, seeing nothing in particular. 'Tell me more of this Boudicca,' he said presently.

'There is little more that I can tell you,' replied Catus. From his tone, it was evident that he did not wish to speak. The girl who was sucking him had started to bob her head up and down furiously and his breathing was becoming heavy and stilted. Suetonius waited patiently. Suddenly, inevitably, Catus' expression broke into a grimace and Suetonius knew that he was pumping his cream down the young girl's throat. 'This woman has a mouth like a goblet full of live eels,' his friend muttered as she slowed her movements to a stop.

Catus took a long, deep breath as the girl sat back on her heels. She smiled gently. A small trickle of sperm slipped from the corner of her mouth. She regarded the two men through wide blue eyes. Suetonius considered that, were it not for the telltale sliver of cream on her chin, she could have been taken for the most innocent of virgins. Catus would miss these Celtic women when he returned to Rome.

The girl rose to her feet and turned her back on them. She walked slowly into the mêlée of writhing bodies until she was grabbed by a lusty young soldier who took no time at all to impale her with his hard prick.

Suetonius looked away. 'Let us go into the tent,' he said, rising to his feet. 'There are too many distractions here and we must talk.'

Once inside the tent, the two men sat together on the long couch. The noise outside was already starting to abate. The soldiers were tiring of their pleasurable labours at last, and would soon fall into drunken slumber.

'Now that I have your undivided attention, Catus Decianus,' said Suetonius with a wry smile, 'perhaps you will tell me what you know of the warrior queen.'

'I spoke truthfully, friend,' replied Catus as he stretched his weary body out on the couch. 'Little is known of Boudicca apart from legend and the terrifying accounts from those who have met with her in battle. She and her hordes fight with merciless purpose. They are all mad, quite mad.'

'You say that there are many soldiers in her army?'

'Far too many to count. Their numbers blotted out the very ground from our sight as they swooped down on us. We stood no chance at all.'

'But surely they are a rabble? Untrained, unskilled and –'

'How many men are under your command, Suetonius?' Catus interrupted.

'Four hundred or so of the best soldiers of Rome.'

'Boudicca is reputed to have an army of over one hundred thousand.'

Suetonius took a sharp intake of breath. He pondered for a moment. 'If we cannot defeat her by force, then she must be vanquished by stealth and cunning.'

'And just how do you propose to do that?' Catus regarded his friend with a benign expression.

'That I do not know,' Suetonius replied, 'but I have two weeks of marching ahead of me. That will allow me sufficient time to draw up a plan.' He looked down at the ground beneath them as clouds of uncertainty and fear began to muddle his thoughts. His orders were clear; the rebellion must be put down, and he had just two short weeks to think of a way to do it. 'Will you accompany me, Catus?' he asked.

'I am ordered to return to Rome.'

'Make a small diversion. Please, my friend, your company will be welcome and your advice may well be very necessary.'

'The road to Londinium passes through Verulamium. I will accompany you that far, but then must take my leave of you. You must deal with the warrior queen on your own.'

Suetonius regarded his friend closely. 'You're afraid of her, aren't you?' he said, barely believing his own words.

Catus nodded. 'Yes, I am afraid,' he said, 'and so will you be, when you see her. She is possessed. Take great care, my good friend.'

'We will march to Londinium first. I will send orders to the second legion based to the south-west to meet me there. Then we will find this warrior queen and deal with her severely.' Suetonius stood up and drew himself up to his full height as if to demonstrate his determination to his friend.

'As I have said, Suetonius,' Catus whispered gently, 'take great care.'

Two

The darkness of night began to fall over the bleak marshy landscape as the mist drifted in from the sea like a ravenous prowling animal. Boudicca, Queen of the Iceni, watched as a solitary tree became gradually swathed in a cloak of fog and its grim skeletal form slowly faded into a memory. She could hear her two serving-girls busying themselves behind her in the bedchamber. It had been a long and arduous day. Rebuilding the fortifications of the village had taken its toll on the battle-weary men and women and the work had been completed in sullen silence.

But the Romans had fled; the battle had been won. The once mighty legion had been reduced to a mere handful of terrified soldiers, who had been sent scurrying away like a pack of whipped dogs. Her only regret was that she had not been able to capture their general, Catus Decianus. She had come close to him just the once in the mêlée of battle and had hated him on sight, despite not even being able to see his face. Tales of his cruelty to her people, especially the womenfolk, had enraged her and she had sworn vengeance, but the coward had been the first to flee.

'Mistress?' Boudicca was snapped out of her thoughts by the sound of a young girl's voice. She swung round to see Sisa, one of her serving maids, standing nervously in the shadows by the open door of her bedchamber.

'What is it, girl?' she demanded.

The young woman stepped forward and her slim, lithe form became illuminated by the flickering flames of the numerous torches set in their brackets on the walls. Boudicca regarded her beautiful face hungrily but took care not to show her desire in her expression. 'Please, mistress,' the girl continued, 'the tribal chiefs are awaiting your presence.'

The queen looked down sternly at the young woman. 'Let them wait,' she snarled, 'I am not yet prepared.'

The girl bowed obediently then turned and walked back into the bedchamber. Boudicca followed, closing the door behind her against the pervasive mist. Her other servant was carefully arranging the furs and hides on the huge bed. She was a lovely young Nubian girl by the name of Micha, whom the Iceni had rescued from the Romans some months previously. Boudicca had grown fond of the quietly enigmatic girl during the short time that she had served her, and was both attracted by and envious of her flawless beauty. She was almost as tall as the queen herself, but with a willowy form that seemed to drift as gracefully as a wild cat when she moved. Her ebony skin shone with a silk-like sheen and bore not the slightest blemish. Her legs were long and her buttocks thrust out arrogantly – an attribute that the queen had noticed was not lost on the men of the court, whom she had often seen gazing lustfully at the pert globes.

Boudicca took a long look at her own reflection in a large polished shield that served as a mirror. She smiled to herself, pleased with her image. She unfastened her cloak and let it fall to the floor. She stood naked, towering over the tiny form of the white-haired serving-girl. Sisa gasped at the sight of her queen's beauty. Boudicca's bright red hair cascaded over her sumptuous form, the tresses reaching the firm swell of her buttocks, which jutted provocatively as though in blatant invitation. She looked at the girl and saw that her gaze was fixed on the huge mounds of her bared breasts. She cupped them in her hands and raised them as if weighing them.

'Perhaps you would have me present myself to the leaders like this?' she sneered.

'No, mistress, I . . .'

'Silence! Fetch my armour. They will see before them a warrior, not a woman.'

The young girl hurriedly opened a large chest and retrieved a number of heavy garments, which she laid out on the bed. Boudicca examined each item of apparel carefully and selected those that she considered were suitable for the occasion. The leaders were her subjects, of course, but they had served her well in battle and were deserving of her respect.

She dressed quickly with Sisa and Micha's help and then stood once more in front of the shield to examine her reflection. She had chosen a short, heavy skirt made from thick strips of leather, which were decorated with bronze studs. She shook her hips and noticed to her satisfaction that, as she moved, the strips swung heavily against her legs to give fleeting and tantalising glimpses of her naked thighs. She turned her back to her reflection and swayed her lower body again. The skirt was sufficient to hide her modesty but nevertheless made it obvious that she wore nothing underneath.

She turned and faced the shield once more. Her tunic was made of thick hide and was festooned with elaborate brooches and gold chains. The massive swell of her firm breasts was, if anything, enhanced by the heavy garment and each of them was tipped by a small cone made of bronze which served to protect her nipples. The sumptuous mounds of flesh thrust massively forward. Boudicca cupped them again proudly and ran her thumbs over the nipple-cups. She sensed the buds hardening under their restricting cover. How long had it been since she had felt the touch of a lover's mouth to her breasts? One, maybe two weeks. The Romans had a lot to answer for.

Her boots were of polished hide and stretched to conceal most of her supremely long legs, finishing just below the hem of the short skirt. She smiled proudly as she admired her reflection. She knew that she looked every bit the warrior while, at the same time, maintaining her enigmatic sexuality.

She turned to face Sisa. The young girl's gaze immediately became centred once more on her breasts. Boudicca took hold of her wrists and put her small hands to one of the heaving mounds. Sisa cupped her breast gently, the fingers of both of her hands barely covering half of its superb size. 'The tunic fits well, doesn't it?' teased Boudicca. The girl seemed to take up a little more courage and ran the palms of her hands over both of the queen's breasts. There was a hungry look in her eyes. Boudicca suddenly grabbed her wrists and pulled her hands away. 'Enough, girl,' she chided. 'Remember that I am your queen.'

Sisa let her arms fall by her sides and hung her head in shame. Boudicca examined the small lithe form before her. The girl's nipples had hardened and were now clearly visible through the thin material of her dress. Boudicca found the sight of her most appealing. The girl was new to the court, and Boudicca had chosen her to be her personal servant on the strength of her waif-like appearance. In a

32

delightful way, she was the complete opposite to Micha. Sisa was innocent and naive, while the Nubian had seen and experienced much in her short life. Soon, she decided, it would be time to initiate Sisa into her circle and teach her the true meaning of giving service to her queen. But not now. The leaders were awaiting her in the great hall and she wished to reward them all for their bravery.

She bent her head forward and kissed Sisa lightly on top of her head. The girl looked up and smiled gratefully. 'Come,' said Boudicca gently, 'let us be about our business.'

Sisa bowed and moved over to retrieve her shawl that had been hastily dropped on to the floor earlier. Boudicca watched appreciatively as the girl bent over to pick the garment up. Sisa hardly bent her knees as she did so and the thin material of her dress stretched across her tight little buttocks, to offer the most enticing sight. Boudicca ran her tongue across her upper lip hungrily. 'Are you a virgin, Sisa?' she asked in a tone that demanded immediate response.

The girl stood upright quickly, swung round and glanced up at her queen's dispassionate expression, then let her eyes fall so that she stared humbly at the floor. Micha giggled knowingly and Boudicca flashed a glare across at her. Micha looked down quickly and continued to prepare the bed.

Boudicca looked back at Sisa. 'Answer me, girl,' she demanded.

The young girl looked up at her nervously. 'Yes, mistress,' she replied, as though ashamed of the fact.

Boudicca liked the way that she had called her 'mistress'. It seemed so much more submissive than 'your majesty'.

'I will teach you,' she continued. 'That is, if you wish to learn?'

Sisa looked up into her eyes questioningly. 'Learn, mistress?' she said quietly.

Boudicca smiled and stroked the young woman's hair softly. 'Later,' she whispered simply. Sisa bowed her acquiescence and the two women walked towards the door.

The four guards who were standing at the doorway snapped to attention the moment that Boudicca and Sisa entered the long passageway that would lead them to the great hall. Boudicca saw that one of them, a young man whom she had not seen before, stared directly at the massive swell of her breasts. She glared at him and, when he finally noticed the severity of her stare, he looked quickly away. She smiled inwardly but gave no outward impression of her amusement. He would be punished for his impertinence.

She strode quickly down the passageway, the others having difficulty in keeping up with her. The soldiers' armour rattled noisily and the sound echoed against the damp stone walls. Sisa scurried alongside her mistress like a pet dog. Boudicca was pleased with her new servant; she would have much sport with this gentle nymph-like creature.

The great hall was bustling with people, soldiers and peasants alike mingling and enjoying jocular conversation. Naked male servants moved among them, carrying trays of wine and food, their nakedness all but ignored by the throng. Two of the queen's guards opened the large doors and rapped their spears hard on the stone floor. The room fell into immediate silence as Boudicca and Sisa entered.

The queen strode purposefully over to the throne at the far end of the hall and stepped on to the dais. She turned and faced the crowd, her expression grim and haughty. Hundreds of pairs of eyes stared back at her, as though waiting for her to give them permission to blink. Suddenly, Boudicca raised her arms triumphantly and smiled. The cheer that rang out was deafening. She turned from side to side to acknowledge their cries, and the roars of approval and adulation rose to a crescendo. Her heart filled with pride. For the first time ever, the Roman invaders had been repelled. The druids had foretold it; the Iceni would vanquish the aggressors for good.

The queen allowed her arms to fall to her sides and waited for the crowd to quieten. Once the cheers had been reduced to a murmur, she raised her head high in order to address the milling throng. 'People of the Iceni,' she began proudly, 'today has been a turning point in our history. You have all served me well. Rejoice in your victory!' The crowd immediately cheered again and the sound rang like sweet music in the queen's ears.

She sat down on the huge wooden throne and Sisa knelt at her feet. A naked servant moved to offer the queen a goblet of wine. Boudicca took the goblet and glanced appreciatively at his thick cock, which was hanging limply from his bushy groin. She looked up at his face but the man stared past her dispassionately. She had taught him well.

Boudicca looked around at the sea of smiling, happy faces and grinned broadly. She held her hand in the air for silence and the cacophony ceased immediately. She paused for a moment, as if deliberately teasing them.

'Let the celebrations begin!' she suddenly cried. Another cheer followed and music was played as the crowd took up their goblets and toasted their victory with the fine wines looted from the Romans. Boudicca sat back in order to watch the badinage. She would take her pleasures later. A young serving-girl rushed past them, laughing loudly as two soldiers chased her. Her large bare breasts bounced provocatively as she scurried through the crowd until the men caught her and dragged her to the floor. Moments later, Boudicca was just able to make out the form of one of the soldiers' backsides rising and falling rapidly as he plundered the willing girl's most intimate treasure. It was as though some unheard signal had been given. Soon, virtually everyone in the room was divesting themselves of their clothing until the floor became a mass of writhing naked bodies.

Boudicca looked down at Sisa, who was watching the mêlée through wide staring eyes. 'What do you think of the ways of the Iceni court?' she asked with a wry smile.

Sisa turned and looked up at her queen. Her expression was a picture of innocent excitement and her face was flushed and her eyes were sparkling. 'It is wonderful, mistress,' she said breathlessly.

'I do not believe that you will be a virgin for much longer,' said Boudicca. Sisa looked down in embarrassment. The queen rested her hand on the young girl's shoulder. 'Do not be so coy, sweet child,' she breathed. 'Soon you will revel in the attentions of many, many men, and I will teach you to use them for your own pleasures.'

'I do not understand, mistress,' said Sisa with a concerned expression on her lovely features. 'Surely a woman is placed upon this earth to give delight to her husband, and to none other?'

Boudicca smiled sympathetically.

'No, sweet virgin,' she said as she ran her fingers through the girl's soft, white-blonde hair. 'Men should be treated as mere playthings. Come, I have something to show you.' The queen rose to her feet and held out her hand. Sisa grasped her fingers and

the two women stepped carefully over the multitude
of thrusting bodies to leave the great hall and re-enter
the passageway. They walked quickly past the royal
bedchamber and then came to a small, heavily barred
door. Boudicca quickly unbolted the door and tugged
it open. She turned to face Sisa.

'Down these steps is the place where I take my
pleasure,' she said enigmatically. She turned and
began to move quickly down the winding stairway.
Sisa followed, still grasping her queen's hand tightly,
like a small child being led on some wondrous
adventure.

They reached the foot of the stairwell and faced yet
another barred door, the area illuminated by a single
flickering torch. Boudicca slid the bolts open and the
old hinges creaked and squealed as she dragged the
heavy door open. She took the torch from its clasp
and entered the cell. Sisa followed immediately,
clearly not wishing to be left alone in the darkness. A
distinct aroma of male sweat invaded their nostrils.

'What is this place?' asked Sisa fearfully as she tried
to peer into the gloom.

'You will see,' replied Boudicca. One by one, she lit
more and more torches that were fixed in brackets
around the walls of the dank cell. As each one
crackled and spat into life, Sisa's eyes became ever
wider as she gazed in astonishment at the scene which
was unfolding before her. The room was filled with
the restrained and shackled forms of men, all of them
naked and all of them looking fearfully at the queen
as she completed her task.

At the centre of the cell stood a long, low table, on
top of which lay a man, his wrists and ankles
shackled to the four corner legs. Against one of the
walls there hung four more young men with their
backs turned to the room, although each one of them

was looking over his shoulder with a terrified expression on his face. Sisa could see that their bottoms were heavily marked and bruised. Other men were strapped across various designs of wooden frames, some of them bent over to present their firm buttocks to her eager gaze, others shackled on their backs with their legs spread widely apart so that their most intimate parts were fully exposed.

Sisa glanced back at the man on the table and saw, to her profound amazement that his cock had thickened and had grown to a superb erection. She looked quickly around the room and discovered that all the men present were rapidly joining him in his state of abject arousal.

'What do you think of my chamber of pleasure?' asked Boudicca. Sisa said nothing, but merely gazed at one thick cock after another, her eyes shining with excitement. 'Choose one,' continued the queen. 'Pick the one who will take away your innocence.'

Sisa backed away fearfully, clutching her arms across her stomach as if to protect herself. 'Oh, no, mistress,' she wailed, 'I couldn't, I just couldn't!'

Boudicca grinned. 'You will, child,' she teased, 'you will.' She walked over to a table and poured some water into a small goblet. She moved back to stand next to the man who was lying prone on the long bench and raised his head with one hand, while offering the goblet to his lips. He drank the liquid gratefully, much of it running down his chin to soak his neck and shoulders. She set the water down and then grasped his thick erection and held it vertically. 'This is a fine specimen, don't you think? Would you not like to impale your virginal body on a staff such as this?'

Sisa shook her head, although she continued to stare at the huge cock that the queen was nonchalantly displaying to her. Boudicca could see that the girl was trembling. She smiled and let the stiff rod fall on to the man's stomach. Moving to the far side of the cell, she took up a thin cane from a rack of similar implements. She swished it in the air and Sisa jumped.

'As I explained to you before,' said Boudicca as she walked back to stand behind the group of men who were shackled facing the wall, 'men are merely playthings, to be used and abused as a woman's pleasure demands.' She flicked the cane across the buttocks of one of the men, causing him to gasp. She looked back at Sisa and noted her shocked expression. 'Do not fear for him, my dear; these men take as much delight in their punishment as I do in administering it.' She grasped the man's waist and tugged his body away from the wall as far as his restraints would allow and then stroked the cane up the length of his hard cock. 'See how stiff it is! It would not be so if he did not take joy in the pain.'

She walked slowly back to stand by the man on the low bench. He eyed the cane fearfully but his cock remained firmly erect. Boudicca dropped the implement to the floor and turned to face Sisa. 'I will prepare him for you,' she said quietly.

The queen stepped over the prone form so that one of her legs stood on either side of the bench. She parted the leather strips of her skirt to reveal the shaven succulence of her pussy-lips to both his and Sisa's gaze. His cock seemed to stiffen even more and became raised slightly from his stomach. She reached out with her free hand and grasped his stiffness, then held it erect while slowly lowering herself to squat above his groin. She looked across at Sisa and saw, to her satisfaction, that the young girl was gazing avidly at the monstrous weapon as the head slipped effortlessly into Boudicca's silky wet flesh. The man groaned as inch after inch was absorbed inside her until she sat down hard on him, so that she held his full length within her body.

'Do not come,' she ordered her hapless victim, 'or you will be thrashed severely. I have a special task for you to perform.' She looked across at Sisa meaningfully, but the sight of her naked pussy holding the immensely long rod within its tight grip held her servant's gaze. She began to move up and down, each time allowing the cock to almost slip out of her, so as to give Sisa the full benefit of the vision of her pussy lips being stretched by the thick rod. She noticed that beads of sweat were beginning to form on the man's brow and she realised that he might lose control at any moment.

She raised herself from him and his cock slapped noisily against his stomach. Stepping over him, she approached the quaking form of Sisa and held out her hand. 'Come, sweet virgin,' she breathed. 'It is time.'

Sisa shook her head. 'No, no, I . . .'

Boudicca grasped her wrist firmly and began to tug her towards the prone man. 'Do not disobey your queen,' she growled. 'I told you that I would teach you. This is your first lesson.'

Sisa seemed to lose her will and she allowed the queen to lead her to the bench like a condemned prisoner. She gazed at the man's stiffness through terrified eyes. 'It is too big!' she complained. 'It will hurt. Perhaps one of the others; one who is not so well blessed?'

Boudicca put the tip of her finger to the trembling girl's lips to silence her protestations and then kissed her lightly on top of her head. She released her grip on her wrist and stepped back a little. 'Remove your smock,' she ordered.

Sisa paused for a moment and then grasped the hem of her dress with shaking hands and slowly raised it up her body, pulling it over her head. Boudicca felt her mouth become dry as she looked upon the frail lithe form of the naked girl standing before her. Her breasts were tiny, although perfectly formed, with cherry-pink nipples that were clearly erect. Her waist was narrow to the point of being thin and her stomach curved gently towards the down-like fur between her slim legs.

'Get astride him,' commanded Boudicca. 'I will see to it that there is no pain.'

Sisa took a deep breath and then moved her leg over the bench. Being that much shorter than her queen, she had to squat slightly in order to spread her legs wide enough to hold her position with her feet planted firmly on the stone floor.

Boudicca could see the lips of her sex plainly now and was pleased to note that they were puffy and slightly parted, as a certain sign of the girl's arousal.

She knelt by the side of the bench and once more gripped the man's thick tool and raised it to aim the head at Sisa's virginal opening. 'Lower yourself slowly,' she ordered.

Sisa obeyed immediately, gingerly squatting lower and lower until the thick bulbous knob brushed against the soft lips of her pussy. Boudicca moved her face closer and rested her head on the man's muscular stomach. She took a long, deep breath and savoured the sweet scent of Sisa's arousal. She moved the head of the hard stalk against the wet succulence of the young woman's sex-lips and watched them open in juicy invitation. The man arched his back and pushed his hips upward as best as he could in his shackled position. The head slipped inside the folds of virginal flesh and the lips closed around it, as if to trap it within their moist warmth.

41

Boudicca noticed a trickle of the girl's juice slip down the back of the long, thick shaft. She pushed out her tongue and licked the nectar from the bone-hard flesh. It tasted honey-sweet. Sisa lowered herself a little more and then gave out a short sharp gasp of pain as her virginity was lost. The queen grasped the cock tightly, in order to prevent deeper intrusion and then raised herself to look directly into Sisa's lovely face. A small tear slid down one cheek. Boudicca rested her free hand on the girl's pert little bottom and then leant forward and kissed her lightly on the mouth. Suddenly, she released her grip of the man's weapon and pushed down hard on Sisa's buttocks. The young girl gasped loudly as the huge cock impaled her tight sheath to the hilt.

'That's it!' cried the queen jubilantly. 'Your virginity is gone and there will be no more discomfort. Relax your muscles and move yourself slowly. Enjoy its size and the way that it penetrates you completely. Be happy, Sisa, for now you are truly a woman.'

Sisa smiled bravely and then looked down as she raised her body slowly. Her eyes widened with astonished delight as she saw the superb length of flesh gradually come into view. The thick ridge under the head appeared and she lowered herself again, as though she were unwilling to allow it to escape from her body. She repeated the movement, but this time forced herself down hard on the man's groin. He groaned, more from shock than from pleasure. Sisa grinned and raised herself until just the tip of his cock was held between her engorged sex-lips and then rammed herself down again. She squealed with delight as the man gasped for breath.

Boudicca moved back, smiling proudly. 'Now, Sisa,' she said, 'fuck yourself as hard and as quickly as you please.' She turned her head and looked into the man's face with a stony, unforgiving stare. 'And you, slave,' she snarled, 'see that you do not come until after my pupil has enjoyed her own release, or it will be the worse for you.' The man closed his eyes and she saw him bite his lower lip. Clearly it was not going to be an easy task for him.

Sisa began to ride his prone form as though she were astride a wild bucking animal. The speed and force of her assault surprised even the queen. She recalled that her own introduction to womanhood had been an altogether calmer affair, a gentle and tender encounter with a young peasant in the swaying grass of a summer's day. She had lain passively on her back as the young man had taken her, and he had proven his own lack of experience with his fumbling approach and lack of control. It had all been over quickly, far too quickly.

She watched hungrily as Sisa slapped her pussy hard against the slave's pubic mound over and over again. The man's face was held in a grimace and she saw that he was digging his fingernails into the fleshy palms of his hands. He would not last much longer under such a forceful assault. Boudicca knew that she needed some satisfaction herself. She picked up the cane and lashed repeatedly across the buttocks of one of the men shackled to the wall and thrilled to his cries of blissful agony. She grasped herself between the legs with her other hand and began to work her fingers in and out of her hot, throbbing pussy. She worked her thumb hard against her little bud and sensed that her release was imminent. She turned her attention to the other men who were hanging helplessly before her and whipped their firm buttocks in turn, while forcing all four of her fingers deep inside herself. The sensations of impending orgasm were building up rapidly inside her loins.

Suddenly, Sisa gave out a loud, piercing shriek. Boudicca dropped the cane and turned to watch the young girl's ultimate delight. Sisa held herself still with the slave's cock buried inside her to the hilt. She stared at Boudicca with wide, manic eyes. The queen matched her stare and forced her fingers and thumb deep into her own cunt, while rubbing her hard little bud rapidly with her free hand. The pain and delight of orgasm tore through both of them simultaneously.

Boudicca felt her legs give way and she fell to her knees on the cold stone floor, still grasping and probing her soaking sex-lips. Sisa squealed again and then began to pound her small, lithe body up and down at a furious rate. Boudicca watched in fascination as the huge cock became a blur under her ferocious demands. The slave threw his head back and roared and Sisa slipped back and allowed his cock to spring free. She watched as though hypnotised as the semen jetted from the big, throbbing rod to soak his muscular chest and shoulders. She leant forward and put the tip of her finger into a small pool of the cream and slid it a little over his bronzed skin. She sat back and put the finger to her mouth and licked at gently with the tip of her tongue. Boudicca smiled to herself as she struggled to her feet. This girl would certainly be a compliant and willing pupil.

Sisa looked down at the slave's sweating body. His cock, although wilting slightly was still large and it glinted in the torchlight, its gnarled surface soaked with her wetness. She turned to face Boudicca. 'I still can't believe that I had all of that inside me,' she mused.

Boudicca ran her fingers lovingly through the young girl's tousled blonde tresses. 'You did, Sisa,' she breathed, 'and I swear that you could have taken another, just as large at the same time!'

'Is such a thing possible?'

'Very much so, and there are many more diversions that you will experience and enjoy in the forthcoming weeks.'

Sisa clambered from her straddling position and stood next to her queen. Boudicca put one arm around her shoulders and hugged her tightly, while pressing her free hand against the soaking lips of the girl's pussy. She kissed her lightly on the mouth and then looked meaningfully into her wide eyes. Sisa closed her eyes and pressed her groin hard against the queen's hand. Boudicca caressed the soft soaking lips tenderly. 'Many, many more diversions,' she breathed.

The mist over the fens was far denser than she had ever known it before and the moonlight played tricks as it danced its silvery path through the swirling clouds. Boudicca walked slowly along the grassy trail. It was a road that she knew well, the road to the place of the druids. She was naked, but the cold didn't seem to touch her. He was calling her, the one they called Arman.

A solitary tree threw its ghostly shape before her as suddenly as if it had appeared from the depths of her imagination. It seemed to drift silently past her as she moved purposefully onward. His voice seemed to whisper to her like the sound of the breeze playing through the gnarled branches of the old tree but the words were clear: *come to me, Boudicca, Queen of the Iceni, come to me.*

She heard a sudden sound coming from behind her, a scurrying, scratching noise. She stopped dead and held her breath. A pair of badgers ambled past her, their eyes fixed ahead as though they hadn't seen her. They melted quickly into the mist. She began to walk forward again.

The trail began to rise steeply. She knew that she was nearing the cliff-edge. She listened for the sound of the sea but heard nothing. She moved cautiously, although she knew in her heart that she would not come to any harm.

Suddenly he was there, standing by the ethereal shapes of the old stones. She stood still, as if waiting for instruction. The figure stepped forward, its ghostly shape shrouded by the swirling mist. He held out his arms as if beckoning for her to come to him. She remained motionless but somehow she seemed to be drifting closer and closer to his shadowy form. Other figures appeared out of the mist, their bodies swathed in long white cloaks and their heads covered by shapeless hoods. They surrounded her and appeared to be closing in on her menacingly. She suddenly remembered her nakedness and hurriedly put one arm across her chest and the other hand between her legs in a vain attempt to hide her physical attributes from their gaze.

'Welcome, Queen of the Iceni, welcome to our temple.' His voice was as enigmatic as his form and seemed to drift through the still air like a cloud. He stepped forward and drew back his hood. His face was inches away from hers. His deep blue eyes appeared to be boring into her very soul. She had spoken with Arman many times before, of course, but they had always met at her fortress and always in the company of her soldiers. This was entirely a different matter.

He smiled: a broad comforting smile. Boudicca let her arms fall to her sides and took a deep breath. She saw his eyes fall to gaze at the full swell of her breasts and felt a familiar warmth between her legs. She felt a sudden sense of pride in her body and stood with her legs apart and her hands resting squarely on her hips, with her back arched and her chest thrusting forward. He reached out and stroked one of her nipples with the backs of his fingers. The bud hardened under his delicate touch and she shivered slightly.

'Why have you called me?' she asked. Her voice faltered and drifted into the mist. He took her hand and led her through the circle of hooded figures until they came to a huge stone altar. Suddenly, she found that she was lying on the altar and the druids had once again surrounded her. Arman was standing at the foot of the stone table and, from the expression on his handsome face, was clearly enjoying the sight of her prone naked form. He reached forward and grasped each of her ankles tightly. He parted her legs and gazed between them at the open vulnerability of her most intimate parts. She sensed the lips of her sex opening slowly and felt a damp trickle of juice slipping between her buttocks. She cursed her weakness. He leant further forward and she closed her eyes. His warm breath played over her tender sex-flesh. She tried to raise her head to glance down at him but, for some inexplicable reason, she found that she could not move. She looked down but the upward thrust of her large breasts hid him from her view.

She sensed him kiss her pussy and then he began to lap her tender lips. Despite her anger at finding herself in such a vulnerable position, she moaned softly as a warm sensation of gentle delight coursed through her body. He licked and suckled her soft flesh, occasionally drawing the lips into his mouth and nipping them lightly between his teeth. His tongue probed deep inside her, far deeper than anything that she had experienced before. It circled and prodded within her suppliant sheath, while his

47

mouth nuzzled against her outer lips and sucked them hard.

Then he was gone from her. She managed to force her head from the invisible bonds that had seemed to hold it moments before, and rested herself on her elbows. Arman was standing silently, just looking at her. She began to feel angry again. He might be the leader of the druids, she thought, the high priest even, but he had no right to stare at a queen in such a blatant manner. She tried to move from the stone but was strangely powerless to do so. It felt as if the very mist was weighing down on her naked body, keeping her its prisoner.

He drew back his cloak and let it fall from his shoulders. Now he was naked, and suddenly her anger abated and she ached for him to touch her again. The presence of the other druids was forgotten; she simply wanted their leader to take her, there and then on that hard stone slab.

She glanced down at his stomach. His cock jutted firmly from his bushy groin like a rod of iron, the wet head glistening in the moonlight. Boudicca swallowed hard. She had never yearned so much in her entire life for a man to impale her hungry body. She struggled against the unseen force that was holding her and managed to raise her bottom from the stone in blatant invitation.

Suddenly, Arman nodded his head and she was grabbed roughly by the arms and legs. She struggled vainly and was eventually turned to kneel on the altar on her knees and elbows. She knew that Arman would be looking at her bottom now, and was also well aware that the sight of her perfect globes would be enough to enchant him, as had happened with many of her lovers in the past. Nevertheless, she felt debased and totally at his mercy and it was not something that she was accustomed to.

The druids released their grip on her arms but she held her position. She moved her knees further apart and forced her bottom higher. He would see her pussy now, and that other inviting hole. She would make him hunger for her, just as she longed for him to ram his splendid rod deep into her.

There was a long silent pause. The surface of the stone felt rough against her nipples and they hardened to its unyielding touch. There was no sound other than that of her breathing and the steady thumping of her heart. At last, she felt him stroking her buttocks with his fingertips. He traced the shape of the firm globes and then ran his fingers down along the cleft between them. She gasped as he tickled her anus and then moaned softly as he fingered her hot pussy. Her will deserted her like a dream on a stormy night. 'Fuck me, my lord,' she pleaded quietly. 'Please fuck me.'

He moved from her and she felt strangely empty without his touch. She raised her head and looked at the two druids who were standing in front of her. Their hoods hid their faces and their bodies were entirely swathed in their cloaks but she could see, from the telltale bulges in the flowing material, that their cocks were hard and erect. She looked from side to side and over her shoulders at the others. They too sported similar evidence of their arousal, each one standing motionless, waiting for their leader to take his prize.

Suddenly, she felt the touch of his thick cock-head to her sex-lips. She arched her back even more to open herself to him and he slid slowly into her succulent sheath. He held himself still. She couldn't feel his thighs against her bottom and so knew that he had more to give her. She waited for him to start fucking her but he remained motionless. In desperation, she thrust her bottom back towards him and absorbed the full length of his hard stalk. She tensed her inner muscles and gripped him tightly within her. Still he refused to move. She eased herself forward until his cock all but slipped from her and then she thrust back again, once more taking his full size into her body. She realised at last that this was precisely what he wanted.

With steady rhythmic movements, she pushed her bottom backward and forward against him, fucking herself on his long, thick staff. She looked over her shoulder. Arman was standing stock-still with a benign if impassive expression on his face. Boudicca turned her head away again and began to ram herself heavily against him, determined to arouse some passion in her enigmatic lover.

There was a movement in front of her. She raised her head to see that the two druids at the head of the stone table had drawn back their cloaks to present her with the sight of their rampant erections. She reached out and took one of them in her grip and pulled it towards her mouth. She engulfed the stiff stalk between her lips and then reached out again and caught hold of the other. The second hooded man moved forward and pressed the head of his cock against her cheek. Opening her mouth as wide as possible she managed to accommodate both of the hard rods between her lips. She sucked them voraciously, all the time thrusting her backside backward and forward and relishing the feel of Arman's manhood slipping in and out of her hot cunt.

Someone grasped hold of one of her hands and she suddenly found herself gripping another firm erection. She reached out with her other hand and soon slipped her fingers around yet another gnarled shaft.

Using the two cocks for leverage she hammered her backside against Arman's groin. He began to move at last, matching her rhythm with firm invasive thrusts of his own. She sensed the touch of two more hard cocks, each one being pressed against the soles of each of her feet. She felt them rubbing themselves against her and wriggled her toes playfully over the stiff flesh and the softness of their scrotums.

Someone raised one of her legs a little and she sensed Arman moving to one side and withdrawing his cock so that just the head remained inside her pussy. She held her body still, although she continued to pump the erections in her hands and to suck the two lovely cocks in her mouth. She felt her thighs being tugged wider apart and then sensed a heavy pressure against her sex-lips. Arman began to slide slowly into her again but she realised that this time he was not alone. Somehow, they had positioned her so that she now had two thick cocks slipping into the folds of her succulent sheath.

The two men who were now fucking her were unable to fill her with their full lengths, due to the awkwardness of their position but nevertheless the incredible feeling of distension delighted her. She tried to imagine the delightful vision her joyous experience would present to any onlooker. They would see a beautiful naked woman kneeling on a stone altar, two cocks plundering her loins, two in her mouth, one in each of her hands and two more happily being rubbed against the soles of her feet. Eight men, seven of them complete strangers, daring to use her in this way! The thought thrilled and excited her. This was something that even Sisa would never believe.

She was coming, and she knew that the orgasm would tear her apart. The feelings were building up to a crescendo within her ravaged loins. The men seemed to sense her urgency and they all began to thrust heavily against her. She felt one of the rods rubbing against the soles of her feet begin to throb and then sensed the warmth of the man's cream slipping between her toes. Almost immediately, one of the cocks that she was steadily pumping with her hands suddenly erupted into orgasm sending a jet of hot juice streaking across her back. She massaged the throbbing stalk lovingly and caressed the softening head with her thumb as more semen trickled through her fingers. She heard the man moan softly and then he pulled away as the tenderness became too much for him to bear.

Arman and the other druid continued to pound in and out of the stretched flesh of her pussy. Suddenly, one of them pulled from her and, although the remaining stalk was long and thick, she felt somewhat empty. She felt the now familiar warmth of the jet of male release soak her bottom just as the two men who were fucking her mouth came simultaneously. She swallowed their creamy offerings gratefully until they had no more to give. The men moved from her and Boudicca released her grip of the other cock that she had been rapidly masturbating as, once more, the palm of her hand became soaked.

She raised her head and glanced over her shoulder. The hooded figures had all disappeared into the mist, leaving just Arman standing behind her, thrusting heavily into her aching sex. She could see that her bottom and lower back were streaked with copious amounts of white oily fluid. She reached back and massaged the cream into her skin and grinned suggestively as he increased his pace and started to hammer his long cock in and out of her. Her orgasm was still threatening to burst within her but, for some reason, she couldn't take herself over the edge, no matter how much she strained the muscles of her lower body. She felt used and debased, feelings that she had never experienced before and which now excited her in a strange erotic way. It was as though she was being sacrificed, here, on this pagan altar to their gods.

Suddenly Arman rammed his cock as deep as it would go inside her hot sheath and he held himself still, gripping the sides of her buttocks tightly and digging his fingernails into her flesh. She felt his thick rod thumping within her and knew that he was filling her honeyed depths with his cream. She came at last and the sensations tore through the nerve-endings within her pussy, seeming to shoot like bolts of lightning throughout her thighs and buttocks. She arched her back and opened her mouth to scream, but no sound came save for a loud gasp of delight.

Arman began to pound in and out of her again as she was carried over the edge into the glorious oblivion of total joy. She felt out of control; he could do anything that he wanted to her. She could feel the head of his prick thumping against her cervix and the sensation thrilled her intensely, so much so that she realised that she was going to come again.

She reached under herself with one hand and clawed at her soaking pussy-lips with her fingers as the stabbing in her loins once more rose to fever pitch. Arman appeared to realise her need and he thrust his slowly wilting cock in and out of her as rapidly as was possible. This time, the scream came. It was more a shriek of delight, piercing the still night air and echoing against the surfaces of the old stones. Her nipples rubbed against the roughness below her as her breasts bounced rhythmically in time with the pounding of her lover's groin against her bottom.

Eventually, it became too much for Arman and he slipped out of her. Slowly, the joyous after-effects of her delightful release subsided and Boudicca collapsed on to the cool surface of the stone altar, panting heavily. Arman knelt at her side, stroking her long red hair lovingly and gazing into her eyes. Boudicca felt as though she wanted the moment to last forever.

'You must leave this place,' he said quietly. 'You must march on Verulamium.'

His words seemed strange, especially spoken at such a blissful time. Boudicca raised her body stiffly and sat on the edge of the altar. She looked down at herself. Her long nipples were red-raw from chafing against the stone and her pussy-lips were engorged and puffy. She looked back at Arman's face. 'What do you mean?' she asked breathlessly.

'The citizens of that sorry place have joined forces with the Romans,' continued Arman as if nothing had happened between them. 'They must be routed before they can prepare to attack your people.'

She looked deeply into his eyes. 'How do you know this?' she asked. Arman merely smiled and she knew that she would gain no further information. She looked around and peered into the mist. 'Where are the others?' she enquired after a moment.

He looked puzzled. 'What others?' he said. 'There is only you and I.'

Boudicca jumped to her feet and walked over to one of the tall stones. She strained her eyes and peered into the swirling fog but she saw nothing. She swung round and regarded Arman angrily. 'You know there were others,' she barked, 'many others! Where are they now?'

He smiled benignly and sat on the altar and patted the stone lightly. 'Come, sister,' he said in a gentle tone, 'come and sit with me.'

Boudicca walked slowly towards him as if some strange powerful force were drawing her to his side. Arman slipped his arm around her shoulders and she turned her face to him. Her anger drifted into the night as their lips met. She felt weak and completely at his mercy. Surely she couldn't have imagined it all? Her jaw ached from sucking two thick cocks simultaneously and her sex-lips tingled. She felt him cup one of her huge breasts and then he pinched her hard nipple. The pain thrilled her. It was as though the seduction was just about to commence.

She felt light-headed and unsure of her reality. She lay back on the stone table and parted her legs. She gazed at him as he moved to kneel before her. His cock rose magnificently from his groin. Had she imagined it? He bent his head and pressed his mouth against her soaking sex-lips and she felt him begin to lap hungrily. She closed her eyes in order fully to savour the sensation as he suckled her cunt with renewed vigour.

Somehow, the stone altar appeared to feel softer against her back. His tongue flicked rapidly over the hard bud of her clitoris. She felt as if she were floating on some gentle cloud, drifting through the mist towards some unknown destination. She pushed her hips upward but could still only feel his fluttering tongue playing over her aching pussy. The softness beneath her seemed to envelop her entire body and she began to feel the dampness of her sweat as it ran in little rivulets across her skin.

She wanted his cock inside her again. It would be real, this time. She needed to wrap her long legs around his thrusting body and dig her heels into his firm buttocks and tear at his back with her fingers. Above all, she wanted to come.

The slippery touch of his long tongue gradually

became lighter until it was barely noticeable. Boudicca opened her eyes. A torch flickered faintly on a nearby wall. She sat up suddenly and looked around. As her vision cleared, she realised that she was no longer lying prone on the stone altar. She was alone in her bedchamber. Her lover was gone. He had faded into the night with her dream.

Three

The thin drizzle cloaked the distant hills like a shroud and Suetonius watched impatiently as the soldiers wearily laboured to set up the encampment. The rain was trickling down the back of his neck but he had become immune to its irritation. His horse snorted and blew out a cloud of steamy breath that hung momentarily in the air like a ghost before fading into nothingness. Suetonius drew his soaking-wet cloak around his body. His tent had been the first to be erected and the fire would have been lit inside it. Soon he would be warm again.

'Doesn't the sun ever shine in this pitiless land?' It was Catus who spoke as he drew up alongside his shivering colleague. Suetonius regarded him with a frown as water dripped from his eyebrows. He shrugged. The question clearly didn't require an answer. 'What is this place?' continued Catus as he surveyed the dismal scene before them.

'It is known as High Cross,' replied Suetonius. 'We are close to halfway from our destination.'

'Halfway? We have been marching for days! Your men will be good for nothing when they reach Londinium.'

'It will be worth it, when we arrive. The people of that good city are friendly and welcoming and the women are particularly accommodating.'

57

Catus slipped from his mount and his boots sank into the mud. He cursed under his breath and struggled to stand on a clump of grass. 'I could do with the company of an accommodating woman right now,' he grumbled as he kicked clumps of mud from his heels.

Suetonius grinned. Similar thoughts had not been far from his own mind. He slipped from his horse and took care not to step into the quagmire. He patted Catus lightly on the shoulder. 'Come, friend,' he said, 'our tent is ready. Let us bathe and attempt to warm our bones.'

The two men trudged through the mud and headed for the relative haven of the hastily erected shelter. Once inside, they saw that the soldiers had done their work well. A small fire was flickering in the centre of the tent, the smoke from the damp wood drifting lazily to the roof where it hung like a storm cloud before floating out through a small hole cut in the canvas. The area was filled with the thick, sweet aroma of burning pine. Two guards were preparing a bath by filling it with steaming water from jugs brought in by a procession of serving women. Suetonius and Catus divested themselves of their soaking cloaks and sat on a bench to wait for the work to be completed.

Suetonius watched the women with less than dispassionate interest. 'I'll have a couple of these fine women stay to bathe us,' he said with a grin. There was never a shortage of local women to be had whenever and wherever the legion made its encampment.

Catus laughed. 'Why only two?' he said, 'it has been three days since I last tasted the flesh of a woman. Have them all stay.'

Suetonius stretched himself stiffly. His body ached

from the long ride across the windswept hills. 'No, two will be sufficient,' he said. 'I am tired. I need to sleep.'

Catus gripped his already rising cock and pulled the loose skin roughly over the stiffening shaft. 'I'd like to see them all kneeling in a row, six tight little bottoms waiting to be impaled by my hard rod!' He rubbed himself rapidly and his stalk rose to full erection.

The women set the jugs on the ground, their task completed and waited for further instructions. Suetonius regarded them thoughtfully. Their clothes were ragged and their faces were dirty, but they were all attractive in their own way. The thought of having all six of them was tempting – but he knew that he simply would not be up to the task. He also knew that if Catus were honest with himself, nor would he. He pointed nonchalantly at two of the women and they bowed their heads while the others were quickly escorted from the tent by the guards.

Catus jumped to his feet and walked over to the two women. They raised their heads as he moved around them and looked at him through wild staring eyes. They would know their duty. Suetonius recognised the face of one of them. She was about twenty years of age with long straggly brown hair. He remembered that she had pleasured him with her full mouth, some days previously. The other woman was a little older but no less attractive. Her hair had been cut short almost to the scalp and her near-naked body was heavily tanned as evidence of years of hard work in the fields. She had no doubt joined the Romans as they had marched, as had many of her compatriots, eager for the promise of good food and adventure to relieve the drudgery of their miserable lives.

'What are your names?' asked Catus. The women remained silent. He grabbed the younger woman's hair and yanked it roughly. 'I said, what is your name? Speak!' The girl merely whimpered in response. Catus released his grip of her hair in exasperation and turned to the other woman. 'What about you? I like to know the name of a woman before I fuck her.' The girl's eyes widened at his words and Suetonius could see that her expression indicated that the thought did not displease her.

'Nina,' she said quietly.

'Nina,' parroted Catus as he put his hand to one of her breasts, which was barely covered by the thin rag that served as a dress. He looked into her eyes and she held his stare proudly. 'A feisty one, I feel,' he said with a grin.

'The other is known as Maya,' said Suetonius as he suddenly recalled the young girl's name. 'She is unable to speak.'

Catus turned to her and stroked her face gently with the back of his hand. 'Really?' he said. 'How utterly perfect.' He reached down to touch her small breasts, but the girl shrank back with a look of terror on her grubby face. He laughed and walked over towards the bath. He washed his face quickly and then turned to stand in front of the women. His cock was once more flaccid but nevertheless hung heavily between his legs. 'Bathe me,' he ordered simply.

The two servants immediately filled jugs from the bath and poured the water over him as he stood there. Suetonius watched as they soaped his friend with their hands and noted with some amusement how his cock thickened and rose under their delicate ministrations. The older woman gripped his rod and rubbed it slowly, while soaping his backside with her other hand. Catus reached down and unfastened the rope that held her dress in place. The garment fell to the floor and she moved behind him and emptied more water over his back, then wriggled her body against him.

Maya suddenly seemed to gain courage and knelt before him and stared at his thick erection. She took hold of his now fully erect cock and soaped it liberally with both of her hands, while Catus roughly tore the tattered dress from her slim body. Suetonius noted that her small buttocks jutted provocatively as she knelt and he could see the inviting promise of her sex-lips between her thighs. He recalled the delightful sensation of her tongue fluttering around his own stalk when she had held it within the warm wet envelope of her mouth. He had intended to fuck her, of course, but had surrendered to her expert sucking and licking and had filled her mouth with his cream. Tonight, it would be different. He would ram his huge cock deep inside her pussy and make her squeal.

He stood up and quickly began to remove the remainder of his uniform. Catus stood with his hands high above his head as the girls now washed his armpits. From the expression on his face he was clearly enjoying the sensation. Suetonius removed his skirt and now stood naked before the others, his cock hugely erect.

Nina was the first to notice him and her eyes widened as she stared at the swollen shaft between his legs. She moved from Catus and filled a jug with water from the bath. She smiled as she walked over to Suetonius and he gazed lustfully at her large firm breasts, which bobbed heavily as she moved.

'My lord?' she said sweetly.

He nodded and she poured the warm water over his shoulders. She took up the soap and rubbed it rapidly between the palms of her hands and then

61

smoothed it over his chest and back. Her touch was delightfully sensuous. He closed his eyes to savour the sensation and she continued to soap him from head to foot, while carefully managing to avoid touching his genitals. She was teasing him and he knew it, but he didn't complain. The feeling of having the day's sweat and filth removed from his body was pleasurable enough, at least for the present.

He opened his eyes and looked across at Catus. Maya was still kneeling before him and gently sucking his hard stalk. He looked back at Nina. His cock was jutting forward immensely, the head inches from her belly. She soaped her hands liberally and then began to caress the lather into his hairy groin. She smoothed the soap around his thick stalk and then slowly moved her palms along its length, before gripping it tightly with both hands. His cock throbbed heavily and a stream of his fluid jetted from it to soak her stomach.

He knew that he would not be able to last long while undergoing such delightful ministrations. He caught her by the wrists and pulled her hands from him. She looked at him quizzically but he patted her arms and moved to kneel behind Maya. He watched her for a few moments, seeing her head bob backward and forward as she sucked his friend's cock, and then he shuffled forward and pressed the head of his stiff rod to her soft, open sex-lips. He heard Maya's muffled groan as he slid the long thick shaft into her succulent, hot sheath, until his groin was pressed hard against her pert little backside. He fucked her slowly, not wishing to come. He wanted to prolong the delightful sensation of the tight fleshy grip around his aching cock.

Apart from her initial groan of pleasure, the girl didn't appear to notice as he plundered her welcoming depths. She continued to suck Catus as though she were oblivious to the fact that she had a huge stalk moving steadily in and out of her cunt. Suetonius eased himself from her and rose to his feet. Maya continued to orally pleasure Catus without giving as much as a brief glance over her shoulder. He slapped her bottom playfully and then turned to face Nina.

Nina looked up at him and smiled. Her eyes were shining with lust. She crouched down in front of him and once more began to caress his cock smoothly with both of her soapy hands. He watched as she opened her mouth; then he took a deep breath as she took the bulbous head between her lips. He throbbed again and sensed her tongue moving against his hard stalk as she swallowed. She began to rub his stem rhythmically with her hands whilst she sucked him. He sensed her tongue lapping around him and her thick lips gripped his hardness firmly, as if trying to draw him deeper within their heavenly clasp.

He heard Catus groan and glanced round to see Maya frantically rubbing his friend's cock as his juices jetted from him to soak her face. It was too much for Suetonius. He grasped the back of Nina's head and forced himself forward so that over half of his length slipped into her mouth and down her throat. He came with a low moan and thrilled as she swallowed his cream, the undulating movements of her throat muscles heightening the glorious sensations. Nina rubbed his stem rapidly and squeezed his balls tightly with her other hand as if to draw every drop of juice from within his body.

Eventually, he pushed her away and his cock flopped heavily against his thigh. His legs were trembling and his heart was pounding inside his chest. It was the only way to bathe.

* * *

Suetonius peered from the tent in disbelief. The sun was streaming down from a cloudless sky and, for once, the aspect of the landscape was anything but grey. He cursed his misfortune. It could have been the first good marching day that the legion had experienced since setting off on the long trek from Mona, but they had to wait until General Plutius joined them with his forces from the north. It would have been foolhardy to venture to Londinium alone, if the Iceni army was as large as Catus had informed him, but nevertheless the delay was maddening.

He turned back and re-entered the tent. Catus and the two serving-girls lay asleep on a blanket, oblivious to the cacophony of noises coming from outside as the camp began to awaken. Nina was lying with Catus' limp cock in her mouth and with Maya's face buried between her legs, while Catus himself was resting his head on the soft furry cushion of Maya's pussy. Suetonius smiled to himself. He had drifted off into a deep sleep almost immediately after filling Nina's lovely mouth with his seed but Catus was never one to be denied his pleasures. Suetonius had woken during the night to be met with the sight of his friend firmly impaling Maya's pert little bottom with his thick stalk, while Nina was happily lapping her tongue between his buttocks. He had been tempted to join them but had thought better of it. He had genuinely needed to rest.

He reached down and took up a bucket of icy water. 'Catus,' he called. 'Catus Decianus!' His friend barely stirred. Suetonius unceremoniously threw the contents of the bucket over the sleeping trio, who immediately jumped into consciousness and struggled from the ground.

'By the gods! What the . . .' Catus spluttered.

Suetonius laughed raucously. 'Come, friend, it is morning. We have much to do.'

Catus angrily grabbed a piece of white linen and used it to dry himself off before wrapping it tightly around his loins. 'Curse you, Suetonius Paulinus!' he barked, 'Could you not have merely shaken me awake?'

'Where is the fun in that?' laughed his friend. Catus growled back at him and stepped out of the tent to take a piss. Suetonius looked back at the two girls, who were huddled together on the wet blanket. Nina smiled at him nervously but he ignored her. They didn't look so attractive in the cold light of day.

Catus returned and retrieved his skirt from the haphazard pile of clothing on the floor. He removed the linen from around his waist and Nina reached up and touched him lightly on the thigh. He pushed her hand away and threw the rags that the girls had worn the night before at her, then summarily dismissed the pair of them with a casual wave of his hand. The two naked women grabbed their dresses and scurried out of the tent.

'I thought that you might wish to indulge yourself again,' said Suetonius, somewhat taken aback by his friend's callous attitude.

'I tired of them quickly,' said Catus disdainfully. 'They are just whores.'

Suetonius shrugged and busied himself by polishing his sword while Catus dressed. His thoughts returned once more to Boudicca, Queen of the Iceni. He tried to imagine her as Catus had described her: tall, with long red hair and massive breasts. The lack of further detail enabled him to conjure up a vision of his own of her flawless features and sumptuous body. He allowed his hand to wander up his skirt and he fondled his lengthening cock as he formed a mental picture of this strange wild woman submitting her lovely body to his every demand. He imagined her shackled to a bench, her long legs splayed wide apart and her huge breasts bouncing heavily as he fucked her mercilessly.

'Have you ever impaled a Nubian woman?' Catus spoke suddenly, snapping him from his fantasy.

Suetonius pulled his hand from his skirt quickly. 'Er, no; no, I haven't,' he replied.

'You should, my friend; it is well worth it.'

'What is so different about the Nubian women, apart from the colour of their skin?' In truth, Suetonius had rarely seen one of these exotic creatures, except in the slave markets of Rome, and he hadn't really thought about it.

'The colour is an attraction in itself. The sight of flawless sable skin can turn a man's rod to iron.'

'I take it that you have had such an encounter?' said Suetonius lamely.

Catus sat down on the bench next to him. It was obvious that he was itching to tell his tale. 'Only once, sadly,' he began, 'but it was an experience that will stay with me for the rest of my life. It was back in Rome. I was staying at the house of a friend, the merchant Maximus Lubus. We were about to eat a meal when this vision of perfection entered the room carrying a tray of fruit. She was tall, and her skin was as black as the night. She wore little, save for a simple white dress that barely covered her shapely form. Her breasts were large and firm and the nipples could be clearly seen – long, thick buds that begged for attention. But it was her bottom . . . oh, that bottom! It was large but in no way plump. It seemed to jut out from her in the most enticing fashion. It was almost arrogant in its firm swell.'

'Your preference for a woman's rear is well known, Catus,' laughed Suetonius.

'Indeed,' continued his friend, 'but this was like no

other behind that I had ever seen before. I simply couldn't help but stare at it as she walked around the table, serving us with the fruit. Her buttocks moved as though they possessed a life of their own. I ached to reach out and touch them and to feel the firmness of those delectable globes.'

'So what happened?' asked Suetonius, warming to the story himself.

'She came next to me and bent to serve me. Her scent was intoxicating. It was a mixture of exotic oils and the aroma of pure woman. I was tempted to touch her but decided that my host might take offence. She bent further forward and I caught sight of the deep cleavage between her breasts. My eyes became transfixed by the two melon-sized globes. She coughed lightly and I looked up at her face and, at first, thought that she had realised that I had been gazing at her in such a brazen and unashamed manner. I looked down in embarrassment and saw to my horror, however, that my pego was standing rigidly to attention, completely free of my toga. She could see it, too; there was no way that she could have missed it.

'I covered myself quickly and grabbed a bunch of grapes from her tray and then turned my back to her, as though nothing had happened. She continued to serve the other guests and then was gone from the room. The meal was ruined for me; conversation was hopeless. All I could think of was her wonderful bottom and those lovely big breasts.'

'What was her face like?' asked Suetonius wryly.

Catus laughed. 'I did see her face, friend, despite what you may think of me. Her eyes were large and of the deepest brown. Her cheekbones were high and regal and her mouth was large, with the thickest pouting lips that I had ever seen. She was, my friend, quite the most beautiful creature that I had ever set my eyes upon.

'I retired to my bed soon after the meal was over. I had drunk too much wine and was feeling exhausted. I lay on my bed and tried to sleep, but I couldn't get the picture of the Nubian serving-girl out of my mind. I decided I had to do something for myself, or I knew that I would not get any sleep at all. I threw back the sheet and began to rub myself. I closed my eyes and pictured the sight of my lovely Nubian kneeling before me on the bed and presenting her wonderful bottom to me. I tried to imagine what it would be like to force my cock between those two sumptuous globes and to penetrate her sweet arsehole.

'Suddenly, I had the distinct feeling that I was not alone. I grabbed the sheet and covered myself and then sat up. It was her. She was standing at the door holding another tray, this time carrying a bottle of wine and a goblet. I was sure that she must have seen that I was pulling myself, but she gave no indication that that was the case. She walked slowly towards me, her wide mouth turned into a luscious smile. "I thought you might like some more wine," she said, in a voice that sounded like the song of an angel. I told her that I had had sufficient but she set the tray down on a table and turned to face me. I looked up and down at her sumptuous form. Her nipples seemed even more prominent than before and I could just make out the dark promise of the curls between her legs, through the thin material of that little white dress.

'She asked me if there was anything else that she could do for me. By the gods, was there? I wanted to order her to tear off her dress and sit on my face so that I could lap between her perfect buttocks, but I merely shook my head. I had never been at a loss for words in the presence of a woman before, but the beauty of this vision standing before me entranced me.

'She stood silently for what seemed like an eternity. My cock was so hard it was aching. Suddenly, she sat down on the edge of the bed and started to pull the sheet from my body. "What are you doing?" I asked, but she simply smiled and removed the sheet altogether. I just lay there, looking down stupidly at my erect dick. She glanced at it also, then looked back at my face and smiled again. It was then that I knew that my dreams were about to be fulfilled and I prayed that I would not come before I had had the chance to penetrate her lovely body.

'She bent forward and kissed me lightly on the mouth. Her lips felt like a deep, warm cushion against mine. She pushed her tongue into my mouth and pressed her lips harder against me; I circled her long neck with my arm and hugged her tightly. I felt her fingertips stroking my chest and then they moved slowly down over my belly. She inched nearer and nearer to my cock, which was so hard I felt that it would burst. I ran my free hand down her long, slim back as I felt her circle my raging stalk with her fingers. I traced the firm swell of her buttocks. At last I was touching it, that perfect bottom! My cock throbbed under her gentle caress. She moved her face away from me and I looked down. A thin streak of cream was trickling over her fingers as she steadily pumped my rod. I was so close to coming that I felt like crying.

'I gripped her wrist to stop her rubbing me. My cock throbbed again and a jet of sperm shot from the end and streaked along the full length of her forearm. She looked into my eyes, her expression one of abject disappointment. I reassured her by telling her that I hadn't come and then she let go of my cock and raised her arm to her mouth and licked my juices from her skin. We kissed again. The feeling of her lips against mine was truly wondrous. The softness of her fleshy mouth appeared to engulf mine and her tongue worked miracles as it lapped around my own. I let my fingertips trace the cleft between her buttocks and she moaned softly as they brushed against her anus. Even through the material of her dress, I could feel every contour and every delightful detail.

'I moved my hand down further and tucked it under the hem of her garment. I was now touching the bare skin of her thigh. It felt silky smooth, as though her body had been lightly oiled. I moved my hand upwards until my fingertips were able to trace under the curve of her bottom and then I pushed my fingers between her thighs. I brushed them lightly across the soft fleshy lips of her pussy. To my delight, I discovered that they were soaking wet.

'She moved from me and stood by the bed. She grinned broadly and I could plainly see that her eyes were shining with lust. She reached down and gripped the hem of her flimsy dress and then slowly pulled the garment up to reveal her naked body. Removing the dress completely, she tossed it on the floor and then stood looking at me, as if seeking my approval. Her body was superb in every way. Her breasts thrust forward without a trace of sag, despite their size, and her nipples jutted like ebony studs from large puffy areolae. Her narrow waist accentuated the broad sweep of her hips, which framed the dark curls between her long, curvaceous legs. This was a body that had been created for just one thing – to be fucked.

'I reached out and gently stroked her belly with the

backs of my fingers. Her skin shone with a glorious sheen that seemed to glow in the soft light of the moon, which bathed the room with its silvery glow. I took hold of her hand and coaxed her towards me. She knelt on the edge of the bed and glanced down at my hardness, then looked back at my face. Her smile was mischievous and intoxicating. I would have died for this enticing stranger at that moment.

'She moved me to lie on my front and then knelt between my legs. She began to stroke and knead the flesh of my back as if to massage away the aches of the day's labours. I felt her lick my shoulders and then she moved her tongue slowly down my spine, while at the same time smoothing the palms of her hands over my skin. She cupped my buttocks with her hands and then eased them apart with her thumbs, just as her tongue reached the top of the cleft between them. I gritted my teeth, once more terrified that I would lose control and soak the bed beneath my groin.

'Her tongue tickled the hairs between my buttocks as it slipped steadily downwards. I took a deep breath just as the tip of her tongue touched my anus. She licked around it and then I felt her pushing it inside my tight hole. If ever I was close to an unwanted ejaculation, it was at that moment. The joy of feeling the long tongue move quickly in and out of me, coupled with the knowledge that soon I would be giving her the same pleasure was almost too much to bear.

'After some delicious moments, she drew her tongue from inside me and lapped gently over my balls, then licked upwards along the full length of my cleft. She turned me to lie on my back. I propped myself up on the pillows and we kissed, a long and passionate embrace. I tasted myself on her lips and it felt good.

'Presently, she moved back from me and gazed once more down at my bone-hard cock. She was kneeling between my legs and her breasts were hanging heavily, the nipples almost touching my thighs. She took hold of my stalk and bent forward so that her luscious mounds were crushed against my legs. I watched as she pushed out her tongue and licked the ridge of my cock; then she parted her lips and engulfed the head within her hot mouth. The sight of her thick black lips enveloping my rod was an image that I will take to my grave. The stark contrast between our skin-tones made the scene all the more erotic.

'She sucked me gently at first, clearly aware that I could come at any moment, and then arched her neck and pushed her head forward until my entire length was held within the fleshy grip of her mouth. I had never been served in such a way before! I wondered how she could manage to breathe with my thick dick down her throat, but she was evidently quite expert at the task. She pressed her lips against my groin and I could feel her swallowing against my flesh. I desperately wanted to come, to fill her sweet, sucking mouth with my cream, but I also wanted to fuck her more than life itself.

'As if sensing my need, she raised her head and let my cock slip from her wet mouth. She kissed the tip and smiled up at me. I stroked the short black curls on her head lovingly. Due to the way that she was positioned, I could see the firm swell of her delightful bottom. I reached over her back and fondled the tops of her buttocks. I felt her take my cock into her mouth again and I lay back against the pillows to watch her. Such a vision! I cannot begin to describe how I felt as I gazed at her, seeing her head bob up and down as she fucked her face with my hard stalk.

'Eventually, she raised herself once more and then moved to lie beside me on her stomach. I ran my hand down her back, over the thrusting curve of her bottom and then down along her thighs. I moved to kneel between her legs and gazed in awe at her wonderful arse. I bent forward and kissed her buttocks in turn, then began to lick the sumptuous globes. The taste of her fresh sweat invaded my senses. She shifted herself to a kneeling position and pushed her bottom against my face. I licked her hot cunt and then let my tongue slide up and down over her anus. I heard her moan softly. She clearly took as much pleasure in such treatment as I had when she had done the same thing to me.

'I pushed my tongue into her and she gasped with delight. I tongue-fucked her arse for some minutes, while fingering the sopping lips of her pussy. I found her hard bud with the tips of my fingers. It was far larger than any that I had known before. I rubbed it rapidly, while continuing to slip my tongue in and out of her bottom. She came in seconds. Her body shook and she groaned loudly as her juices soaked my chin. I continued to rub her until her moans of joy became whimpers and then I sat back. I stroked her wet bottom gently and waited for her to calm herself.

'She looked over her shoulder and thrust her backside upwards. "Fuck me," she said. "Fuck me now!" I was not accustomed to receiving orders from a servant but this was one I fully intended to obey. I shuffled forwards and aimed the head of my cock at the open lips of her cunt. I pushed inside her in one slow and easy movement until her flesh engulfed my full length. I held myself still, gripping her buttocks tightly. I could feel my cock throbbing inside her. I bit my lower lip hard and tore my gaze away from her backside. I looked around the room and focused on anything that could take my mind off her for the moment.

'Gradually, my need for release eased and I began to slowly fuck her. She matched my movements exactly, pushing her bottom backwards and forwards gently. I looked down. Her arsehole was wet with her juices and my saliva. I eased my thumb into the tight little sphincter and she moaned again. I eased my cock out of her completely and then plunged it back in to the hilt, causing her to gasp with delight. I repeated this movement over and over again, watching with fascination as her cunt-lips seemed to snap each time at the withdrawing head of my tool, as though desperately trying not to release it from her heavenly grip. I reached under her and found her hard bud with my fingertips. I rubbed it rapidly, while hammering my cock in and out of her pussy. Her moans rose into a crescendo of cries as she came again. She gripped the head of the bed and squealed with delight and I knew that I had served her well. I rammed my stalk fully into her and held still, gripping her tightly by the waist.

'At last, she calmed down and I began to move gently in and out of her again. I eased a finger into her bottom and then another and another. Slowly, I sensed the muscles of the tight little hole becoming relaxed and I knew that she was ready. I slipped my fingers out of her arse and bent down to soak her inviting sphincter with my saliva. I aimed the head of my cock at her ultimate prize and pushed forward. It slipped into her as easily as it had entered her hot cunt. She was evidently well used to such pleasures. I inched forward carefully until the full length was held within the grip of her wonderful sheath. My cock throbbed again and my juices helped to ease my movements as I began to fuck that wonderful bottom.

I slapped one of her buttocks hard with the palm of my hand and she yelped with delight. I slapped her again and again, seeing her dark skin begin to redden. The more I smacked her bottom, the more she moaned with pleasure.

'She began to move against me with an urgency that thrilled me. It was clear that she was thoroughly enjoying every moment; I began to hammer into her like a man possessed. My stalk felt harder than it had ever done before and I knew that soon I would be lost. Her buttocks rippled enticingly as I pounded my groin against them, and I could hear her breasts slapping together rhythmically in time with my thrusts. I could feel that wonderful tightness at the root of my cock and the entire length became inflamed with the need for release. I fucked her faster and faster as the surge within my stalk grew to a gut-wrenching climax. I came deep inside her fabulous bottom and the thumping within my cock seemed to go on forever as I filled her tightly gripping sheath with my hot cream. I sensed her clawing at her pussy with her fingers and heard her groan loudly as she joined me in my ecstasy.

'Gradually, my stalk began to wilt and I eased it from within her tightness. We lay together on our backs, staring at the ceiling. We were both covered in sweat and gasping for air. My cock ached and felt damp between my legs. I turned my head and looked at her. Her breasts rose and fell heavily as she breathed. She was truly a beautiful woman.

'After a while, she slipped from the bed and retrieved her dress. I watched as she pulled the garment over her head and then as she smoothed the material over her wonderful body. She bent over and kissed the end of my cock lightly before giving me one last smile and then she left as silently as she had arrived. I lay my head back on my pillow and pondered over the events of the previous moments. It had been amazing but it had been over too quickly, far too quickly. Trust me, Suetonius: you have not fucked until you have savoured the delights of such a woman.'

Suetonius sat quietly as he considered his friend's tale, resting his sword heavily across his lap in order to stop his stiff erection from bursting from under his skirt. 'That was quite a story,' he said eventually.

'And a true one, friend,' said Catus. 'I have often longed to repeat such an experience.'

'Did you not see the woman again?'

Catus regarded him as though he had said something incredibly ridiculous. 'Of course not,' he answered. 'I had fucked her. Why see her again?'

Suetonius shrugged. His friend's complete disdain for members of the opposite sex was as legendary as his prowess as a soldier. 'I had an experience many years ago which I would dearly love to repeat,' he said after a moment.

Catus seemed uninterested. He walked over to the front of the tent and raised the flap. 'I can't believe that the sun is shining,' he said.

'Do you want to hear my story?' said Suetonius in an exasperated tone.

Catus returned and sat on a bench opposite him. 'Of course, friend,' he said with a grin, 'but I can't believe that it will surpass the tale that I have just told you.'

'It may not surpass it, but my experience was different in many ways. For one thing, it involved three women, and they were as alike as peas in a pod.'

'Three women? Triplets?'

'Indeed.' Suetonius sat back proudly, eager to begin his tale. 'They were part of a troupe of acrobats from the Orient. They visited the palace of Caesar two years back and gave the most illuminating performance. The men were extremely strong, despite being slight of build, and their feats bordered on the impossible. But it was the three girls who captivated the audience with their dancing and cavorting. They were identical in every way, with their long black hair, their lithe little bodies and their angelic faces.

'The suppleness of their bodies was astounding. Some of the positions that they were able to bend themselves into defied belief. Their slim forms were entirely swathed in tight white silk which revealed every crevice and every curve. They would stretch themselves on to their backs or curl their legs under themselves so that the shapes of their tiny little pussies were clearly displayed for all to savour. By the end of their show, my cock was as hard as bone.

'I had found favour with Caesar that year and considered that I was able to make my desires known to him. I approached him and quietly suggested that I would dearly like to spend some time alone with one of the triplets. He agreed to my request but demanded that I take my pleasure with all three of them, and there and then, in full view of the court. I had never as much as fucked just one woman before an audience, let alone three, and the thought delighted me. The men of the troupe were approached and, I assume, were paid handsomely, for there was no complaint. The three girls were brought before me. They bowed low and then stood together in a row, their faces flushed with excitement.

'I signalled for them to remove their costumes. They obeyed immediately. Their breasts were tiny and their nipples were small and dark brown. Their bodies were remarkably slim, without appearing to be emaciated, and their legs were long and appealingly muscular. The most delightful thing about them, however, was that their little pussies were all completely devoid of hair. Their sex-lips were already engorged with their excitement and were all pouting invitingly.

'I stood up, kicked off my sandals and removed my toga. My cock was standing stiff and proud. The three girls stared at it, their expressions a mixture of wonder and delight. I heard someone say, "He'll split them in two!" and I smiled vainly. I have always been delighted that fate had dealt me such a magnificent weapon.'

'Go on with your story,' said Catus wearily.

Suetonius grinned. He was well used to his friend's envy. 'I stepped down and stood in front of the three girls. One of them reached out cautiously and slipped her fingers around the root of my stalk. Her hand looked tiny against me. The other two followed suit, until I had three small hands gripping my cock at the same time. I reached down and slipped a finger of each hand into a soft, wet pussy. I stirred the juicy flesh around, as if preparing it for what was to come. Not to be outdone, the third girl let go of my cock and raised herself up in one practised movement, until she was sitting astride her two sisters' shoulders, with her legs splayed wide apart and with her stretched cunt inches from my mouth. The crowd cheered as I bent my head forward and licked the sweet juice from her puffy lips, while I continued to finger the other two girls.

'The girl that I was licking let her body fall backwards until she gripped her sister's ankles. I chewed and guzzled her sex-lips with renewed vigour and delved my tongue deep into her hot little pussy. The other girls were squirming on my fingers and rubbing my cock rapidly. Suddenly, the girl on their

78

shoulders flipped her legs back and landed squarely on her feet, then fell to her knees behind the others. She pushed between the two girls and took the head of my erection into her small mouth and began to suck me expertly. Her sisters knelt on either side of her and proceeded to lick the sides of my shaft. After some moments of this delightful treatment, each of them raised one of their legs high so that they both stood with one foot on the floor and the other resting against my chest. I dipped my fingers into the open purses of their pussies while all three of them continued to lick and suck my rampant erection.

'The triplets moved with amazing precision and grace. It became quickly apparent that this was not their first performance of such an intimate nature. They bade me to lie on my back on the marble floor and one of them sat astride me. She took the full length of my cock inside her hot little cunt without the slightest grimace or complaint. She leant right back and began to nuzzle and suck the toes of one of my feet. My cock was so hard that the position hurt me somewhat but I endured it, more from the novelty of the situation than anything else. The other two girls squatted over my face with the fronts of their bodies pressed close together and lowered themselves so that I had the delightful task of licking two shaven pussies simultaneously. Their juices flowed copiously and soaked my mouth, chin and neck.

'The girl who was sitting on my lap eased herself from me and my cock slapped hard against my stomach. Immediately, a second girl slipped her body down over my chest and absorbed my stalk inside her hot little sheath. The third girl pressed her pussy hard against my mouth and I sucked her wet flesh greedily. She came with a muted squeal and then fell from me. The first girl took her place immediately and I repeated the action with her until she, too, climaxed in my mouth, while the third girl happily bounced her lithe body up and down on my hard rod.

'After a few moments, we all disentangled ourselves and stood up. One of the girls immediately turned her back to me and bent forward to present me with a tantalising view of her cute little bottom. I stood behind her and aimed the head of my prick towards her open sex-lips –'

'You mean you didn't fuck her arse?' interrupted Catus, with an astonished look on his face.

'You know that is *your* preference, friend. Each to their own.'

Catus shrugged. 'I know what I would have done,' he said glumly. 'Anyway, pray continue.'

'As I said, the girl was bending over in front of me with her legs held straight and slightly apart. I eased my cock slowly into her soft, hot sheath until my groin pressed against her tight little bottom. It was then that it happened. The girl bent herself double and tucked her head between her legs and, the next thing I knew, she was licking my balls! I couldn't believe it. The sensation was astounding and the sight of her stretched pussy and curved body was something to behold, I can tell you!

'I fucked her gently, not wanting to stop her from lapping her tongue over me. One of the other girls put her hands on the top of my head and suddenly raised herself so that she was sitting squarely on my shoulders, with her pussy once more offered delightfully to my mouth. I accepted the invitation with pleasure and started to lick the soft lips of her sex and flick my tongue against her hard little bud. My joy was completed when the third girl began to lap against my backside.

'I couldn't hold back any longer. I felt that

wonderful, unremitting surge build up between my legs and I began to thrust heavily in and out of the tight little cunt that so wonderfully gripped my throbbing stalk. I came with a muffled groan and bit the succulent lips that were pressed against my mouth, which caused the girl to squeal with pain and delight. The sperm jetted from me to fill the hot sheath as I rammed in and out of her sister.

'Eventually I was done and I staggered back to my seat and acknowledged the rapturous applause of the audience. The girls' tasks were by no means over, of course. My demonstration had merely been a taste of things to come. Soon there was not a clothed body in the hall and I watched with detached interest as the triplets demonstrated their talents with as many lusty males as they could manage.'

Catus slapped his friend heartily on the back. 'A fine story, Suetonius, true or not.'

Suetonius shrugged. 'Believe what you like,' he said with a wry smile.

Four

A wave of nervous apprehension coursed through Boudicca's body as she once again trod the long winding path towards the grove of the druids. The dream had been too real; she needed to learn the truth. Above all, she had to understand why she had submitted so readily to Arman's sexual demands, and why she had seemingly enjoyed being subjugated by so many men at one time.

The night sounds of the wooded area surrounded her and the air felt distinctly cold. She shivered and drew her long cloak about her and, for a brief moment, seriously considered that she might return to the encampment. Her need to satisfy her burning curiosity was too powerful, however. The words spoken by Arman in her dream had seemed so real. She had to know if her vision had been prophetic or merely the wanderings of her exhausted mind.

This time, there was no sign of the mist billowing in from the sea as she approached the ancient stones. Arman was standing in their shadows, drinking from an ornate goblet and talking amiably to a hooded colleague. Boudicca stopped short and waited. After a few moments, Arman must have sensed her presence for he swung round suddenly to face her. Recognising her, the two men fell to their knees and bowed their heads in subservience. The queen smiled proudly to herself. The dream had been ridiculous. There was no way that these men would have had the courage to take her body so roughly or treat her with such apparent disdain.

'My queen!' exclaimed Arman as he rose to his feet. 'To what do we owe such an honour?'

Boudicca stepped forward and held out her hand. Arman took hold of her fingers and kissed them lightly. 'Greetings, Arman,' she said. 'I have need of your counsel.'

'Why did you not send for me, my queen? I would have come to your side immediately.'

'There was no time. Come, we must speak privately.'

Arman waved his colleague away and offered Boudicca his arm. She rested her hand lightly on his wrist and they walked towards the altar. She eyed the rough stone nervously, remembering the feel of its cold, unyielding surface rubbing against her nakedness in her dream. She tugged her cloak protectively across her chest.

Arman sat on the altar and beckoned for her to sit beside him. It seemed strange to her that he should treat such a holy object with such apparent disregard and she decided to remain standing. The druid looked up at her and the moonlight caught his piercing stare. Boudicca felt her mouth become dry. 'The Romans have fled,' she began hoarsely. 'Should we follow them and see that our lands are freed of their tyranny forever?'

'Why ask me?' replied Arman casually. 'I am no soldier.'

'You are wise, and you have consort with the spirits of the dead. Who better to advise me?' Boudicca said the words with little conviction, knowing that she would never normally seek such counsel from the druids. She just had to hear what he said and to see if his words matched those in her dream.

'You must take the capital. That should be your prize. As long as the Romans hold the city, there will be no victory for you.' Arman's advice was obvious but it was not what she wanted to hear.

'What of Verulamium?' she asked suddenly.

'What of it?' Arman spoke quickly, and Boudicca sensed that he was hiding something.

'I have heard stories about that wretched town,' she answered. She was goading him but was also taking care not to put words into his mouth. He looked down at the ground uncomfortably. 'Speak, druid,' she commanded. 'What do you know?'

Arman looked back up at her. His expression was one of both concern and confusion. 'I had a dream, my queen,' he began slowly, 'a dream so clear that it seemed to break the boundaries of reality. In this dream I spoke to you and told you of the people of Verulamium, and of how they have chosen to fall in with the Romans. But it was just a dream, nothing more.'

'What else happened in your dream?' asked Boudicca, her heart pounding in her chest. Arman looked startled.

'Nothing, majesty, nothing more!' His protest was too vehement and his voice was trembling.

'You are lying! What else?'

'I cannot say, majesty,' he pleaded. 'You would have me put to death!'

Boudicca smiled to herself. His weakness pleased her. How he had appeared so enigmatically powerful in her own vision astounded her. 'I will see to it that you are thrashed if you do not speak the truth,' she barked.

Arman shook his head. 'I cannot, I cannot,' he

whimpered. Boudicca grasped the hair at the back of his head and tugged it back. Their eyes met and, for a moment, she felt the strength of his frightened gaze draining her. She released her grip and stepped back.

'I will not harm you if you speak the truth,' she said, quietly. The softness of her words seemed to calm his uneasiness.

'We kissed, majesty,' he said, his voice quivering with emotion. 'I embraced you and we kissed.'

'Is that all?' Boudicca waited for his reply but Arman looked back at the ground and said nothing. 'I said, is that all?' she repeated angrily. He glanced up at her again and she felt a sudden surge of warmth between her legs as their eyes met. She took a deep breath, determined not to show her discomfort.

'We made love, my queen,' he said at last. 'Here, on this altar.'

There was a long silence. Boudicca saw that his hands were shaking and she felt a warm satisfaction in her power over the man. She determined to satisfy herself by subjugating him completely. 'I had the same dream,' she said. He looked up at her quickly, a startled expression on his face. 'In my vision, it was not only you that took me,' she continued. 'There were others. Is that how it was?'

Arman nodded. 'All the druids took you, majesty,' he said quietly, as though ashamed. 'All of them.'

Boudicca suddenly felt an uncontrollable surge of desire coursing through her body. She unfastened her cloak and let the heavy garment fall open to reveal her nakedness underneath. She drew back the cloak and held it against her waist. 'Is this how you saw me, Arman?' she asked in a haughty regal tone. He stared at her and his mouth fell open. She thrust her huge breasts forward proudly and grinned as she saw him gaze at them through wide, lustful eyes.

'M-majesty,' he stuttered, 'you are beautiful!'

'Have your druids come to us,' she ordered. 'Have them stand and watch while I take you upon the altar.' Arman said nothing, but simply continued to stare at the massive swell of her firm mounds. 'Fetch them!' she barked. 'Fetch them all.'

He jumped quickly from his seat and scurried into the darkness. Boudicca slipped the cloak from her shoulders and smoothed it carefully over the stone altar, then lay herself on top of it and adopted what she considered to be a provocative pose in readiness for her lover. She touched herself between her legs. She was wet, very wet, and more than ready to impale herself on his thick shaft. She wondered if it would be as big as it had appeared to be in her dream. She imagined him lying prone on the altar, while she pounded her body up and down on his groin, his eyes transfixed by her shaven pussy or her breasts. She would be in complete control and would give him no quarter. His priests would watch while she enslaved their master with her sexuality.

She caressed herself gently between her thighs and began to pull at the fleshy lips of her sex. The nerve endings became inflamed with desire and the agonising need to be chafed by the rough surface of a long, thick cock engulfed within their succulent grip. She stared impatiently into the darkness. Why was he taking so long? She needed him – now. She wanted his body beneath her and she yearned to feel his hardness inside her, stretching her as it probed her intimate depths.

The moments became long minutes and still Arman did not return. The mist was beginning to drift in from the sea and the moon gradually faded into a shimmering, ghostly light. Boudicca sat up and wrapped the cloak around her. She peered into the gloom but there was no sign of movement. 'Arman! Where are you?' she called.

There was no reply. The mist thickened rapidly and she began to feel somewhat afraid. She cursed her decision to come to the grove alone. 'Arman!' she cried again. 'Arman! Come to me! I command it.'

She stared again into the thickening swirling mist. Suddenly she saw them. Their forms were as shadowy as ghosts: tall hooded figures appearing from the fog like creatures returning from the realm of the dead. Boudicca gripped her cloak tightly to her throat. 'Arman? Is that you?' she called. Her voice drifted into the mist and was lost forever.

The tallest of the figures stepped forward and stood at the foot of the altar. He drew back his hood to reveal his face. It was Arman, as she had expected, but his expression was now strangely powerful and the stare in his eyes seemed to be piercing into her mind with an almost irresistible force. Boudicca swallowed hard and then took a deep breath. The coolness of the air in her lungs seemed to give her new-found courage. She lay back on the altar and allowed her cloak to fall once more from her shoulders. 'Arman,' she said in a strong tone, 'order your druids to surround the altar and then come to me.'

Arman nodded to the others and they moved slowly around her to form a circle. Boudicca smiled. It was just like her dream. Soon they would all fuck her. She would lie back on the stone and they would take her, one after the other. Her pussy and her mouth would be filled with their cream, and her desperate cravings would be satisfied. Suddenly, she realised what she was thinking. This was not how it was supposed to be! *She* was in control here, not some group of nameless, faceless priests!

She made as if to rise from the stone, but Arman quickly moved forward and rested his hand heavily on her shoulder. She looked up into his piercing blue eyes and her will failed her. Without being asked, she lay back again on the altar and let her legs fall slightly apart to reveal her vulnerability to them all. She rested her head on the hard, cold surface and closed her eyes. Her legs seemed to take on a life of their own, parting slowly until they were splayed obscenely. She felt the coolness of the mist playing across the engorged lips of her pussy. Its ethereal caress soothed her.

Suddenly, she sensed a gentle warmth blowing against her hot sex. She raised her head to see Arman kneeling between her outstretched thighs, his face almost touching her aching pussy. He was staring at her intimate treasure, admiring it. She found an enormous rage building up inside her but could not move. She knew that she wouldn't be able to resist.

But this was wrong. This was not how she had planned it. She had intended to tease him, to drive him to distraction with her body and her sensuous touch until he begged for her to allow him to penetrate her, but now she was powerless to do anything but lie there and wait.

She saw him push out his tongue and felt it lap playfully around the lips of her cunt and then trace its way down the long divide between her sex-lips. She jerked her body as the tip touched her anus and then he slid it upward again until he found her hard bud. He pressed his lips against her pussy as though he was kissing her mouth and his tongue delved inside, circling and probing within her hot flesh. She rested her head back to savour the sensation and arched her body so that her mound pressed hard against his sucking mouth.

Then he was gone from her. She raised her head again and looked at him. He was standing again at the foot of the altar, his face stern but his eyes filled with lust. He drew back his cloak and let it fall to the ground. His cock jutted upward firmly, the tip wet with his arousal. He nodded to the other druids. Immediately, they all drew back their cloaks to reveal their erections while their bodies and heads remained hidden. They began to rub themselves steadily. Boudicca looked all around her. Each of the men was doing the same thing, masturbating while staring through hidden eyes at her nakedness. She shook with a mixture of fury at their impertinence and an incongruous desire to be fucked by any or all of them. They stood dispassionately, however, gently massaging their stiff rods in ghostly unison.

She looked back at Arman. He stood motionless with his hands by his sides and his cock still firmly erect. A small trickle of semen was slipping down the length of his stalk. Boudicca desperately wanted to move over to kneel before him, take his cock into her mouth and suck the delicious cream from him, but she felt that to do so would be a sign of subservience. She remained prone and passive, waiting for him to play his game.

At last, Arman moved to kneel on the stone between her splayed legs. His cock jutted from his groin like a thick spear, ready to enter the succulence that lay inches from the shining purple head. Boudicca felt the tell-tale trickle of her juice running down along the cleft between her buttocks and knew that he would be able to see her arousal for himself. She hated finding herself in such a vulnerable position but, at the same time, craved for his stalk to thrust deep inside her body.

He moved closer and she felt the tip of his cock touch her sex-lips. She sensed them parting in open

90

invitation and cursed the way that her body was surrendering itself to him. She looked around at the others. They were all continuing to rub themselves, each one matching the others with a steady rhythm that seemed unreal in its uniformity.

The thick head of Arman's cock entered the silky purse of her cunt and she stiffened the muscles of her thighs to grip him inside her, determined to milk him quickly. He pushed the full length slowly into her until their groins met and then he held still for a moment. She could feel his thick rod throbbing heavily within the folds of flesh inside her hot sheath and knew that his arousal was intense. He began to move cautiously in and out of her. Boudicca responded by thrusting her hips heavily upward. His expression turned into a grimace and she knew that she had him. She thrust again and again, all the time watching his face. He gritted his teeth and his cock seemed to grow longer and thicker inside her. Boudicca grabbed hold of his backside with both hands and managed to worm a finger deep into his anus. That was the end for him. With a mighty roar, he came and his stalk throbbed deep inside her, the effect being to bring her to a sudden and delightful climax of her own. She sensed that she could feel the heat of his cream as it filled her and she tore at his buttocks with her fingernails until he could give her no more.

Arman pulled from her and knelt, panting between her splayed legs. Boudicca grinned. She had won. She had taken control. Suddenly, however, Arman gripped her thighs and held her tightly so that she was unable to move. He nodded to the others and almost immediately she felt the splash of hot come as a jet of semen shot across her breasts. Another and yet another followed this, until she realised that all the men who were circling her were spending over her prone body. The fluid streaked over her legs, her stomach, her breasts and her face. It was the final insult. She struggled furiously but to no avail. Arman held her until the last droplet of semen had soaked her. Despite her anger, she found herself becoming aroused and excited by this strange turn of events. Her pussy throbbed and she wished that she hadn't forced Arman to finish so quickly.

Their duty done, the druids quickly filed off into the night, their ghostly forms rapidly being engulfed by the mist. Only Arman remained. He handed her a rag with which to clean herself and then he, too, turned and disappeared into the darkness.

Boudicca sat up slowly and began to use the cloth to remove the copious streaks of white fluid from her body. A trickle of cream slipped down from her cheek to her mouth. She licked her lips and savoured the taste before wiping the reminder of the juice from her face.

Suddenly, she had the uneasy feeling that she was not alone. She looked up and saw a large black horse standing close to her. At least, she thought, Arman had the decency not to force her to walk back to the encampment after her ordeal. She donned her cloak and then moved awkwardly over to the beast, her limbs aching from holding her position on the altar. She eased herself on to the animal's back. Her hot pussy pressed against the horse's firm hide and it felt soothing. As she coaxed the animal into a light trot, the movement of its muscular back aroused her intensely, so much so that she determined that she would not sleep that night until she had savoured the feeling of at least one more bone-hard cock slipping into her insatiable sex-flesh. And this time, it would be on her terms.

* * *

The thick sea-mist cleared almost as soon as Boudicca steered her mount away from the grove of the druids. The moon was full, bathing the flat landscape with its silvery sheen and highlighting the skeletal forms of the occasional tree that stood ghostlike against the blasted landscape. The queen kicked the horse into a gallop. She clung tightly to the animal's mane, holding her bottom high from its back and feeling the soothing rush of the night air against her skin as her cloak billowed behind her.

The encampment was close and it did not take long for her to reach it, at such a speed. Deciding that she needed more time alone to reflect on the events of the evening, she rode past the fortified walls and headed out into the fens. The beast seemed to fly through the long grass and the bracken, its hooves crashing against the hard ground and occasionally sparking against stones. The faster she rode, the more her anger increased. She couldn't understand how she had allowed herself to submit to Arman's demands, especially as she had gone to him with the express intention of subjugating him.

After some time she slowed the horse to a walk. The animal's broad back rubbed heavily against her pussy, its sweat mixing with the juices that seemed to be flowing from within her like water from a spring. She hugged the beast's neck tightly and slid her crotch up and down its undulating spine. The heat within her grew to an intensity that she was beginning to find unbearable: the simple burning need to be fucked. Suddenly, she turned the animal and forced it once more into a gallop, heading back to the encampment.

The soldiers at the gate showed little surprise as their queen slipped from the steaming mount and pushed past them to enter the fortifications. They were used to her regular sojourns into the night. She headed straight for her quarters and entered, slamming the heavy door behind her. The scene that met her eyes pleased her greatly. The Nubian servant Micha was kneeling on the floor, happily sucking the stiff cock of a sturdy young man. Behind her, another youth was busily plundering the dark secrets of her plump ebony bottom with his equally hard, thick rod.

Micha made to disentangle herself when the queen entered but Boudicca indicated, with a wave of her hand, that she should continue. Micha contentedly obliged. It wasn't the first time that her mistress had witnessed her revelries. The young men seemed a little nonplussed at first, but soon relaxed as Boudicca lay back on the couch to watch. She eyed the firm rippling buttocks of the boy who was arse-fucking Micha with keen interest. She let her cloak fall open and began to finger herself. Her hand quickly became soaked with her juices. Raising one of her legs, she eased all four fingers and her thumb inside her succulent lips and then pushed hard until her hot sheath enveloped her entire hand. She clenched her fingers into a fist and started to steadily pump her arm backward and forward. The youth lying on his back was watching her with an avid and startled gaze. He had clearly never before seen a woman pleasure herself in such a manner.

The other young man was moving rapidly against Micha by now, his belly slapping noisily against her buttocks. Boudicca tried to imagine the delights that her serving-girl must be enjoying, never having been tempted to savour the joys of anal penetration herself. Micha, on the other hand, had always appeared to have a preference for such delights and, from the look on her face, she was clearly enjoying every moment. Boudicca forced her fist as deep as possible inside her aching cunt until her stretched lips gripped her tightly around her forearm. The feeling of complete fullness was excruciatingly wonderful. She rubbed her bud with the fingers of her other hand and the muscles of her groin tightened as her longed-for orgasm began to build up inside her. She tickled herself rapidly and raised both of her legs high, at the same time plunging her fist in and out of herself.

Suddenly, the youth behind Micha pulled from her and Boudicca could see the full length of his superb erection. She watched as he gripped the root of his stalk tightly and then he gasped as jet after jet of white fluid shot from the thick mushroom-shaped head to streak across the shining, sable skin of the girl's bottom. The contrast between the glistening fluid and the deep black hue of Micha's flawless skin proved too much for her to resist. She pulled her hand from herself and almost leapt over to them. She pushed the panting boy out of the way and dived her face down on to Micha's upturned backside and began to lick the bitter cream from her sweating flesh. The taste thrilled her and the gentle aroma of pure woman invaded her senses.

She paused for a moment and stared at Micha's perfect rear. The dilated greased little hole seemed to be inviting her attention. She bunched her fingers and eased all four of them into the tight sphincter. Micha moaned loudly as Boudicca pushed in to her knuckles. The young man she had been sucking moved away from her and the next thing that Boudicca felt was her cloak being raised up from behind her. She forced her bottom upward in readiness for whatever he chose to do to her. Within moments, she felt the touch of his cock against her engorged sex-lips. He pushed into her with one simple

95

movement until his groin pressed against her buttocks. Her self-fisting had opened her up considerably and, for a moment, she could barely feel his stalk inside her.

He began to move in and out, circling his hips as he thrust forward so that the tip of his cock prodded her silky flesh, sending spasms of gentle, blissful pain coursing throughout her lower body. For such a young man he was clearly expert at his task. He fucked her slowly with a steady pulsating rhythm that matched the beating of her heart. She stiffened the muscles of her upper thighs to grip him tightly and felt her inner flesh closing around his probing length. The pace of his movements increased slightly but he continued to circle himself around, sometimes pushing upward, other times downward or side to side.

Boudicca pushed her fingers in and out of Micha's anus, hearing the young servant moan happily. She licked the remaining cream from Micha's bottom and then moved her face down so that she was able to lick the girl's lush pussy. Micha reached under herself and began to rub her little bud rapidly as Boudicca dipped her tongue between the moist lips of her hot cunt and pressed her mouth hard against her. She sucked the luscious flesh between her lips and prodded her tongue rapidly in time with the movements of her fingers slipping in and out of her tight bottom.

Micha came with a squeal and her body jerked and shuddered as the spasms tore through her. The young man started to thrust his cock rapidly into Boudicca's tender wetness and she knew that her own release was imminent. She stiffened her thigh muscles again and felt his hard gnarled shaft rubbing violently against the soft tightness of her sex-flesh and she came at last.

The exquisite sensations tore through her and her thighs quickly became soaked as her fluids of delight seemed to gush from within her. Her lover pulled from her and the next thing that she felt was the heat of his sperm as it splattered over her bottom. She reached back with her free hand and smoothed the cream over her skin. The young man did the same, soaking his fingers and then massaging the wet lips of her pussy with the palm of his hand. His touch was calming, serving as a perfect end to her moments of pleasure.

Boudicca eased her fingers slowly out of Micha's bottom and sat back on the floor. The serving girl slipped forward to lie on her stomach with her head resting on her arms. The queen rose to her feet stiffly and drew her long cloak around her nakedness. The two young men looked at her questioningly, as though awaiting some sort of command. She said nothing, however, and turned swiftly and left the room. Her immediate need had been satisfied, but she was not finished yet.

As the guard unbolted the cell door, Boudicca felt a warmth within her body that she was beginning to think had deserted her. Her need to punish all men for what Arman and his druids had done to her seethed in her mind as she opened the door and stepped into the gloomy room. The guard followed her into the cell and banged the door shut behind him, the sound echoing noisily against the damp stone walls.

There were two Roman soldiers in the cell, prisoners taken earlier that day. They were standing, shackled by their wrists, so that their arms were drawn high above their heads, with their backs against the wall at the far end of the room. A single torch illuminated the area around them and accentuated the terror in their eyes as she approached them. They had been stripped of their uniforms and now hung naked from their shackles, their feet barely touching the floor. They were both young and their bodies were tanned and muscular. She regarded them with a contemptuous look on her face. They would make ideal playthings.

'Do you know who I am?' she asked haughtily. The men nodded fearfully. Boudicca grinned cruelly. 'Then you will know of my reputation, and of how the Iceni treat vermin such as you.' She turned and nodded to the guard, who handed her a long-handled whip of the type normally used to steer the horses that towed her chariots of war. She looked back at the hapless prisoners. They were trembling visibly, their eyes focused on the vicious looking lash. 'Turn them,' she commanded.

The jailer stepped forward and roughly forced the two men to face the wall. Boudicca eyed their strong backs and small bottoms with mounting excitement. 'They are unmarked,' she chastised. 'How is this?

'They are awaiting your majesty's pleasure,' replied the guard in a gruff voice.

She smiled and stepped behind the first prisoner. 'What is your name, soldier?' she said as she stroked the end of the whip-handle up the inside of his thigh.

'Marcos, your majesty,' he replied in a quaking voice.

'And you?' said Boudicca, addressing the other man.

'Claudius,' he replied. His voice was deep and self-assured.

'An emperor's name for a common soldier,' she teased. 'How nice.' She moved the whip-handle higher and ran it between the younger man's buttocks. He gasped as she pressed the end against his anus. She turned to the guard. 'Oil this one,' she ordered.

The guard immediately took up a small stone bottle and poured the contents over the young Roman's backside. Boudicca smoothed the viscous fluid over his taut buttocks and applied it liberally between them, especially over his tight little hole. His breathing became laboured. She put the end of the whip-handle to his anus and pushed it gently into the puckered hole. He gasped aloud as inch after inch was slipped inside his oiled sheath. She reached around his body and gripped his penis, finding to her delight that it was thickening rapidly.

Moving the handle slowly in and out of him, she coaxed his erection to full hardness with expert manipulation of her fingers and felt it throb within her grip. She eased the rod from within him and looked up at the other man. He looked back at her with a horrified expression on his face and she noticed that his cock was hanging limply from his bushy groin.

Boudicca stepped back and raised the whip high above her head. The second man turned his face away from her and she noticed him stiffen his buttocks in readiness for the lash. She brought the whip down forcefully and the leather cracked across his bottom. He took a sharp intake of breath but didn't cry out. She whipped him again, harder this time, but still he refused to utter a sound. After the lash cut him a third time, she threw the whip down in exasperation. 'Turn them again!' she barked.

The guard did as asked. Boudicca picked up the whip again and faced them. To her delight, she saw that both of them now sported fine, thick erections and she realised why it was that Claudius had not cried out. He clearly enjoyed the kiss of the lash. She played the vicious strand of leather over Marcos' cock and watched as it began to droop. He was evidently afraid that she was about to lash him there, in that most tender of places. She moved over to Claudius and did the same thing to him. His erection became stiffer, if anything. She coiled the long strand round and round the root of his stalk and then suddenly pulled it tight. Claudius winced with pain. The plum-sized head of his cock turned purple and the veins in the long shaft were becoming more and more pronounced. She knelt down in front of him and stared at his cock as it seemed to grow ever larger. Fearing that she might cause him permanent damage, she quickly uncoiled the whip, but his rod remained just as hard. She gripped him tightly by the root and found that her fingers barely encircled his girth. She stood up, still holding his erection within her grasp and stared straight into his eyes.

'If you come, Roman,' she hissed, 'I will have the guard flay you until there is no skin left on your back.' The prisoner swallowed hard and nodded. Turning, she set down the whip on the floor and then stood to face the men as they watched her fearfully. She unclasped her cloak and let it fall to the floor. Their eyes widened as they gazed at her naked beauty. The younger man's cock thickened and rose again. Although it was nowhere near as large as that of his comrade, it was nevertheless a more than adequate specimen.

Boudicca cupped her massive breasts with her hands and raised them high. She licked each nipple alternately until they stood out sharply from her swollen areolae. She let the sumptuous mounds fall to her chest and then caressed herself suggestively between the legs. The two men stared at her crotch, their cocks as stiff as two spears as she pulled and fingered between her soft, wet lips.

Boudicca smiled and walked over to them. She grasped each of their hard stalks with her hands and squeezed them gently. 'The first one of you to come will be left here to rot. The other will be released.' She turned to face the jailer, who was eyeing her hungrily. 'Come, guard,' she mewed. 'Let us give our guests a demonstration of the Iceni way of taking pleasure.'

The guard gasped as the meaning of her words became clear. 'Majesty,' he protested, 'but you are the queen!'

She walked up to him and began to unfasten his tunic. 'I am also a woman,' she breathed, 'and you are going to fuck me.' She bared his powerful chest and wrenched the tunic from his shoulders. He struggled quickly to remove the remainder of his clothing and then stood before her, naked save for a pair of tattered leather boots. Boudicca reached out and grabbed hold of his cock, then dragged him to stand with her in front of the shackled prisoners. She turned to face them. 'You will watch everything,' she ordered sharply. 'If I see you turn your heads or close your eyes, it will be the worse for you!'

With that, she knelt before the guard and nonchalantly took his cock into her mouth. She rubbed the exposed length of his stalk slowly while she sucked the thick head, tasting the bitter-sweetness of his fluid against her tongue. She moved her head backward and forward and the guard responded by thrusting gently against her. Cupping his balls with her free hand, she let go of his rod and arched her neck slightly, then pushed her face forward. His long cock slipped over her tongue and down her throat until her lips were pressed against the bush of hair at his crotch. She drew back until she held just the head between her lips and then repeated the action, this time swallowing hard to afford him the most delightful of sensations. His masculine scent was strong and arousing and she could sense the lips of her pussy opening in readiness for joys to come.

She allowed his cock to slip from her lips and then she stood up and faced the two Romans. Their erections remained firm but their faces were filled with anguish. Boudicca smiled cruelly and turned her back to them, moving to stand in front of Marcos. She bent over until her hands touched the floor with her legs fully straight and widely spread apart, then moved back until she felt the tip of his cock touching her bottom. She wriggled her backside provocatively, feeling his erection rubbing against her buttocks, and then moved from him to stand with her back to Claudius. She bent over once more and moved back to him until the massive swollen head of his thick rod touched against the lips of her pussy. She was sorely tempted to allow him to enter her, but that would have spoilt the game. Instead, she wriggled her bottom again and moved back against him so that his shaft rested between her firm buttocks. Rubbing herself up and down against him, she stiffened and then relaxed her creamy globes over and over again, in the full knowledge that she was teasing him unmercifully.

Tiring of this, Boudicca moved from him and stood between the two men with her back pressed against the cold stone wall and her legs parted invitingly. As the guard approached her, she grasped hold of both of the erections at her sides and began to rub them gently. The guard stood before her and aimed his wet stalk at the open lips of her pussy. He sank into her quickly and immediately began to fuck her with all the finesse of a wild animal. He grasped her breasts and kneaded the firm flesh painfully whilst he hammered in and out of her. Boudicca rubbed the two cocks furiously, anxious to see an end to the game, knowing that she was about to come herself.

Suddenly, the two prisoners groaned in unison. She gripped the ends of their cocks tightly and felt their seed filling the palms of her hands. Almost immediately, the guard roared as his cream was pumped into her lushness and she came with a long, low moan. The guard continued to thrust in and out of her until he was spent, then he stepped back and staggered across the room to squat on a small stool. Boudicca released her grip of the two wilting erections, put her hands to her mouth and licked the warm fluid from her fingers.

Retrieving her cloak, she quickly donned it and once more took on the haughty expression of a queen. She glared at the two Romans. They clearly thought that they had outwitted her by coming in unison. 'A clever trick,' she said with a sneer, 'but there was no winner. Now you must both remain here until I decide what is to be done with you. Guard, open the door!'

The prisoners watched her with dejected expressions on their faces as she swept from the cell. She smiled smugly to herself. It had been good.

Boudicca lay back on the long ornate couch as Sisa gently massaged her feet. The frail waif-like form of the young girl looked particularly appealing under the soft light of the flickering torches. Boudicca reached down and ran her fingers through her servant's long white-blonde hair. It was freshly washed and bore a delicate scent of wild flowers. The girl glanced up at her queen and smiled.

'Did you enjoy it, when you gave up your virginity

to that wretched slave?' Boudicca spoke gently as she conjured up an image of Sisa's lithe body impaled on the man's huge rod.

'Yes, mistress,' replied the girl as she continued to caress the queen's feet. Her soothing touch felt heavenly. Boudicca closed her eyes and relaxed herself completely. It had been a long march that day and Londinium was but a few short miles to the south. She needed to rest before the battle that was to come.

'Mistress,' Sisa began cautiously. Boudicca opened her eyes and regarded the young servant coldly.

'What is it, girl?' she demanded. Sisa seemed reluctant to continue and she stared down at the queen's feet and rubbed them roughly. 'What is it?' repeated Boudicca, somewhat curtly.

'Mistress, I need more.' The reply was short but delivered with considerable emotion.

'More? What do you mean?'

'The feeling of the slave's staff within my body; the way that it stretched my . . . my *place* . . .'

Boudicca could see that the girl's hands were shaking. 'Your *cunt*,' she barked, 'say what you mean, girl.'

Sisa looked up, startled at the queen's crudeness. Her lips moved as though she were attempting to force words from her mouth that were totally alien to her.

'You must feel no shame in the use of such language,' continued Boudicca. 'You have had a big cock up your little cunt, the first of many.'

Sisa stared into her eyes with an earnest, imploring expression on her lovely face. 'But that is what I want, mistress,' she pleaded. 'I have dreamt of nothing else, these past few days. As my horse moved its broad back between my legs, I rubbed myself against the hardness of its back and thought continuously of that hard stalk pushing deep into my ... my cunt.' The word slipped from her lips in a whisper and she looked down quickly.

Boudicca smiled and caressed the long, flowing tresses of her hair again. 'It is a beautiful word, do you not think?' she breathed. Sisa looked up at her face and nodded. Her eyes were wide and sparkled in the torchlight. Boudicca ran her hand down the girl's back and allowed her fingertips to stray briefly across her small, pert buttocks. 'I have much to teach you,' she said warmly. 'There are many joys that await you, many delights, some so wonderful as to defy your imagination. Do you really wish to learn?' Sisa nodded and resumed her gentle massage of the queen's toes. Boudicca sat up and pulled her hands away. 'Take off your dress,' she breathed.

'Mistress?' said Sisa, taken aback.

'Remove your dress,' repeated Boudicca with an encouraging smile. Sisa nervously gripped the hem of her small garment, slowly pulled it up over her head and let it slip to the ground. The heavy walls of the tent fluttered noisily with a sudden breeze, which startled her. She glanced around anxiously as though expecting to see someone entering the confines of the royal enclosure. 'Do not be alarmed,' said Boudicca. 'We will not be disturbed.'

She gazed in admiration as Sisa's nakedness was revealed in all its delicate perfection and she knew that she wanted her. She was also well aware that she could command the young girl to obey her every whim and force her to submit to her carnal desires, but that was not how she wanted it to be. She needed Sisa to offer herself to her willingly and to have her beg for her intimate caress.

Boudicca purposely allowed her gaze to move

slowly down Sisa's lithe form until she gazed pointedly at the fur between her legs. The girl immediately covered herself with her hand. 'Move your hand away, Sisa,' said Boudicca in a quiet, undemanding tone. 'Do not hide that precious treasure from my gaze.' Sisa nervously moved her hand away and rested it against her thigh, as though ready to cover herself quickly again, should the need arise. Boudicca smiled. 'Do not be ashamed to show yourself to me,' she continued. 'You are no different to me, even if I am your queen.'

As if to give credence to her words, she raised the loose smock that covered her nakedness and bared her lower body. She parted her legs slightly to ensure that nothing was hidden from the young girl's eyes. She knew that her sex-lips would be engorged and would be pouting thickly, their succulence enhanced by the fact that her mound had been freshly shaven. Sisa stared at the brazen display, her eyes wider than ever. To her delight, Boudicca saw her apprehensively run the tip of her tongue across her small mouth.

'Raise your leg, Sisa,' she said in a more authoritative tone. 'Let me see what you are hiding. Remember, I watched while you impaled yourself on that slave and you showed no shame or reticence then.'

'That was different, somehow,' protested Sisa. 'I was nervous about what was to happen to me at first and, when I held that wonderful thing inside my body, I could think of nothing else but the exquisite feelings that I was enjoying.'

'Open your legs, Sisa,' repeated Boudicca persuasively. 'Show me.' The girl slowly lifted her leg until she rested her foot on the edge of the couch. Boudicca bent forward and stared between her slim thighs. The tiny mouth of her pussy seemed barely able to admit a probing finger, let alone a long, thick cock. Sisa's entire body was trembling. Whether it was from fear or lust was difficult for her to discern.

'It really is quite beautiful,' breathed the queen as she leaned her face closer to Sisa's groin. 'Do you often touch yourself there?'

'Mistress?' queried the girl, her voice barely above a whisper.

Boudicca sat back and regarded her kindly. 'You know what I mean. Do you fondle yourself? Do you close your eyes and rub your fingertips against that little bud of yours until you come?'

'I – I don't understand,' complained the girl.

'Don't lie, girl,' said Boudicca angrily. 'Surely you have tickled those soft lips as you dreamt of some handsome young man touching you in the same manner?'

'No, mistress, I have never . . .'

'Then let me teach you. Lie opposite me on the couch.' Sisa obeyed immediately, lying so that she faced her queen. 'Open your legs wide,' continued Boudicca. 'Let your foot rest on the floor.' As Sisa did as instructed, Boudicca noticed that her tiny sex-lips parted slightly and she detected a faint dampness on the down-like hair that surrounded them. 'Now,' she said, 'watch what I do.'

She reached down and parted the lips of her pussy with the fingers of one hand to reveal the wet hole between them. She dipped two fingers of her other hand into her warm sheath and then smoothed her juices over her hard clitoris. She began to rub herself gently with a steady circular motion. The sensation thrilled her immediately, particularly so as she was being so closely observed. 'Now you do the same,' she said breathlessly.

Sisa reached down and began to caress herself

inexpertly. Boudicca watched as she stroked her fingertips up and down the full length of her pouting lips, occasionally slipping them inside to dampen them with her own juice. What quickly became all too evident was that she had little idea as to how to stimulate herself.

Boudicca leant forward and took hold of Sisa's wrist. 'Let me show you,' she breathed. Holding the girl's wrist firmly, she directed the fingertips to touch the folds of flesh at the top of her pussy. Sisa gasped with delight. Boudicca released her grasp of the girl's arm and sat back to watch as she began to rub her bud rapidly. 'Do you like that?' she said with a grin. Sisa merely nodded and closed her eyes tightly. Her fingers became a blur as she became more adept at her self-caress and her breathing became stilted.

Suddenly, her body stiffened and she gasped out loudly. Rubbing herself even faster, she gripped the side of the couch with her free hand and gasped again, then gave out an involuntary cry as her orgasm took over her senses. Boudicca watched happily as the girl slowed the movements of her fingers until she let her hand fall limply against her thigh and she fell back heavily on to the cushions.

There was a long silence, broken only by Sisa's laboured breathing. Eventually, she became calm and opened her eyes. The gentle innocence of her expression became clouded with guilt.

'You learn quickly,' said Boudicca.

'It was wonderful, mistress. It was the same feeling that I had when I . . . when . . .'

'When you were fucked,' said Boudicca firmly.

Sisa giggled like a child. 'Such a word, mistress! How can you say such things?'

'They are very special words, my sweet girl. Fuck – cunt – cock. But use them sparingly. At the right

108

moment their sound will be music to a lover's ears. You have such an innocent way about you. If you stare into a young man's eyes with that lovely, watery gaze of yours and whisper, ever so gently in his ear those magical words, "please fuck me", you can be certain that no man will have the strength to resist.'

Sisa smiled and looked down. She blushed noticeably and her hand strayed once more to caress herself between her legs. Boudicca realised that the girl was staring at the shaven heaven of her own pussy. She leant forward and kissed Sisa quickly on the top of her head. 'Touch me,' she whispered.

Sisa looked up at her face with a startled expression. 'Mistress?' she protested. Boudicca kissed her again, this time on her cheek. She took hold of her small hand and directed it towards her groin. At first there was a little resistance, but then Sisa seemed to relax and give in to the inevitable. Boudicca thrilled as the girl's fingertips touched the engorged lips of her pussy. 'It is very wet, mistress,' said Sisa as she stroked the soft flesh, 'and it is so beautiful. Perhaps I will shave myself.'

Boudicca shook her head. 'No, Sisa, for you it is unnecessary. That delicate coating of fluff between your legs hides nothing.' She let go of Sisa's hand and lay back to enjoy the gentle fingering of her warm wetness. Opening her legs as wide as possible, she tugged at her sex-lips with her fingers to reveal her innermost charms to the young girl's excited gaze. 'Kiss it,' she breathed.

This time, there was no protest. Sisa moved her head slowly forward and down until her face was inches from her queen's aching cunt. Boudicca could feel the warmth of her breath playing across the throbbing lips. 'Kiss it, lick it,' she implored, 'and then I will do the same for you.' She felt the wetness of Sisa's tongue lapping around her sex-lips and sensed her juices flowing from within her to soak the young girl's face.

Sisa took to her task like an expert. Soon, she was flicking the tip of her tongue across the hard bud of Boudicca's clitoris, which caused her to buck her hips in rhythmic response. For a brief moment she was no longer the Queen of the Iceni. She was the prisoner of her arousal, completely at the mercy of this serving-girl with her fluttering tongue and sucking mouth.

She came within seconds and grabbed Sisa's head and forced her face hard against her throbbing mound. Sisa continued to lick her until she was fully sated, clearly wishing to satisfy her queen completely. Eventually, she raised her head and looked directly into Boudicca's eyes. Her expression remained that of an innocent virgin, despite the fact that her face was soaked with the juices of her queen's delight. Boudicca stroked her features tenderly. 'Now lie back,' she purred.

Sisa moved to lie on her back with her legs splayed wide apart. Boudicca knelt between them and moved her face towards the open, pouting lips of the young girl's pussy. She breathed deeply and the sweet musky aroma invaded her senses. She kissed the inviting lips and then opened her mouth and took them between her teeth. She sucked the soft flesh into her mouth and lapped wetly over its succulence, then dipped her long tongue deeply between them into the hot little hole.

Sisa mewed contentedly as Boudicca tongue-fucked her and then she groaned as the queen allowed the tip of her tongue to flick rapidly over the bud. Boudicca pressed her teeth hard against Sisa's mound and nipped her clitoris between them. Moving her head slightly in order to enable her to breathe easily, she fluttered the tip of her tongue rapidly over the little button until Sisa suddenly squealed and came. Her juices flowed from her like wine from a goblet, filling Boudicca's mouth with its sensuous taste. She lapped hungrily, circling her tongue round and round the wet lips until she was sure that Sisa could take no more, and then she moved from her.

She looked down lovingly at the small naked form of the trembling girl. Sisa gazed up at her. A small tear of joy trickled from her eye and she smiled weakly. Boudicca leant forward and kissed her full on the mouth. Sisa responded immediately, her tongue slipping between her lips and her arms becoming wrapped tightly around her neck. Boudicca moved to lie on top of her and the young girl curled her legs around her waist. She could feel the hot wetness of Sisa's pussy rubbing against her stomach. The kiss became more and more urgent until, with a muffled cry, Sisa came again. Her fingernails dug into the queen's shoulders and her soaking mound pressed hard against her belly as the tremors of delight coursed through her body. Boudicca responded by pushing herself firmly against the tiny writhing form until Sisa collapsed back on to the cushions, fully sated.

It had been a most worthwhile lesson.

Five

'Just one more day's march and Londinium will be within our sights,' said Catus, stretching himself on his stirrups as he gazed into the distance. Suetonius slipped from his mount and rubbed the aching muscles of his inner thighs. It had been a long and arduous ride. The sun was already beginning to sink behind the hills, throwing the bare branches of the distant trees into sharp relief. In the valley below them, the tents were already erected and the vast army of soldiers was bedding down for the night.

'I don't like it,' mused Suetonius as he surveyed the scene. 'The men are too vulnerable here. What if the Iceni hordes swoop down on them from the hills while they slumber? They wouldn't stand a chance.'

'There are guards posted on every hilltop,' answered Catus with a reassuring grin. 'You worry too much. You have become more and more timorous, the closer we have come to meeting with Boudicca. I fear that you are losing your nerve, friend.'

Suetonius glared up at him. 'It is a wise general who remains cautious, Catus,' he snapped. 'You know these fiends. The forests could be full of them. They could be waiting for nightfall, ready to tear the throats out of the men as they sleep.'

'That is not their way, Suetonius. The Iceni fear the

demons of the night. They believe that if they are slain after the setting of the sun, their spirits will remain forever to wander aimlessly in perpetual darkness.'

'Then why do we not simply attack them at night?'

Catus heaved his leg across the broad back of his horse and jumped to the ground. 'Would that it could be so easy, friend,' he said with a wry smile, 'but they also believe that if they are shielded by the boundaries of their own encampment, no matter how temporary, then they will be protected from such an eternal damnation and would fight like devils.'

'They are a strange people indeed,' muttered Suetonius as he nevertheless eyed the distant forest with mounting apprehension. 'How do you know so much about their ways?'

'As Procurator, it was my business to know these people and to try to understand them, in order to keep them under the control of Rome.'

'You didn't do a particularly good job, did you friend?' teased Suetonius.

Catus looked down at the ground sullenly. 'While Prasutagus, the King of the Iceni, lived there was no problem. They seemed to be a weak and submissive people and their women were always more than willing to submit themselves to whatever was demanded of them. I tell you, friend, I have never enjoyed as much sex before in all my life as in the past short years. I rarely spent the night alone and usually I was in the company of two or more of those delightful young creatures.' He gazed wistfully into the distance as memories of past pleasures filled his mind.

'So what happened?' asked Suetonius curtly.

'As I told you, when the king died, his vicious widow, Boudicca, took control. She refused to hand over her lands to the Emperor, as was lawfully decreed, and she caused her people to rise in revolt. The newly erected temple to Claudius was destroyed in a single day. For some reason, its destruction was pivotal to their anger and they tore the great building down to its very foundations. Fired by this, the rabble turned on my army. My men had become lazy and unfit and were no match for the seething mass of hysterical savages who attacked them. As you know, I was lucky to escape with my life.' His words trailed off and his expression became clouded.

Suetonius rested his hand on his friend's shoulder. 'Soon you will have your revenge, Catus,' he said quietly.

Catus shook himself. 'Come, friend,' he said jovially, in an obvious attempt to lighten the mood of the moment, 'let us go to our tent and find ourselves a couple of pretty little whores to take our minds off such matters. A nice tight little arse will soon rid me of these troublesome thoughts.' The two men strode purposefully down the hill, tugging their reluctant mounts behind them and laughing uproariously.

The two naked women sitting huddled together on one of the rugs strewn across the tent floor couldn't have been more different. The younger of them, whom Suetonius and Catus had been told was known as Risa, was remarkably slim, to the point of boyishness while the other, whose name they had not yet learnt, was very plump with a huge bottom and large bouncing breasts. Suetonius nevertheless found the shapeliness of the older woman's body the most appealing.

He signalled with a nonchalant but demanding wave of his hand for her to come to him. She moved over to him like a whipped dog and knelt obediently at his feet, with her gaze firmly fixed on the ground.

115

'Look at me, woman,' he said, in a cruel uncompromising tone. The girl looked up at him, caught the leer in his eyes and quickly looked down again. 'I said, look at me!' he demanded.

She moved her face up slowly until her eyes once again met his. He smiled, but his expression lost none of its callousness. She stared at him through wide terrified eyes, her body trembling and her large breasts heaving massively.

Suetonius reached down and cupped the huge globes with his hands. 'You have fine big tits,' he mumbled through clenched teeth as he kneaded the heavy, fleshy mounds. The girl looked away from him, as though ashamed.

Her face was not unpleasant: round, with rose-tinted cheeks and a full wide mouth. Suetonius drew back his cloak to reveal his nakedness. The woman stared at his erect cock as though it was the first one that she had ever seen. He gripped the root firmly so that the long stalk swelled remarkably and the head took on the size and colouring of a fully ripe plum. 'Suck it!' he ordered.

The woman seemed hesitant.

'I said, suck it!' he barked again. She moved her face cautiously forward until it was barely an inch from the end of the huge rod. Nervously, she pushed her tongue out from her pursed lips and licked the tip. She drew back and looked imploringly back up at him.

Suetonius was enjoying this. It was evident that the woman had never paid oral homage to a lover before and he revelled in his power to have her do anything that was demanded of her. He leant forward and spoke quietly but in a clear, insistent tone. 'Open your pretty mouth and take it inside. Lick it and suck it, and take care not to chafe it with your teeth.'

116

The woman moved her face forward again and this time she opened her mouth wide to take the huge head of his cock within her thickly pouting lips. At first, she made no other movement, and then he began to feel her tongue sliding wetly against his engorged flesh. He glanced across at Catus. His friend was naked and lying on his back with the younger woman spread-eagled across his face, so that he could lick her small bottom while she sucked and rubbed his thick erection.

Suetonius watched them enviously. Risa was clearly an expert at the task, unlike her older colleague who was making little effort to stimulate him other than by gently licking his flesh. He pushed her away angrily so that she fell back on her big bottom with a shocked gasp. He grabbed her by the hair and forced her to face the others. 'Watch your friend!' he ordered. 'See how it is done.' The woman dutifully observed the other's deft performance and the expression on Risa's face suggested that she felt proud that her ministrations were being so closely noted. She worked on Catus' cock, slurping and guzzling the thick rod while at the same time rubbing the exposed shaft and squeezing his balls with her free hand. The scene of delightful debauchery soon proved too much for Suetonius.

Moving to kneel between his friend's legs, he presented his long, thick stalk to the younger girl's face. Her eyes widened when she saw it and she happily let Catus' rod slip from her mouth and immediately closed her lips around Suetonius' hardness. Despite its girth, she managed to accommodate over half of its length inside her small mouth and he sighed with pleasure as he sensed her tongue circling around it in a sensuous sucking movement that seemed to be trying to draw the very seed from within his body.

He also noticed that she was not neglecting Catus, who was still lapping noisily against her nether regions. She rubbed his stiffness rapidly while continuing to suckle Suetonius as though he were the only man there. She began to bob her head up and down quickly on his hard rod and made excited mewing sounds as she savoured his taste.

He turned to look at the other woman, who was sitting glumly on the ground. 'See how it is done, woman?' he gasped. 'Learn from your young friend!'

Suddenly, the older woman burst into tears, pulled herself up from the ground and ran, sobbing, out of the tent. Normally, Suetonius would have been furious at her impertinence but Risa was using her mouth so expertly on him that he simply shrugged and ignored the outburst. He stroked the young woman's soft brown curls with all the tenderness of a true lover.

Suddenly, he heard Catus utter a muffled groan and he felt a warm dampness splash over his thighs. Realising that his friend had come, he eased his cock from Risa's mouth and quickly wiped the cream from his legs with a small strip of cloth that had been lying on the ground beside them.

'By Jupiter's teeth!' exclaimed Catus, 'I couldn't stop myself! What with the exquisite taste of this girl's sweet honeypot and the way she used her hand, there was nothing that I could do!' He pushed Risa's lithe little body from on top of him and struggled to sit up. He glanced down wearily at his flaccid penis. 'You'll have to deal with her until I can raise this sorry specimen again,' he said, with a laugh.

Suetonius was only too happy to oblige and, from the happy expression on the young woman's face, Risa shared his delight. He sat back and she knelt between his legs and took hold of his cock with both of her hands. She kissed it lightly on the tip and then looked up into his eyes. Her face was a picture of excitement.

'My lord, it is a monster.' She spoke quietly with an accent that was new to him and he nodded in proud acceptance of the compliment. Grasped by her tiny hands, his shaft did indeed appear enormous. Risa licked around the head and prodded the tip of her tongue against the fleshy glans before running her tongue down along the full length of his cock and then fluttering the tip around his balls, tracing their shape while she gently caressed his firm staff with both of her hands.

Careful not to stop her in any way, he lay on his back and raised his legs slightly so that Risa was able to lick under his heavy sac in the tender place between his balls and his anus. He had always enjoyed the touch of a woman's tongue there and Risa didn't disappoint him. She flicked the tip of her tongue against him and then, to his utmost joy, she began to lick the sphincter itself. At first, she just lapped over the hole but then she prodded inside him, moving her tongue in and out with a gentle, steady rhythm. He closed his eyes to savour the incredible sensation. 'Oh, Catus,' he groaned, 'she's licking my arse! She's licking my arse!'

'I dare say that she would enjoy similar treatment herself,' said his friend. Suetonius raised his head and looked across at Catus, who was sitting behind the girl and staring with unconcealed admiration at her upturned bottom. Suetonius ignored him and closed his eyes again while pulling his legs higher to afford the girl easier access to his most intimate region. Her tongue felt incredibly long as it plundered ever deeper into his anus and his cock swelled to full erection as she rubbed the hard flesh rapidly with her hands.

Suddenly, he grasped hold of her by the wrists to stop her pumping him. It had been close, almost too close. Risa sat back, a look of dismay on her lovely features. He looked at her mouth. He found it hard to believe that such sweet, innocent lips had been pressed against his bottom. His cock throbbed involuntarily and a small jet of clear fluid shot across his chest. Risa immediately leant forward and licked the juice from him, then sat back and regarded him with an enigmatic smile on her face.

Suetonius sat up and gripped her under the arms, then lifted her up bodily until she was squatting on her heels across his groin. He let go of her arms and raised his cock so that the tip of the thick head touched the wet, open lips of her pussy. She sank down on him cautiously until the entire length was gripped by her hot, undulating sex-flesh. She leant forwards and gripped his shoulders tightly with her hands, then began to move her lower body up and down rapidly. Suetonius didn't need to move; she was doing everything that was necessary.

'Now there's a truly wondrous sight,' joked Catus. 'That dick of yours is almost as thick as one of her legs.' Risa was having no problem whatsoever in accommodating Suetonius' hard weapon, however. She rode him as though she were astride a wild stallion, gasping with delight as she thrust herself heavily against him. He knew that, at this pace, he would not be able to hold back for long and he grasped her tightly by the waist in order to slow her down. The woman was having none of it. She thrust even faster, her groin thudding against his pubic bone over and over again as she absorbed everything he had to offer without the slightest indication of discomfort.

The inevitable happened and he came, deep inside

her hot little cunt. Risa had shown no sign of having an orgasm herself but, at that moment, Suetonius could not have cared less. She pounded up and down on him until his wilting cock finally slipped from inside her and then she fell on his body, panting like a fleeing animal.

'This vixen stays with us!' announced Catus with a laugh. 'There is much sport to be had with this one, much sport indeed.'

The sky over Londinium looked oddly beautiful with the billowing clouds reflecting a thousand shades of red in the slowly fading light of the evening. But it was not the setting of the sun that created the romantic image that lay before the Roman army on that cool spring morning. The ashes of the once proud and prosperous city spread before them, fires burning furiously as they consumed what was left of the town.

Suetonius and Catus surveyed the miserable scene in shocked silence. There was not a single person to be seen moving among the blackened embers; the entire population was either slain in battle or had fled to the hills. Close by them, a dog foraged in the ruins, its coat filthy with soot and its eyes clouded by the sadness of the moment.

Suetonius looked across at Catus. 'These devils must be caught,' he said in a quiet, trembling voice. 'They must be made an example of.' There was nothing more to be said. The two generals turned their mounts and headed slowly back to the encampment.

Risa busied herself by putting the tent into order whilst Suetonius and Catus sat glumly staring at the small fire. Despite the fact that she wore nothing but a tiny thong drawn tightly about her narrow hips the men showed no interest in her. The sight of the ruined capital had dimmed their ardour, at least for the moment.

A sudden, urgent noise came from outside. Suetonius looked up as a young soldier rushed unheralded into the tent. The man fell to his knees before them, his head bowed.

Suetonius stood up, angry that the soldier should have entered the tent unannounced. 'What is it?' he demanded.

The young man looked up at him. He was panting heavily and his face was coated with fresh sweat. 'My lord,' he gasped, 'the Iceni are bound for Verulamium!'

Catus jumped up from his seat. 'Verulamium? You have seen them?'

The soldier nodded. 'Yes, my lord. They are making camp near the city. But they are many. Their numbers stretch as far as the eye can see!'

Catus swung round to face Suetonius. 'We must go after them!' he said excitedly. 'We must attack before they can rout the city.'

Suetonius shook his head. 'The men are tired from the march and, besides, we should wait until the legions arrive from the south-west.'

Catus paced across the tent, waving his arms in frustration. 'How can we wait? The people of Verulamium are loyal to the Emperor. If we don't march, they will be massacred! You have seen what these animals did to Londinium.'

'We wouldn't have a chance,' replied Suetonius wearily. 'You yourself said that a single legion of the finest Roman soldiers was no match for them.' He waved the messenger away and the young man scurried from the tent. Suetonius leant close to Catus, anxious that no other person, not even Risa, should hear his words. 'We must use stealth, friend,' he whispered. 'Somehow, we must infiltrate their camp and get to the queen. Once she is dead, the rebellion will fall apart.'

'We?' breathed Catus. 'You mean you and I?'

'We can trust no other. The task is too important to be entrusted to mere soldiers.'

'You are asking a great deal, Suetonius. Remember, I am supposed to be bound for Rome.'

'You are not afraid, are you?' Suetonius knew the answer to his question, but he was also well aware that he needed his friend at his side. Too much depended on the success of the mission.

'I have told you before,' countered Catus angrily, 'nothing would give me greater pleasure than to wreak vengeance on that foul vixen, Boudicca.'

Suetonius smiled and patted Catus on the shoulder. 'We will rest for a few hours, then head north under cover of the night. Two fast horses should have us near Verulamium by daybreak.' He glanced across at Risa, who was now crouching in a corner of the tent and nonchalantly combing her long brown curls. 'Let us have Risa ease our tension before we sleep.'

Catus looked over at the girl and grinned. Suetonius knew that, even under these sombre conditions, his friend would be unlikely to resist such a temptation. Risa suddenly noticed that they were both leering at her. 'My lords?' she said, her face a picture of innocent promise.

'Come here, girl,' ordered Suetonius.

The young woman got to her feet and walked slowly over to the two seated men. Her tiny breasts bobbed enticingly as she moved and her hips swayed gently. She stood before them, a slight smile on her face. Suetonius put out his hand and touched her pussy through the thin material of the thong with the tips of his fingers, while Catus stroked her small firm buttocks lovingly.

'Ooh, my lords!' she purred. Suetonius pulled the cord that held the thong in place and the wispy material drifted to the ground. He gazed at the girl's bared pussy and remembered how it had accommodated his huge stalk with such apparent ease, the night before. He put his fingers to the delicate pouting lips and caressed them gently. They were already becoming damp. Risa slipped down to kneel on all fours before him and then reached under his skirt and grasped his thickening erection. It rose quickly to its full magnificence as she rubbed it with her small hand.

'My lord,' she breathed as she gazed at his cock, 'it is so big!' She bent forward and licked the head, tracing its shape with the tip of her tongue, then lapped gently down the long gnarled shaft to the root. Suetonius found the touch of her wet mouth against his raging hardness the most delicate and sensuous feeling that he had ever experienced. It was more than apparent that Risa loved to use her mouth in this way and that she had much experience of giving oral pleasure to men, despite her youth.

He saw Catus move behind her and watched as he knelt down and pressed his face against her upturned bottom. He could tell from the movement of his head that his friend was licking the girl's backside, but Risa didn't seem to notice, so intent was she on her task of pleasing Suetonius. She wormed her tongue under his heavy sac and raised his balls on its soft platform. She glanced up at him and smiled broadly, then engulfed his balls in her mouth, her lips closing to enclose the hairy flesh tightly. He sensed her tongue fluttering around the sensitive skin as she began to suck him, not too hard, but just enough to send a warm, soothing sensation coursing throughout his lower body. He heard her give a tiny, muffled moan and looked up to see that Catus was now moving his fingers in and out of her from behind. He couldn't see, from this angle, whether it was her pussy or her anus that Catus was invading, but he had a pretty shrewd idea.

Risa allowed his heavy sac to fall from her lovely mouth and then licked all the way up his long stem until she once again playfully tickled the head with the tip of her tongue. He watched as she prodded the wide slit at the end, her efforts sending little jabs of pleasurable pain shooting down his bone-hard length. After a few moments of this delightful torture, she opened her mouth wide and took him in. Arching her neck slightly, she swallowed at least six inches of his fine weapon, while continuing to rub the exposed stalk with steady strokes of her hand.

He felt the head of his cock touch the back of her throat and feared that she might gag. Instead, she arched herself more and, despite the thickness of his rod, he felt it slipping down her throat. He could sense her swallowing against him, the sensation causing his cock to throb as the urge to spend deep into her mouth began to build up within his groin. She let go of the root of his cock with her hand and cupped his balls. She squeezed the tender plums tightly and moved her face forward until her lips pressed against his hairy mound.

'By the gods, she has taken the lot!' he exclaimed.

Catus looked up, pausing from his steady plundering of her rear, and saw that his friend's superb length had indeed become entirely engulfed within the young girl's mouth. 'Take care, friend,' he said with a grin, 'that sweet mouth will suck you dry.'

Suetonius knew that he was right. Much more of this blissful treatment was bound to make him come and he desperately wanted to fuck Risa's delightful little cunt again. He caught hold of her hair and slowly pushed her head back, easing his long cock from the heat of her mouth. She looked up at him, her wide eyes shining and the tip of his rod less than an inch from her lips. For a moment, he had the urge to plunge his stiffness once more into her mouth, but thought better of it in the full knowledge that he would come as soon as he felt her tongue sliding against his hard flesh. He pushed her away and sat back. The girl immediately grabbed hold of his penis and tried to force it back into her mouth.

Catus dragged her away. 'She would tease you, my friend,' he said as he held on to the struggling girl. 'She wishes to drink your semen and deny you entry to that tight little hole between her legs, just as she did with me. She should be punished for her disobedience!'

Risa stopped struggling the moment that Catus spoke these last few words. Suetonius looked into her eyes. The pupils were dilated and her expression was one of near manic lust. The idea clearly delighted her.

He grabbed hold of her and wrenched her lithe little body across his lap. He looked down at her small inviting buttocks and then parted them with his thumbs. The skin surrounding the puckered little hole was red, as testament to Catus' earlier ministrations, and her pussy glistened with the juices of her arousal. He raised his hand high and looked up at Catus. His friend grinned and licked his lips. Suddenly, Suetonius brought his hand down sharply and slapped his rough palm against the firm little globes. Risa yelped with delight and he spanked her again. The flawless white skin of her bottom began to redden as hc struck her once more.

'Harder!' she shouted. 'Harder!'

He was in no mood to refuse her ardent request. He slapped her again and again with all the force that he could muster. With every blow, the girl shrieked with joy and wriggled her body against him, the wetness of her pussy soaking his groin and thighs. Clearly defined imprints of his fingers appeared on her quivering buttocks as she continued to beg for more and more.

'This one needs the kiss of the lash,' grunted Suetonius, his arm beginning to tire as he slapped her bottom as hard as he could for the last time.

'Later,' panted Catus, 'but first, hold her still.' Suetonius gripped the girl tightly by the waist and Catus wrenched off his skirt and then positioned himself behind her. He gripped her thighs and pulled her towards him so that her stomach rested against Suetonius' lap and then he parted her legs widely. His cock jutted forward, the head pointing directly at the open succulence of her pussy. He plunged into her with one violent stabbing movement. Risa gasped loudly. Catus gripped her hips and began to hammer into her as though he hadn't had a woman for months. The sight of his friend's thick shaft thrusting rapidly in and out of the girl's luscious sex-flesh, coupled with that of her rippling hot buttocks, was having a marked effect on Suetonius.

'Hold still, Catus!' he barked. 'I must have her, before it's too late!'

Catus laughed and pulled from her. 'We will both have her,' he announced. He grabbed her roughly and forced her to stand astride his colleague's thighs. She lowered herself slowly and Suetonius almost came as her hot flesh engulfed his cock. Risa gripped his shoulders and stared lustfully into his eyes as she started to move her body slowly up and down, absorbing and reabsorbing his stiff stalk. Then she held herself still, with just the head of his cock gripped by her tight pussy lips.

Catus moved to stand behind her. Suetonius assumed that he intended to enter the tiny puckered hole of her bottom, but he was wrong. He felt the hardness of his friend's cock press against his and then he realised that Catus was easing his thick shaft into the same tight orifice. Risa groaned and closed her eyes as the two rods slipped deep into her pussy simultaneously. Suetonius felt her juices dribbling down the exposed length of his stalk as they were forced from her hot sheath by the double intrusion. He thrust his hips upwards until the full length of his cock filled her.

Catus started to thrust in and out of her rapidly. Suetonius felt Catus' hard flesh rubbing against his own aching rod and knew that he wouldn't be able to hold back much longer. He held himself still with his pole fully embedded inside her and let his friend do the work. Suddenly, he felt a mighty surge within his groin and knew that he was lost. 'By the gods, Catus,' he groaned, 'I am coming!'

Catus immediately thrust wildly in and out of the girl, as if determined to join his friend in blissful release. Risa's small body shuddered and shook under the violence of the assault, and it was clear from her expression that she was close to her own orgasm. Suetonius managed to worm his hand down between them until his fingers touched her hard clitoris. He rubbed it rapidly, determined to make the end of their blissful union perfect. His cock stretched inside her and an intense pressure built up within the full length. Risa suddenly squealed as her climax ripped through her and, almost immediately, his cream erupted from him. Catus let out a mighty roar and Suetonius fancied that he could feel the steady thumping of his friend's hardness against his own spurting cock.

Gradually, the two men eased from her. Risa remained standing astride Suetonius, her body trembling and her face flushed. He looked down at the ravaged lips of her pussy. A thin trace of semen slipped from between them to form a small white pool on his wilting cock. Seeing this, Risa bent over him and lowered her face to his groin, then delicately licked the cream from his tender flesh.

It was a perfect end to a long and arduous day.

Six

The Iceni encampment was less than ten miles from Verulamium but Boudicca had realised that her army sorely needed to rest before mounting an attack on the city. The townspeople would know of their presence, of course. They were far too many to remain hidden in the thick forests that cloaked the undulating countryside. The Roman garrison would certainly have been alerted and it was more than likely that messengers would have been sent to seek reinforcements from other legions in the vicinity. Without doubt, word would have spread concerning the destruction of Londinium. Time was of the essence, but the queen was wise enough to accept that her exhausted rabble of peasants needed to become refreshed before wreaking vengeance upon the traitorous citizens.

The weather had turned unusually warm for the time of year and the majority of the Iceni people had chosen to lie under the stars. Boudicca had had a small tent erected for herself and she sat within its shelter, quietly contemplating the coming foray as she stared into the dying embers of her fire. The only other source of light in the tent was a single brightly burning torch clasped to the handle of a long spear set firmly into the ground. Its flames cast ghostly shadows against the tent walls, like the spirits of the valiant men of her army who had fallen in battle. She stirred the embers with a piece of charred wood, sending sparks rising to be enveloped by the darkness above her head.

She began to think of Arman, the leader of the druids. She thought first of her dream, and then of the reality of their subsequent meeting when he had taken her as his own. There had been many other men in her life, of course, but none had affected her in the way that her enigmatic, mysterious lover had. She had the uncontrollable urge to touch herself between the legs as she pictured an image of his strong naked body and his long, thick cock. She sensed the taste of his sex-flesh on her lips and remembered the arousing manly odour and the gnarled hard texture of his wonderful length as it had slipped inside her mouth.

She allowed her fingertips to play against the soft wet lips of her pussy and her nipples hardened against the rough material of her smock. She dipped her fingers into the warmth of her sheath and coated them with her juices, then rubbed them gently against the stiffening bud of her clitoris. He had completely and effortlessly subdued her and she had been more than happy to submit herself to his demands, like an innocent, unknowing virgin. He could have done anything that he chose, that night in the druids' grove. He could even have taken her in that secret forbidden place, that tiny, tight treasure between her buttocks that, so far, she had denied to any of her previous lovers.

She thought hard about that and touched her anus lightly with the tip of a finger. Easing it in slightly she tried to imagine what it would feel like to have a thick, rampant stalk plunging mercilessly in and out of such a small restricting hole. Surely it would hurt?

She pushed the finger in further and circled it slightly. The muscle that had at first gripped her so tightly seemed to relax, and she found that she was able to move her finger easily. The sensation was strangely compelling and she felt the lips of her pussy opening in total submission to an invisible lover.

She eased the probing finger out of herself slowly and the ring of muscle tightened again, as if to force the intrusion from her. Soaking her fingers with her juices, she then pushed two fingers into her arse, all the way to the knuckle, and was surprised at how easy it was. She slipped them out again and replaced them with three bunched together to form a small probing spear. Lying back, she brought her knees over to rest against her chest and forced the fourth finger inside her virgin sheath. She began to plunge in and out of herself and imagined the intrusion to be that of her beloved Arman's fine thick weapon.

Putting her other hand to her soaking sex-lips, she started to rub herself frantically, while rapidly finger-fucking her tight arsehole. She thought about Micha and of how her lovely young serving-girl regularly accommodated the longest and thickest of cocks in that very same place without complaint. Soon, Sisa would experience the same delights. Micha would see to that. In a strange way she felt envious but knew, in her heart, that she could only permit Arman to take her in such a base and degrading manner.

Boudicca pictured herself kneeling on the altar, her bottom presented to him in blatant invitation as he stood behind her, his wonderful cock stretched to the limit, ready to impale her. She saw him move forward and slowly, carefully ease his full length into her tightness. Just the thought was enough. With a mute stifled cry, she came, as visions of that ultimate joy filled her mind. The muscles of her anus constricted to grip her fingers tightly as the tremors of release sparked through her lower body and she imagined that Arman's seed was jetting into her forbidden depths. She vowed there and then that she would do it; she would give herself entirely to him.

Gradually, the feelings of pure ecstasy abated and she eased her fingers from within herself and struggled to sit. She smoothed the smock down over her thighs and took a long deep breath. There was a sudden sound of movement coming from outside. Composing herself, she looked up to see Sisa and Micha enter. The two serving-girls bowed reverently and then sat at her sides. Boudicca felt the warm trickle of her juices slipping from within her hot pussy and wondered, for a brief moment, whether they could know what she had been doing, just moments earlier. It was impossible, of course, but in an odd way she found the thought highly arousing. She looked at each of them in turn and noted the remarkable differences in their appearances. Sisa's long blonde hair cascaded over her narrow shoulders whilst Micha's thick black curls clung tightly to her shapely head. Sisa's flawless skin was as white as alabaster, her body freshly washed and scented and her small smock still damp from the river. Micha's complexion was as dark as the night and glistened in the torchlight. Only their mouths were similar, both of them full and pouting sensuously.

Boudicca touched Sisa lightly on the shoulder. Her dress felt cold and wet. 'You should both remove your clothes,' she said. 'You'll get a chill.'

The girls obeyed immediately and draped the tiny garments over the back of a roughly shaped chair that stood nearby. The sight of their naked bodies reflecting the flickering torchlight thrilled the queen immensely. The two girls stood beside her again and looked down coyly at the ground before them. Boudicca reached out with her hand and raised Micha's face, then leant forward and kissed her gently on the mouth. The girl's lips parted and she delved between them with her tongue, while allowing her hand to slip down and cup one of her firm breasts. She felt the nipple harden against her palm and she squeezed the soft flesh gently. She turned to face Sisa. The young blonde immediately moved to her and kissed her passionately on the lips. Boudicca hugged the two girls to her and stroked their cool bodies lovingly. She glanced down between Micha's legs. The thick black hair glistened with dampness. She looked over at Sisa. She, too, was showing signs of arousal, the pink rose-petal lips of her pussy opening slightly under her queen's gaze.

There was no need for words. Boudicca relaxed her grip on the two, lithe bodies and quickly drew off her smock to reveal her nakedness to the eager young girls. She wrapped her arms around them both again and cuddled them tightly. Micha bent her head and took one of her queen's long nipples into her mouth. Sisa did the same with the other nipple and the two of them began to suckle her like babies at the breast. They were anything but motherly feelings that Boudicca felt within her heart, however. She ran her hands down their backs and fondled their bottoms, Micha's plump and thrusting, Sisa's small and pert. Boudicca searched out their wet pussies with her fingers and circled the tips against the tender flesh.

Micha responded by arching her back and pushing her bottom out further, while Sisa merely moaned quietly as she continued to suckle her queen's breast. Micha's fingers found the hot lushness of Boudicca's sex-lips and she began to delve within their relaxing grip, which caused the queen to shiver involuntarily. She eased her own fingers deep into the Nubian's fleshy sheath and twisted and turned them inside her, while pressing her thumb firmly against her tight little anus. The muscles of the sphincter relaxed immediately and the thumb entered her to the knuckle.

She attempted to repeat the action with Sisa, but found her tiny hole so tight that she feared that she might hurt the girl and, instead, continued to gently massage her pussy-lips. Sisa's fingers now found their way to Boudicca's cunt and she thrilled as the two girls expertly manipulated her aching flesh, each one of them alternately delving all of her fingers into her. She longed for them to go deeper, to slip their hands into her entirely. She opened her legs wide.

Micha was the first to sense her need. She allowed Boudicca's nipple to fall from her mouth and then pulled Sisa's fingers from within her and coaxed her to caress the queen's hard button with her fingertips. Boudicca watched happily as Sisa tickled her tender little spot and then took a deep breath as Micha bunched her fingers and thumb together and gradually began to slip her hand between the succulent folds of sex-flesh. It hurt slightly, but it wasn't the first time that the queen had been pleasured in this way and she relaxed the muscles of her groin until her outer lips gripped the girl's wrist tightly.

She felt the girl turning her fist inside her as if she was exploring every fold of her hidden depths and the feeling of total fullness, coupled with the thrilling sensations caused by Sisa's stimulating touch, brought her rapidly to the point of orgasm. When her climax came it was gentle, with waves of euphoria floating through her brain as she drifted into the ecstatic oblivion of blissful release. She gasped and fell slightly forward. Micha eased her hand from inside her and the two girls looked up at her through bright, shining eyes, clearly pleased that they had delighted their beloved ruler.

Boudicca lay down on her side and motioned for Micha to lie close to her so that she could lick the dark folds of her sweet pussy. Sisa moved to join them and positioned herself in order that Micha could lick between her legs, while she managed to arch herself so that she could nuzzle Boudicca's throbbing cunt. The three women lay in a perfect circle of love, each sucking and being sucked, with their hands roaming over each other's bodies. Micha held her leg high to allow Boudicca an unobstructed view of her pussy. The black lips were engorged with her lust and the lighter-coloured folds inside were parted slightly to reveal the pink succulence of her most intimate secrets. Her taste was delicate and her juices flowed copiously to soak her queen's face as she lapped hungrily at the tender flesh.

Sisa, meanwhile, was flicking the tip of her tongue lazily across Boudicca's stiff bud. Occasionally, she delved deep inside her and sucked the lips into her mouth, nipping them between her teeth. Boudicca moved her position slightly and licked Micha's other puckered hole. She heard the girl moan softly. She stiffened her tongue and prodded it against the dark circle of flesh. She sensed the muscle relax and pushed her tongue deep into Micha's bottom and then deftly slipped it in and out, fucking her lovely arse with her mouth. She thought again of Arman, and imagined him doing the same thing to her. Micha groaned loudly, the sound muffled by the softness of Sisa's sex-lips against her mouth. It was more than apparent that she was enjoying Boudicca's tender intrusion.

After a while her jaw began to ache and she

withdrew her tongue from the tight grip of the girl's anus and resumed her delicate lapping against Micha's delicious little pussy, resting her head against her thigh. The three women lay in this position for some time, each enjoying a wonderfully intoxicating sense of rapturous relaxation. Boudicca felt no desire for orgasm; the simple closeness of their shared intimacy was enough.

After some time, the three women moved apart and sat in a circle around the cooling fire. Boudicca looked lovingly at her two companions. Their eyes shone and their pussies glinted with desire. Their gentle lovemaking had been delectable but she was aware that they, like her, needed more. She got to her feet and pulled her smock over her body, quickly smoothing it down to conceal her voluptuous form. She moved to the tent flap and raised it, then stepped out into the night.

Three soldiers were standing guard outside. They held themselves suddenly erect when she appeared from the tent. Boudicca looked at each of them carefully. Two of them she knew well; they had both been the source of pleasure to her on many previous occasions. The other was a stranger to her. She pointed at him and spoke in a low, authoritative tone. 'You,' she said, 'come inside. I have need of your services.'

The other men looked across at their colleague and grinned knowingly as he stood with a bemused expression on his face. Boudicca turned and stepped back into the tent. The soldier followed immediately. She held the flap open for him and then let it fall shut as soon as he had entered, as a clear signal to the others to remain outside.

The young man stood stock still, his eyes wide as he stared at the two naked serving-girls who were kneeling before him. Boudicca regarded him with a wry smile. He was little more than a boy, about eighteen years of age and with the fresh-faced look of an innocent farm worker. His sparse uniform did little to conceal his strong muscular body, and his skin was tanned from years of working in the fields.

His eyes darted from one girl to the other and then back to the queen. There was a look of confused terror on his handsome face. His expression became even more fearful when the queen stooped and picked up a vicious-looking whip. 'These young ladies are my serving-girls,' she said as she slowly drew the lash across the palm of her hand, 'but tonight it is you who will serve them. You will do whatever they ask of you. Refuse anything and you will be flogged.'

The young man looked back at the two girls. Micha smiled broadly back at him but Sisa let her eyes fall coyly before looking back up at him with a sensuous sidelong stare. A smile began to play across his lips as he realised the delights that were likely to be in store for him. He glanced back at Boudicca and the grin disappeared from his face as he eyed the whip nervously. 'What would you have me do, majesty?' he asked hoarsely.

'Firstly, when you are within the confines of this tent, you will address me as mistress,' Boudicca replied in a firm tone, 'and secondly, you will remove your clothing.'

The young soldier wasted no time in pulling off his ragged battle-torn garments and casting them to one side. He stood naked, his cock hanging limply from his groin. Boudicca used the stock of the whip to raise the flaccid flesh and looked at it contemptuously. 'Why so small?' she sneered. 'Have you not got two beautiful girls kneeling before you, their bodies offered to you in naked submission?' He looked back at the girls. Sisa sat back on her haunches and parted her thighs to give him a perfect unobstructed view of the silky, glistening treasure between them. Micha turned herself and crouched on her hands and knees. He stared at the plump ebony globes of her bottom and licked his lips. His cock began to stiffen. Boudicca rubbed the underside of the rapidly rising stalk with the end of the whip-handle until his erection stood proud and firm.

'A fine weapon after all,' breathed Boudicca. 'See that you use it well, and do not be in a hurry to spend. Now, go to it!' The soldier immediately fell to his knees between the two girls. Sisa reached out and grasped his erection and he slipped his hand between her legs to fondle the moist promise of her fleshy opening while, at the same time, he stroked Micha's firm buttocks. He stared at the Nubian's bottom, clearly never having seen such a prize before. Boudicca watched as he traced a line along the dark cleft with his fingertip until it rested against her anus. Micha moaned contentedly. Encouraged by this, he eased the tip inside her and twisted it slightly. She breathed in sharply and pushed her bottom out even further in blatant invitation. He pushed the finger all the way in and she sighed heavily.

'Would you have him take you there?' said Boudicca in a whisper.

'Later, mistress,' replied Micha, 'but first, I need to taste him.' She moved forward and allowed his finger to slip from her, then turned to face him. Sisa let go of his cock and he raised himself up on his knees and presented his jutting stalk to Micha's face. She gave him a sultry, hungry glance and then moved forward, opening her mouth widely. The soldier gritted his teeth as her thick lips closed around his stiff rod.

'Take care, soldier,' warned Boudicca. 'If you come

before you have satisfied both girls' needs, the lash will sting you until you bleed!' Her words must have calmed his ardour, for she noticed that his cock wilted slightly, despite the fact that the head was being expertly suckled within Micha's fleshy mouth. Sisa moved behind him and put her lovely face to his bottom. She began to move her head up and down and Boudicca realised that she was licking along the crease. His stalk thickened once more and Micha started to move her face backward and forward rapidly. The young man closed his eyes tightly, his expression becoming twisted in a pained grimace.

'Watch her!' ordered Boudicca.

'Please, mistress, I cannot!' he replied, through gritted teeth.

'Watch her!' she repeated angrily. 'Watch that beautiful mouth suck your big cock while another nymph laps hungrily at your bottom!' She had chosen her words purposefully, knowing the effect that they would have on the poor wretch. He looked down. Micha leant back a little so that his full length was exposed and pushed out her tongue in order that the head of his cock rested on its silky platform. She looked up at him through wide demanding eyes. Sisa parted his buttocks with her thumbs and Boudicca could see that she was wriggling her tongue in and out of the dark sphincter of his arse.

'Mistress, forgive me!' he gasped suddenly. Boudicca grinned as his cream jetted from him to form a thick white pool on Micha's outstretched tongue. The girl held the exquisite pose for a few moments and then engulfed his rod within her mouth and sucked and swallowed all that he had to offer. Boudicca could see that she was thoroughly enjoying the taste and texture of the boy's semen but she was, nevertheless, furious that he had spent so quickly. He had to be punished.

Micha let the flaccid tool slip from her pouting lips at the same time as Sisa gave him a final long lick between his buttocks. Then the two girls sat back on the ground to await their queen's pleasure. The soldier stood stupidly before them and glanced fearfully at Boudicca, who regarded him with a stony stare.

'You were ordered not to come so quickly,' she hissed. 'Why did you disobey?'

The young man began to tremble uncontrollably. 'Forgive me, mistress,' he repeated as a small tear appeared at the corner of one of his eyes. 'I could not help myself. The dark one sucks so beautifully and, when the other licked my rear, I was lost.'

Boudicca took up the whip again and used the handle to raise his wilted penis. 'See how small it is again,' she teased, 'and yet it stretched so long and so thickly, just moments ago!' She let the soft flesh fall and turned to face the girls. 'It is of no use to us in that state,' she said, contemptuously. 'What shall we do with him?'

'Whip him,' replied Micha immediately, her eyes widening dramatically at the thought. 'Maybe the sting of the lash will cause him to rise again.'

'A fine idea,' said Boudicca as she turned once more to face the hapless boy, 'but first we must express our total disapproval. Lie down on your back, soldier, and do not move.'

The young man did as instructed. Boudicca looked down contemptuously at his prone form and then tossed the whip to the ground. Sisa and Micha got to their feet and moved to stand at her side with expressions of excited curiosity on their lovely faces. Boudicca stepped across him so that she stood astride his groin and raised her long smock until she bared her lower body. The soldier stared at the exposed beauty of her shaven pussy and she noticed his small cock twitch slightly. Holding the smock tightly underneath her arms, she reached down and tugged the lips of her sex apart. His eyes widened enthusiastically.

Suddenly, she let go a stream of piss and the hot, steaming liquid soaked his genitals and stomach. Micha squealed with delight and immediately squatted across his chest and let go a torrent of her own to soak his upper body. Boudicca looked meaningfully across at Sisa, who was watching the demonstration through startled eyes. She nervously moved to stand at the young man's head and, after some seconds of straining, the fluid began to trickle from her down-covered lips. The trickle quickly became a steady flow and he closed his eyes to the stinging water as his face became drenched. His cock began to thicken noticeably.

'See!' gasped Micha excitedly. 'It is rising again.' She and Boudicca stepped back and watched as Sisa's flow became reduced to a trickle once more and then finally stopped. The young girl's face was flushed, more from arousal than embarrassment.

'Turn on to your front!' barked the queen. The soldier obeyed immediately and lay on his stomach on the wet ground. Boudicca retrieved the whip and Sisa and Micha stepped back. She raised the lash and waited for a moment. She saw the boy clench his fists and stiffen his buttocks. He had evidently guessed what was about to happen to him.

'Whip him! Whip him!' sighed Micha hoarsely.

Suddenly, Boudicca brought the lash down. The sharp crack of leather against skin rang loudly around them and the soldier yelped with pain. A thin red stripe appeared across his firm bottom. She brought down the scourge a second time, and then a

143

third. Micha grabbed herself between her legs and began to slip her fingers inside her pussy, her expression becoming one of near manic lust. Sisa merely watched the thrashing, white-faced and trembling. Another three cuts were administered in quick succession and the marks of the lash criss-crossed over the young man's buttocks. With each cut his complaints became less urgent, as though he were becoming numbed to the agony.

Boudicca whipped him twice more and then let the crop fall to the ground. 'Turn over,' she commanded. The soldier struggled painfully until he lay on his back. To her delight, she saw that his cock was now fully erect, with the head purple and glistening with his juice.

She smiled cruelly as he looked up at her through terrified eyes. She reached down and grasped the hem of her smock and then raised the garment over her head and cast it to one side. Instantly, the terror faded from his expression as he gazed upon her sumptuous nakedness. His cock throbbed and a small jet of his cream shot over his stomach.

'Take care, soldier,' she warned. 'Fail us again and you will not see the morning.' She had no intention of harming him, of course, but knew that the threat would be sufficient to calm his ardour for the time being. She knelt at his side and grasped his thick stalk. As she gently massaged the stiff pole, she looked deeply into his eyes. 'You are to fuck us all,' she whispered, 'and you will not come until we are completely sated. Do you understand?'

He nodded and she saw him swallow heavily. She bent forward and took the head of his cock into her mouth. He throbbed again and she tasted the sweet saltiness of his semen against her tongue. She moved her head back again and smiled at Micha. 'Take him in the way that you desire the most,' she purred. Micha immediately moved to squat over him with her back to his face. Boudicca held his stiffness erect and the girl lowered herself slowly until the tip of his rod touched her pussy. Micha squeezed the muscles of her groin and her juices slipped from her to soak his long weapon and then she moved forward slightly until the head was pressed against the dark promise of her other little hole. She sank down slowly, gradually taking him inside her tightness. He groaned and Boudicca felt him throb within the grip of her hand as she clutched him at the root and she knew that his fluid would serve to add further lubrication.

She let go of his cock and watched closely as the final inches slid into Micha's bottom. The girl leant back, content for the moment to hold him deep within her. Boudicca pushed out her tongue and lapped hungrily against the exposed lips of her hairy little pussy. Micha's juices flowed from the engorged lips and soaked her face. Her musky scent was strong and filled Boudicca with the desire to delve deeper until she drew the thickly pouting lips between her teeth.

Sisa, meanwhile, had squatted over the young man's face and Boudicca could hear her moans of pleasure as he licked her hot cunt. Micha started to move her body up and down, absorbing and re-absorbing his thick stalk inside her arsehole. Boudicca watched in fascination as the dark ring moved against his gnarled pink flesh. She never ceased to be amazed at Micha's preference for such an unnatural intrusion but, from the girl's rhythmic groans of joy, it was clear that she was thoroughly delighting in the experience.

Boudicca moved to sit astride one of the soldier's ankles and pressed her wet sex-lips hard against the bone. She bent forward again and suckled Micha's oozing cunt once more, dipping her tongue in and out of her and then flicking it rapidly over the girl's hard bud. Micha came suddenly and rammed her body hard down on the soldier, taking his full length deep inside her bottom. Her cries of pleasure were matched by those of Sisa as she came in his mouth. Boudicca licked rapidly against Micha's saturated sex-lips until she was certain that the girl could take no more and then she sat back, once more pressing her pussy hard against the boy's ankle. For a brief moment, she felt a pang of envy as the two serving-girls struggled from on top of their lover, their salacious needs temporarily abated.

Sisa brought over a strip of damp cloth and carefully bathed his hard cock and then licked gently along its full length. She gripped the root and made to squat over him, but Boudicca was having none of it. She grabbed the girl by the arm and pulled her roughly away. 'Don't be so selfish!' she teased. She squatted on the balls of her feet across the prone young man. 'Hold your stalk erect, soldier,' she ordered. 'I have need of it.'

From the expression on his face, it was evident that the boy was astonished that he was about to actually fuck his queen. He gripped his cock and held it vertical, the tip inches from the open glistening lips of her pussy. She lowered herself down until the head was enveloped by her succulent folds of sex-flesh and waited for a moment. He stared at the sight of his long rod dipping into the haven of her intimate charms. Suddenly, she rammed her body down on him and took the full length inside her hot sheath. He gasped as the air was knocked from him. Boudicca repeated the action over and over again, simply using him to sate her lust. His rod speared in and out of her, the ache within her loins building rapidly to a crescendo of delight. She came with a loud cry and forced herself on to him, then circled her hips in a frenzy of joyous abandonment, rubbing her clitoris against the roughness of his hairy mound. Gradually, her movements became less urgent until she finally raised herself and let his cock flop heavily against his stomach.

Boudicca sat back against some cushions, her breasts heaving massively and her pussy tingling. The soldier looked at her, his expression a mixture of lust and wonderment. Sisa and Micha knelt at his side, clearly eagerly awaiting a continuation of the game. 'Now, my fine young man,' said Boudicca, 'fuck these two like they have never been fucked before.' The girls giggled childishly and turned to kneel beside each other on their hands and knees. The soldier raised himself and gazed at the offered perfection of their bottoms, Sisa's pert and small, and Micha's plump and demanding. He moved to kneel behind them and gripped Sisa's hips. He inched forward and Boudicca watched as his long shaft sank slowly into her fleshy pussy.

Sisa lowered herself to rest on her elbows as he began to steadily fuck her. The young man reached out and stroked Micha's upturned bottom, his fingertips tracing between her buttocks and teasing her anus and the soft suppliant lips below. The temptation proved too much for him and he eased his cock from inside Sisa and shuffled across behind Micha, then plunged it into the welcoming warmth of her inviting cunt. He moved rapidly in and out of her, his stomach slapping against her rippling buttocks.

After a short time, he moved again behind Sisa and entered her once more. This time he fucked her with wild, urgent thrusts, until she cried out as her orgasm ripped through her waif-like body. Satisfied that he had done a good job, he returned to Micha and rammed his hard stalk into her bottom. She gasped as he filled her tight sheath and then moaned melodically in time with the rapid pounding of his cock in and out of her anus. Sisa moved behind him and wrapped her arms tightly around his upper body, pressing herself hard against him and riding him like a wild stallion. Boudicca could see that she was rubbing her groin against his buttocks and the dampness of her juices trickled down the backs of his thighs.

Micha came with a loud scream and he humped her furiously, so much so that Sisa fell from him and lay sprawled on her back with her legs wide open. Micha fell forward; the soldier slipped from her and immediately swung around and dived on top of Sisa. He rammed his cock into her with one sudden lunge and she gasped with delight and raised her legs high into the air. She reached up and grabbed her ankles, then pulled them back until both of her legs rested against his shoulders.

The wet sounds of their lovemaking filled Boudicca's ears as the young man plunged again and again into the sweet succulence of the girl's sex-flesh until, at last, he could hold back no longer. He pulled from inside her and gripped his cock by the glans. He looked fearfully across at Boudicca but she merely smiled and nodded. Relieved, he rubbed himself rapidly until jet after jet of white, creamy fluid shot from the swollen head to streak across Sisa's small breasts and lovely innocent face.

Micha moved across and the young man watched in blissful astonishment as she proceeded to lick the sperm from her friend's body. Boudicca smiled to herself, knowing that the young soldier would not forget this day for the rest of his life.

148

Seven

The sun was just beginning to rise over the hills as the small group of travellers slowly approached the Iceni encampment. Suetonius drew his cloak around himself as he trudged through the muddy field and clutched the reassuring bulge of his dagger, which had been carefully hidden within the folds of the garment. He glanced nervously across at Catus, who was holding the old horse by its bridle and steering it along the barely defined path. Risa sat astride the beast, her long brown curls fluttering in the slight breeze. It felt strange to see her there, mounted in almost regal fashion while he and his colleague walked with considerable difficulty through the clinging mud. Normally, it would have been she who had led the horse while he, as supreme commander, would have sat astride the animal.

It had been Catus' idea to bring the girl. He had suggested that her presence would add credence to their deception, as would the selection of the oldest horse that they could find serve to complete the illusion that they were a band of travelling merchants. He knew that Risa was not of the Iceni, of course. Nevertheless, she was a native of this accursed land and could prove invaluable if their identities were questioned. Suetonius looked at her thoughtfully

149

and a mental image of her wriggling body sandwiched between him and his friend as they thrust into her helped to ease his nervousness. He had never known a woman such as Risa. She had been so willing and compliant that there had been no need to shackle or whip her but he knew that, should he demand it, she would happily submit herself to whatever punishment he chose to administer.

They reached the top of the slope and stopped short. Spread before them was the encampment of the Iceni, their numbers blotting out every vestige of the lush landscape for as far as the eye could see. Smoke from their fires billowed into the morning sky, lending an eerie and somewhat ethereal atmosphere to the otherwise dismal setting. There were no guards to challenge them; clearly the Iceni felt safe in their numbers.

'The stories were true,' mused Suetonius as he tapped the hilt of his dagger comfortingly. 'The entire tribe must be here.'

'Many of them are women,' replied Catus, 'but don't let that fool you. Those delicate winsome maidens can be more vicious than their men.'

'We must take great care,' continued Suetonius with little confidence in his voice. 'If we are recognised as Romans, we will be eaten alive!'

Catus laughed. 'They are not quite the savages that you imagine,' he said, slapping his friend heartily on the shoulder. 'They are merely peasants who wish to feed their families and live in peace. It is that mad vixen, Boudicca, who has fired them and caused them to rise against the Emperor. Once she has been subdued, her people will melt into the hills like frightened animals, seeking shelter.'

'I hope that you are right. Come, let us be about our task.' Suetonius strode purposefully down the slope towards the milling throng, Catus following behind as he tugged Risa's unwilling mount.

The ragged and dirty tribespeople barely glanced at the three strangers as they moved slowly among them, their heads bowed and their faces partially hidden by the hoods of their cloaks. Ahead of them stood a large tent, its doorway guarded by three heavily built soldiers. The guards stood suddenly erect as they approached, one of them brandishing a spear menacingly.

'What is your business?' he demanded.

Catus stepped forward. 'We are merchants from the West,' he replied with a surprisingly confident tone. 'We have travelled far and seek rest and food.'

The guard laughed derisively. 'You will find no rest here,' he said. 'A great battle is shortly to begin. You may fight with us, if you have the will to do so!'

There was a noise behind him and the tent-flap was suddenly thrown open. Suetonius gasped at the sight that met his eyes. A woman stood before them, her height and her shock of flame-red hair telling them that this could only be the queen, the infamous Boudicca. Her armoured breastplate glinted in the morning sun, its size and shape giving promise of the sumptuous delights hidden beneath its shining surface. In her heavy boots, the woman was easily as tall as the guards and her legs were incredibly long and shapely. She wore a short armoured skirt that clung to her rounded hips and accentuated the narrowness of her waist. Her body was clearly as superb as Catus had suggested. Suetonius looked quickly down at the ground, lest she should catch him leering at the massive swell of her breasts.

'Who are these people?' she demanded.

'Merchants, your majesty,' replied the guard.

'Merchants?' she said angrily. 'We have no time for merchants!'

'Please, majesty,' said Catus, his voice beginning to tremble slightly, 'we merely wish to rest. Allow us some succour and we will be on our way.'

The queen glared at him and then looked back at Suetonius, her expression cold and filled with cruelty. He felt his cock stiffening under her gaze and shifted uncomfortably on his feet. As if reading his thoughts, she looked down. He followed her stare and saw, to his terror, that the shape and size of his rapidly rising erection was clearly outlined under the thick material of his cloak. He shifted himself to conceal it and looked quickly back at her, praying that she had not noticed his shameful predicament.

The tent-flap moved behind her and a young girl stepped out. She stood next to the queen, her small, slight frame dwarfed by the woman's Amazonian presence. Her hair was long and white-blonde and her face bore elfin-like features that shone with youthful innocence. Another young girl slipped out of the tent and stood next to her. Her appearance could not have been more different. She was only slightly shorter than the queen herself, with a slim but shapely body and skin as dark as the deepest night. He glanced across at Catus and saw with no surprise that his friend was staring wide-eyed at her. He looked back at the girl and watched as she turned to face Boudicca. Her large bottom jutted provocatively under the thin material of her short smock. He looked quickly back at the queen, fearing that his interest might show once more under the folds of his cloak.

Boudicca turned to face the two girls. She waved her hand in the direction of Catus. 'Micha, Sisa, take that one and the girl and see that they are given food and water. I will speak with the other and find out what he knows.'

Suetonius watched enviously as Micha took Catus by the hand and led him away, closely followed by her younger colleague and Risa. He turned to face the queen and stood nervously, wondering if she had seen through his disguise. Her stern expression softened slightly. 'Come, merchant,' she said as she turned and re-entered the tent. The guards parted and he followed her quickly into the relative darkness of the interior.

Boudicca motioned for him to sit on a small chair and then sat on the edge of a rough bed opposite him. Her posture was that of a man, with her legs apart and her back held straight. Her skirt was short and the leather was studded with iron and bronze brooches, the garment falling between her legs to conceal her most intimate treasures from his gaze. Nevertheless, he sensed an innate sexuality about this powerful woman and his erection began to stiffen once more. He shifted his position and crossed his legs in an effort to conceal his discomfort.

'What do you know of Verulamium?' she asked suddenly.

Suetonius thought quickly. 'I have yet to visit the city,' he lied. 'Until now, my business has been in the West. My friends and I seek new adventure in this part of the land.'

'After today, you will find nothing in that foul city but ashes and the bodies of the dead. You would be best advised to head East.'

'Why do you mean to attack Verulamium? Are they not a peaceful people?'

'My reasons are my own,' she snapped as she rose to her feet. She stood before him with her legs apart and her hands resting squarely on her broad hips. He glanced at the bared flesh of her muscular thighs and then looked up at her face. Despite his fear, his cock was now fully erect and was beginning to ache. He had never been in the presence of such a female before. Her powerful dominance seemed to seep from her very pores. For the first time in his life he felt intimidated by a woman and, for some inexplicable reason, he found the situation to be uniquely arousing.

'This land is strange to me,' she said after a moment. 'Do you know what lies to the north of the city?'

'I have heard that the area is thickly wooded and the hills are steep. There is little to be gained from marching in that direction.' Suetonius had chosen his words carefully. He was anxious to keep the Iceni close at hand until his forces could be increased by other legions from the north, rather than have them become straggled across the countryside. Boudicca shrugged and sat down again on the edge of the bed. This time, he caught an all too brief glimpse of her shaven pussy before the tantalising sight was once more hidden from his eyes by the heavy skirt. His cock throbbed and he felt a dampness against his thigh. He cursed his uncontrollable libido, knowing that he had to keep a clear head, but the image of her bared sex-lips was imprinted on his mind forever.

'Perhaps you are right,' said Boudicca quietly and not really addressing him directly. 'I weary of battle. Perhaps, after this day, we will return home.'

'Why trouble yourself with the people of Verulamium? They can surely be no threat to the Iceni.'

Boudicca gave him a long, cold stare. 'As I said, I have my reasons,' she said simply. She stood up again and walked to the front of the tent and peered out.

'The battle has already commenced,' she continued. 'I must join my people.'

Suetonius jumped to his feet. 'No!' he said, a little too quickly. Boudicca swung round angrily and stared at him.

'Why do you care about that wretched city? They are in league with the Romans! They must be punished.'

'I care for such a beautiful queen,' replied Suetonius, relieved that his mind had reacted so swiftly. 'I would not wish to see you harmed.' Boudicca's expression softened and she walked over to face him. She looked down and her eyes widened. He followed her gaze and saw, to his horror, that his erection was firmly pushing the material of his cloak forward.

'Do you hold a weapon there, merchant?' she said in a soft, low tone.

Suetonius pressed himself hard with his hand so that the thing became crushed against his belly. 'No, your majesty,' he protested, his voice trembling slightly due to a combination of lust and the fear that she might discover his hidden dagger. 'It is simply the way my cloak hangs.'

Boudicca reached forward, gripped his wrist and pulled his hand from his stomach. His hard cock fell forward once more and jutted ludicrously under his heavy garment. She grasped the pole and squeezed it tightly. 'Your cloak does indeed hang most curiously,' she said with a wry smile. The ache in his groin grew to a painful intensity as she clasped him harder, digging her fingernails into his bone-hard flesh. She obviously knew what she was holding and there was something cruel in the manner with which she gripped him. He wanted to throw open his cloak and reveal his rampant state to her eyes. Normally, the sight of his erection would be enough to melt the coldest heart but somehow he knew that this was no ordinary woman. Such was the enigmatic power that seemed to exude from her very existence, he felt powerless in her presence.

Boudicca released her fierce hold of his cock and turned to leave the tent. 'I have business in the city of Verulamium,' she said, casually. 'Perhaps, when I return, we can speak some more.'

With that, she was gone and Suetonius was left standing alone with one of the hardest erections that he had ever experienced before in his life. He drew his cloak aside and revealed it. Gripping the thick shaft, he began to pull the loose skin back and forth. He hadn't felt the need for self-gratification for some considerable time, but he felt it now. Something about Boudicca had aroused him in a way that he would previously have thought was impossible. It wasn't just her looks, or even her huge breasts. There was something far more mysterious, even spiritual about her.

He tugged it rapidly, anxious to spend before he was interrupted. He imagined Boudicca standing before him in all her naked glory, her massive breasts thrusting forward invitingly with the nipples hard, demanding to be sucked. He rubbed himself faster as he pictured her turning her back to him and bending over with her long legs splayed apart to reveal the lushness of her soaking pussy. He saw himself approaching her with his thick tool gripped in his hand; then he imagined the sweet sensation that he would feel as her succulent lips folded themselves around the engorged head of his cock. His seed jetted from his throbbing length and hissed as it sprayed over the dying embers of the fire, a truly fitting end to his lonely release.

* * *

Suetonius spent the day wandering aimlessly about the near-deserted encampment. A few children played among the litter of ramshackle carts and discarded weaponry, supervised by a group of elderly women who regarded him with little more than idle curiosity. Catus was nowhere to be seen. Suetonius wondered for a while whether his friend had joined the Iceni in battle in order to compound their deception and to win favour with the queen, but the idea seemed unlikely. It would have meant him fighting his own kind, the Romans who manned the city's garrison.

The weather was turning colder as the sun began its descent in the cloudless sky and he decided to return to the queen's tent. On his way, he gathered some dry branches of wood to rekindle the fire, in the vain hope that a warm welcome might serve to soothe Boudicca and make her more receptive to his desires. He had thought of little else that day. He had been captivated by her, even after such a brief meeting and those few curt words. He had found the need to relieve his tension a second time, once more dreaming of her writhing under his plunging body. He knew that he had to have her, or die in the attempt. His mind was in turmoil. He and Catus had come to kill Boudicca; now all he could think of doing was of fucking her.

He entered the tent and was surprised to find Catus inside, lying on the cot. His friend waved wearily as Suetonius dumped the wood on to the ground. A small fire had already been lit, probably by Catus himself. Suetonius snapped some of the smaller twigs and fed the flames. Smoke billowed thickly at first and then disappeared through a small vent in the roof of the tent.

'Have you had a good day?' asked Catus in a tone of voice that expressed little interest in the answer to the question.

'A fruitless day,' replied Suetonius gruffly. He was angry that Catus had disappeared. They needed to talk, to plan.

'Have I a tale to tell,' said Catus as he pulled himself awkwardly to a sitting position.

Suetonius was in no mood for one of his friend's ribald anecdotes. 'Where did you get to? I searched the camp for hours, but there was no sign of you.'

Catus stretched his arms above his head and yawned. 'I was taken by those two little vixens and given food and water,' he said.

'Is that all? You spent the entire day eating?'

'Not so, friend,' replied Catus with a grin. 'You know me better than that. As I ate, I kept staring at them, trying to decide which of them I found the most captivating. Sisa, the one with the hair that shines like the sun, kept looking at me in the most winsome way and occasionally she gave me the most delightful of smiles. Micha, the dark one, merely carried on with her work and ignored me. I found her haughty disregard for my presence most appealing, and the shape of her perfect bottom, hidden from my eyes by only the flimsiest of smocks, soon caused my pego to rise.

'There was a moment when Sisa crouched on her feet before me to clear my plate. Her knees were spread wide apart and I caught a glimpse of the tiniest virginal pussy that I had ever seen. There was barely a hair to conceal its beauty and I swear the lips glistened with dampness. She noticed the direction of my avid stare and quickly brought her knees together which caused her to stumble and fall back. Her smock rode up as she fell and revealed even more of her lower parts. Instinctively, I held out my hand to help her to sit up. She grasped my wrist with one hand and smoothed down her garment with the other and then looked up at me, her face flushed with pink. She actually apologised to me! She apologised for showing me the most perfect of visions that a man could desire!

'I told her not to worry, and then said that she was very beautiful. Suetonius, my friend, at that moment, I tell you, I meant every word. My rod was as stiff as a sword by this time, as you can imagine. The poor girl looked down at the ground, clearly embarrassed. I put my hand under her chin to raise her head and then looked hard into her lovely blue eyes. Her expression changed and the flush faded. Her small mouth opened slightly and she ran the tip of her tongue across her teeth. I glanced across at Micha and saw that she was watching me closely. She smiled and then looked away, as if she were giving me her permission. I looked back again at Sisa. She was trembling and her eyes were filled with an irresistible youthful innocence. I bent my head forward and offered her my lips. I wanted her to take the initiative, to be the one to plant the first kiss. I closed my eyes and, after a moment, I felt the gentle touch of her lips against mine. It was a nervous, uncertain kiss, which made it all the more delightful.

'I looked deep into her wide sparkling eyes. I remember wondering if this had been the first time that she'd ever kissed a man. It was difficult to tell. She looked so young and so vulnerable – and yet there was an incongruous warmth in the way that she stared back at me, as if she knew that I wanted to fuck her. I knew that I had to be very careful, however. I didn't want to rush things, nor did I want to jeopardise our mission. If she complained to the queen on her return from battle, we could both have been in serious trouble, of that I was certain.

'I merely smiled at her and took a drink of wine.

Sisa looked disappointedly down at her knees and self-consciously tugged at the hem of her smock to conceal her bare thighs. There was a long pause. In the distance I could hear the sounds of battle, the cries of the wounded and the yells of the aggressors as swords clashed against swords and horses reared and charged. In a strange way, it seemed so unreal. Here was I, facing the most beautiful nymph that I had ever seen, my cock jutting firmly upwards under my cloak and there were people dying in the fields within earshot.

'It was Micha who took the initiative. She suddenly walked over and knelt behind Sisa, reached under her and grabbed the hem of her smock and then yanked it quickly up and over her head. She threw the garment on to the ground and then sat down, cross-legged, next to us. She gave me the sort of look that said, "well, what are you waiting for?" and I glanced down between her outstretched thighs. The dark promise of her pussy was clearly visible. I looked back at Sisa. She was now sitting with the same posture as her companion. Her expression was as placid and gentle as before and showed that she had a total lack of concern in the fact that her slim little body had been bared before the eyes of a complete stranger.

'I looked down pointedly between her legs. Her sex-lips were moist and were opening slowly in blatant invitation. "Are you a virgin?" I asked, although I sensed that I already knew the answer. She shook her head slowly, her mouth forming a sensuous pout. I glanced again at Micha. She was clearly intent on staying, to witness the proceedings. She was resting her head in her hands with her elbows on her raised knees. Her legs were now completely bared, the smock having slipped back, and her cunt was displayed to me in the most enticing manner. The tight black curls of hair that surrounded the dark puffy lips shone with the dew of feminine excitement and I wondered if it was not only going to be Sisa whom I would need to satisfy.

'I opened my cloak and let it fall from my shoulders. Sisa smiled broadly as she stared down at my stiff prick. I leant forward again and once more kissed her mouth but this time I forced my tongue between her soft lips. I felt her curl an arm around my neck and she responded to my kiss with all the passion of a woman with considerable experience in the art of love. I reached down and cupped one of her small breasts and then slipped my hand further down over her stomach until my fingers found the softness of her pussy. She was soaking and, although the hole was small, I had the feeling that it would be easy for me to slip all four of them inside her.

'I eased her on to her back, all the time stirring the warm juices of her honeypot. Her tongue darted against mine, slipping sensuously against and around it as though she was suckling a hard cock. I dipped all four fingers into her as far as they would go. She groaned and a rush of her hot breath filled my mouth. I pulled my face from her and gazed into her eyes. She still maintained an aura of total innocence, even though she was naked with my fingers probing deep into her hot sheath. I reached down with my other hand and rubbed her little bud rapidly, while continuing to move my fingers in and out of her. Her breath began to come in short, sharp gasps. She closed her eyes and raised her hips from the ground. I rubbed her faster. Suddenly, she grasped hold of my arm and her expression turned into a grimace. She squealed and her fingernails dug painfully into my wrist. Her juices flowed from her to soak my hand with a veritable river of come and her entire body shuddered with the spasms of her release.

'I could hold back no longer. Once that I was certain that she had calmed herself, I moved quickly between her legs and took hold of my cock, aiming it directly at the open succulence of her cunt. I plunged the full length into her with such force that she gasped loudly. This was not a time for gentleness. I fucked her like an animal, hammering in and out of her like a man possessed by demons. She took the violence of my intrusion with cries of joy, wrapped her arms and legs around my rutting body and forced her groin against me with equal ferocity. She came again and clawed at my back, screaming so loudly that I feared she would draw the attention of the old women in the encampment and have them come rushing to her aid.

'I slowed my movements and then eased my cock from within her. I sat back, in order to regain my composure. Sisa remained lying on her back, her legs wide apart and her fingers gently caressing the bright red lips of her cunt. I watched as she soaked her fingers with her juices and then put them to her mouth and lick them clean. This was certainly no virgin!

'I turned to look at Micha. She smiled, caught hold of her smock and removed it from her body. I savoured the sight of her shining sable skin. It was flawless and seemed to be coated with a shimmering sheen of fresh sweat. My cock throbbed and a droplet of my cream appeared from its angry eye. Micha bent over and took hold of the stalk and then engulfed the head within her hot mouth. I throbbed again as I felt her lapping her tongue over the end, and I knew that she was tasting me. I prayed that I wouldn't come, not yet. I had fucked one, now I needed to fuck the other.

'She moved her head up and down, absorbing and reabsorbing almost the full length of my cock within her suckling mouth. I reached over and slipped the fingers of one hand inside Sisa's pussy while I stroked and fondled Micha's wonderful bottom with the other. Sisa began to rub her clitoris rapidly while I finger-fucked her. It was obvious that she was building up to yet another spend. Micha cupped my balls and then eased a finger beneath them until the tip found my arsehole. She pushed it in slightly and I nearly came but managed, by biting hard on my lower lip, to calm myself. I ran my hand over her thrusting buttocks until the tip of my own finger found her little hole and I eased it carefully into her. To my surprise, it appeared to welcome the intrusion, the ring of muscle barely gripping my knuckle. I pushed a second, and then a third finger inside her. It was clear that she was well used to such delights.

'After a few moments of this splendid torture, Micha let my cock fall from her mouth and then she moved to squat over my lap with her back to me. I took my hand reluctantly from within Sisa and gripped Micha's waist to steady her as she fumbled beneath herself and finally gripped my raging stalk. It was the first time that I had seen her naked bottom. It seemed a little too large for her otherwise slim body but was no less appealing for that. She reminded me of that other Nubian maiden that I had fucked. She had the same fullness of the buttocks and the same sharpness of curves at the top of her thighs, causing her bottom to thrust back in the most wondrous way.

'I felt her pussy-lips close around the ridge of my cock and then she lowered herself slowly, until she held my full length inside her. The heat of her inner flesh was astounding. I rested back on my hands and merely watched as she began to move herself up and

163

down. Her big buttocks rippled as they bounced on my groin. I bent forward and kissed her back, then felt a wet tickling sensation against my balls. I looked round Micha's thrusting body to see Sisa kneeling between my legs, happily licking my taut sac. Micha held herself still for a moment and, as I watched, Sisa drew her tongue upward, along the exposed length of my shaft and then on to the top of her friend's cunt.

'I could see her flicking the tip of her tongue against the girl's prominent bud. Micha was hardly going to move while she was enjoying such delights, so I began to fuck her from beneath. She came within seconds, and I could feel her juices trickling down over my balls to soak me between my thighs. Sisa immediately lapped the fluids from me, as if anxious not to allow a drop to dampen the grass below us. The sensation of her tongue fluttering around my tender flesh was indescribable.

'Micha slowly eased her body up until my cock was freed from the tight grip of her sex-flesh. She grasped hold of it again by putting her hand between her legs and then moved slightly forward. She lowered herself cautiously. I watched with mounting joy as the head of my rod touched her dark sphincter and then disappeared within the tightness of her arsehole. Somehow, I had known that this would happen. A girl with a bottom as perfect in every way as this could not possibly deny a man the ultimate pleasure. She sat down on me slowly until the full length was inside her. Almost immediately, I sensed that Sisa was back with her mouth pressed against her friend's cunt. I could hear the wet sounds as she sucked the girl's juices and I could feel her hot breath on my balls.

'For some moments, I was content to lie with my cock firmly wedged inside Micha's tight rear, but soon I became impatient for more. I gripped her firmly by the waist and raised her body slowly until all but the head of my cock was exposed, and then I rammed her down again on to my groin. She yelped as my rod thrust all the way into her bottom. I repeated the action over and over again, Micha's buttocks slapping noisily against my skin. Sisa somehow managed to continue to suckle her friend's sex-lips as I arse-fucked Micha harder and harder.

'I knew that the end was close for me. The situation had been too exquisite for it to last long. I had fucked two beautiful young girls and now I had my cock rammed deep into the loveliest bottom I could ever have imagined. The surge came quickly. I gripped her waist tightly and forced my stalk as far as it could go into her. She gasped loudly. Sisa must have realised my predicament, for she immediately took my balls into her mouth and sucked heavily on them as I came with a groan of pure joy.

'After it was over, we fell apart and just lay on the ground for some minutes, watching the clouds. The sounds of the battle filled my ears once more, but they were meaningless. My cock was aching and all was right with the world.

'I spent the rest of the day with these two delightful creatures. They caused me to rise three more times until, finally, I had to beg them to allow me to return alone to this tent.'

Suetonius had listened enviously to his friend's ribald tale and his cock was standing stiffly under his cloak. 'They sound most accommodating, these serving-girls,' he said, resisting the temptation to grasp his stalk and ease the pressure of his lust yet again.

'Indeed they were, friend,' laughed Catus as he stretched out again on the cot. 'But what of you?

There are many other willing girls in the camp, I am sure. Did you find one or two to satisfy you?'

Suetonius shook his head. 'I had no such desire,' he replied.

'That is not like you. I am aware that we have to take care, but you once told me yourself that a day without a good hard fuck is a day wasted.'

Suetonius merely shrugged and looked dolefully into the flickering flames of the fire. Catus raised himself on one elbow and looked at him questioningly. 'What is it, friend?' he asked. 'What ails you?' Suetonius said nothing. Catus suddenly sat bolt upright. 'By the emperor's teeth!' he exclaimed. 'You are smitten!'

Suetonius turned to face him and glared angrily. 'Don't be ridiculous,' he growled.

Catus swung his feet from the cot and laughed cruelly as he slapped his friend hard on the shoulder. 'You are!' he cried, 'You are smitten! My story has offended and hurt you. Tell me, which one is it? Which of those two nymphs has stolen your heart?'

'Do you really think I could have any feelings for a mere servant?' hissed Suetonius furiously.

Catus regarded him quizzically for a moment and then broke into a broad grin. 'The queen!' he exclaimed. 'You have fallen for Boudicca herself! This is too perfect. Woo and win her, friend, and our troubles will be over. Besides, I have lost the desire for killing. How could either of us plunge a dagger between those superb breasts? Make her your slave; tame her with that huge pego of yours and her people will yield to the Roman commander.'

'I am not so sure that it will be so easy,' began Suetonius, once more looking into the flames of the fire.

'Of course it will!' interrupted Catus. 'One sight of

that monstrous weapon should be sufficient and, if she resists then beat her until she complies. Sting the royal bottom with the palm of your hand and she will soon yield to your desires!'

'The queen is not one who could be so easily subjugated,' sighed Suetonius sadly. 'Would that she was. Nothing would give me greater pleasure than to cause the skin of her buttocks to redden before I impaled her with my staff.'

'Then do it!' said Catus excitedly. 'Do it for Rome!'

The dark shades of night had enveloped the encampment by the time the Iceni warriors returned from the battle at Verulanium. Suetonius stood outside the queen's tent and watched them as they trudged wearily through the mud. He looked anxiously among them for a sight of Boudicca. He saw her at last, standing triumphantly atop a large chariot pulled by two sweating horses, her long red hair billowing in the breeze as she sped towards him. To his eyes she appeared like a goddess, her frame silhouetted against the flame-red clouds behind her, which gave evidence that the city had been razed to the ground.

The horses reared and snorted loudly as she drew up to the tent, their hooves pawing at the muddy ground. Boudicca slipped from the chariot and stood before him. Her eyes were wide and fired with passion. 'Well, merchant,' she said in a powerful voice filled with emotion, 'the battle is over and the city is ours!'

'What of the Roman garrison?' asked Suetonius, carefully ensuring that he sounded curious rather than concerned.

'The cowards fled into the hills at the first sight of my brave warriors! Those who remained to fight were dealt with quickly. They had grown fat and lazy on the backs of the people.' She swept past him and entered the tent. Suetonius followed her into the warm enclosure. Catus had absented himself, no doubt to seek the favours of the two serving-girls once again.

Boudicca began to grapple with the leather thongs that bound her armoured breastplate to her chest. 'Assist me, merchant,' she ordered. 'My fingers are numbed from clutching my sword.'

Suetonius moved swiftly over to stand behind her and clawed at the knots with trembling hands. The leather had been dampened with her sweat and it had now dried, causing it to constrict so that the knots had become impossibly tight.

'I'll have to cut then,' he said, as he reached for his dagger. Suddenly realising the folly of such an action, he tried again to untie the bonds.

'Use this,' said the queen, handing him a wicked-looking knife. He took the weapon by its jewelled grip and quickly severed the restraining cords. Boudicca eased the breastplate away from her chest and tossed it on to the ground. He stood behind her, staring at her naked back, his hands shaking mere inches from her hot skin. There was a small fresh cut on her body, just above the belt of her skirt.

'You are injured, majesty,' he said. He reached out and touched the scar with his fingertips.

She shivered. 'It is nothing, I am sure. I can feel no pain.'

'Let me bathe it for you,' he insisted, stroking carefully around the mark.

She moved away quickly. 'My servants will do that for me,' she replied. 'They should be here.' She turned to face him, standing shamelessly before him with her breasts bared. Suetonius gazed in wonder at them. It

168

was not only their size that was magnificent. Their upward thrust and their perfect shape thrilled him, as did the sight of her long dark nipples and the deep brown texture of her areolae. He looked quickly up at her face. The queen seemed oblivious to the fact that she was presenting herself half-naked to a man. 'Have you seen the girls?' she continued. 'It really is wicked of them not to be here to welcome me on my return. They will be severely punished!'

'I am sure that they have good reason,' replied Suetonius, his rising lust affording him some bravado. 'Please, allow me to tend to your needs.'

She gave him a sidelong glance and then looked down at the front of his cloak. He knew that the shape of his thickening cock would be discernible under the heavy cloth, but this time he was unconcerned. She would have to know of his desire for her if he was to succeed in his mission.

Boudicca looked back into his eyes and smiled gently. 'Very well,' she said, 'you may bathe me.' Suetonius retrieved a bowl of tepid scented water which lay close to the fire while the queen removed her boots and the remainder of her clothing. She snatched up a piece of cloth and held it against her most intimate part as she turned and faced him. She offered him a brief sensuous glance of her eyes as she moved past him to lie on her back on the cot. She positioned herself with one leg held straight and the other bent with her hand resting on the knee. The cloth was carefully draped across her groin, her only attempt at modesty.

Her provocative pose caused his cock to stiffen completely as he soaked a rag with water. He knelt beside her and twisted and squeezed the rag over her neck. The water trickled on to her, forming little rivulets that cascaded down between her heaving breasts and on to her stomach. He rubbed the cloth over her, firstly between her breasts, then around them and finally over the sumptuous soft globes.

Boudicca closed her eyes and relaxed under his gentle touch. Her mounds moved heavily as he bathed them and he saw that her nipples had hardened remarkably. He became bolder, certain now that she would submit to his carnal demands. He squeezed each breast in turn and then moved the rag down to her stomach. He stroked her softly and she let her leg fall straight with her thighs parted slightly.

Suetonius soaked the rag with water once again and squeezed it deliberately over the cloth that covered her ultimate treasures. He bathed her upper thighs and then, barely daring to breathe, he eased the cloth away from her, baring her completely. He glanced fearfully up at her face, but her eyes remained closed and her expression held a look of benign refreshment. He gazed back at her groin. The sight of her shaven mound delighted him. The lips of her sex were dry and showed no sign of arousal, but he nevertheless felt a compelling urge to kiss them. Nervously, he bent his head towards her and breathed in deeply. Her scent was intoxicating. His lips brushed lightly against her pussy and then he kissed it gently. He heard her take a short, sharp intake of breath and he looked up at her face. She was staring at him through wide startled eyes.

He began to bathe her thighs again in the hope that she would think that the touch to her sex had merely been the accidental brush of the cloth against her flesh. She closed her eyes again and he relaxed. He moved the wet cloth over her pussy and rubbed it up and down. Boudicca sighed and he knew that he had her in his power. He cast the rag to one side and then once more put his mouth to her pussy. He kissed the opening lips again and then traced their shape with the tip of his tongue, before delving between them and sucking the thick flesh between his teeth.

Her juices began to flow and filled his mouth. He swallowed hard and then started to flick the tip of his tongue over her hard bud. She responded by thrusting her hips rhythmically against his chin and moaning softly. She came with a suddenness that shocked him and writhed her body wildly as the spasms of joy coursed through her. He held tightly on to her hips and continued to lick her until she relaxed, then he sat back and gazed down at her with a proud smile on his face.

Boudicca opened her eyes and stared back at him. Suetonius rose to his feet and unfastened his cloak. Careful not to reveal the hilt of the dagger that was hidden in the pocket, he let the garment fall to the ground and stood before her in proud nakedness. His cock jutted forward, the long stalk straining at his groin and the head purple with his lust. He knew that the mere sight of his immense weapon would be enough to cause the juices to flood from her hot cunt. He moved her legs apart and knelt between them. Her sex-lips had parted in open invitation and glistened with her arousal. He gripped the root of his cock and aimed the head at its ultimate target.

Suddenly, Boudicca sat up and pulled herself from him. She drew her leg back and aimed a kick, which connected painfully to his stomach. More shocked than injured, he fell back on to the ground and hit his head sharply on the discarded breastplate. 'How dare you?' she roared, jumping to her feet. 'How dare a mere merchant attempt such a thing? Guards!'

The tent-flap was thrown aside and two burly soldiers rushed in. They grabbed Suetonius immediately and held him firmly by the arms. Boudicca stood before him, her eyes blazing with fury. 'I have welcomed you, fed you, given you warmth and comfort and this is how you repay me! Guards, turn him!'

The soldiers obeyed immediately, roughly dragging him round until he had his back to the queen. He looked over his shoulder in terror. Boudicca walked swiftly to the rear of the tent and stooped to retrieve something from behind a pile of clothing. His eyes widened in fearful confusion as he saw that she now held a long thin cane. He had expected a sword or a knife, fully accepting that he had lived his last day. She moved over to stand once more behind him. He turned his face away and heard her swish the cane in the air, teasing him with its terrible sound. He struggled hard and the guards gripped him tightly, their fingernails biting painfully into the flesh of his arms.

'No man may touch me without my express permission,' she said, her voice trembling with anger.

'But I thought ... you seemed so willing,' he protested.

'Silence, merchant!' she barked. 'You will be punished and thrown out of this place. Hold him tightly!' Suetonius heard the swish of the cane once more. The pain seared through his backside as it made contact with his bare flesh and he gritted his teeth, determined not to cry out. Four more cuts followed in quick succession, the last one delivered with such force that he gasped in agony. The soldiers released their grip on his arms and he fell to his knees. His bottom stung and, to his profound amazement, he found that his cock stretched as hard as before, despite the throbbing pain.

'Take your cloak, merchant, and be gone,' said the queen breathlessly. Suetonius looked up at her through tearful eyes. Even in his pain, he could see that she was beautiful, standing there naked and proud with the cane held high in a threatening manner. Her thrusting breasts heaved dramatically and he could see that the lips of her pussy were engorged and soaking.

He noticed her glance down at his throbbing cock and he tried desperately to understand why she had not let him penetrate her. She was quite evidently highly aroused. He grabbed the garment quickly, before she had a chance to change her mind, and scurried out into the night.

The rabble of exhausted warriors hindered his path as Suetonius clambered over their reclining bodies in a frantic search for Catus. His mind was in turmoil. He knew that he no longer had the will to kill the queen, despite her savage treatment of him, and yet he was also well aware that the Iceni hordes had to be stopped before they ravaged the entire country. With each victory, they would become more manic in their desire to rid the land of every last Roman, and soon they would be out of control.

He reached the edge of the encampment and decided to rest in some bushes until daybreak, before resuming his search for his friend. He pushed his way through the undergrowth, twigs snapping noisily under his rough tread.

'Suetonius! Over here!'

To his profound relief, he recognised the hushed cry as that of Catus. 'Where are you?' he called as he peered into the darkness. 'I can't see you.'

'Here!' repeated Catus. 'Come quickly! I have something here that you must see.' Suetonius pushed his way in the direction of the voice and finally stumbled into a small clear area surrounded by bushes and trees. Catus was kneeling naked on the ground, grinning broadly. In front of him lay Sisa and Micha. The two girls were also naked, writhing together with their faces buried in each other's groins. The air was filled with the sounds of their suckling lips and lapping tongues. 'What think you of this delightful display?' asked Catus. Suetonius fell to his knees and winced with pain as his stinging bottom touched the backs of his calves. 'What happened to you?' his friend asked.

'It is nothing,' he replied. 'Where is Risa?'

'I left her in the company of three soldiers. She is being treated well enough, you can be certain of that.'

The two men sat in silence for some minutes. The girls seemed unaware of their presence as they continued to pleasure each other with their tongues. Suetonius felt his erection begin to stiffen. His need to ejaculate was becoming unbearable. He glanced at his friend's penis. It lay wilted and pathetic across his thigh.

Catus noticed him looking and grinned. 'I have spent three times within the last hour,' he said, 'once in each of their mouths and the last time inside Micha's sweet bottom. I have no more to give. How went it with the queen?'

Suetonius shook his head. 'I had thought that the euphoria of the victory would have made her receptive to my demands, but I received a whipping for my trouble. We have to leave this place.'

'But we have achieved nothing! If you cannot tame her with your rod, then the queen must be killed!'

'No!' said Suetonius vehemently. 'I cannot do it!'

Catus began to struggle to his feet. 'Then I will do it!' he said, reaching for his cloak. 'Her guards will be exhausted from battle. There could not be a better time.'

'Stay, friend,' cautioned Suetonius as he grabbed Catus tightly by the wrist. 'I will not allow it. This is my fight. I must deal with Boudicca in my own way.'

Catus looked at him suspiciously. 'You still yearn for her, friend,' he sneered. 'Your heart is soft and your cock is hard. Would you see the Romans disgraced for the sake of filling one woman with your seed?'

'She is no ordinary woman.'

'She is a woman. That is enough.' He waved his free hand at Sisa and Micha. 'She is no different from these two. Here, sate yourself upon them before your mind becomes addled by your lust.'

Suetonius released his grip of Catus' arm and the two men relaxed. Sisa was lying on top of Micha by this time, happily lapping between the other girl's legs and crushing her pussy against her mouth. 'These two are insatiable,' continued Catus with a smile. 'Surprise the blonde one with that magnificent rod of yours.'

Suetonius gazed hungrily at Sisa's upturned bottom, Micha's tongue playfully delving between the juicy lips of her pussy. His cock stretched to full erection and he knew that he would not be able to hold back for much longer. He also knew that he desperately needed to feel the slippery grip of a woman's sex-flesh around his bone-hard stalk or he would go mad.

He slipped his cloak from his shoulders and shuffled on his knees to kneel behind the young blonde. Micha's eyes widened when she saw the size of his erection and she reached out and grasped it tightly. She rubbed it gently up and down for a moment and then aimed the head at the other girl's open sex. He pushed forward and the huge knob slipped inside. Sisa raised her head and took a deep

175

breath as she realised what was happening to her. He heaved himself forward and forced in as much of his length as she could take, while Micha lapped greedily at his exposed stem and balls.

'Ooh . . . aah,' was all that Sisa could say as he filled her with his thick cock.

He began to fuck her slowly, anxious to prolong the pleasurable intrusion as much as possible, and Micha returned to her task of licking Sisa's clitoris. Sisa buried her face once more between Micha's legs and he watched her head bobbing up and down in almost perfect time with his steady, careful thrusts.

The more that he fucked the slim, lithe body, the more that she was able to take of him until, at last, she accommodated the full length of his weapon. He held himself still with his cock deep inside her, feeling it throb; thankfully, it eased the pressure of his desire. After a moment, he slipped from her and moved round to position himself between Micha's legs. He lay on his back and lifted the dark girl's legs over his body and then moved over on to his side, until his cock was inches away from Sisa's mouth. She left off from licking Micha's cunt and took him between her lips. She sucked as deep as she could, her tongue circling and lapping against his hard flesh, and then she moved her head back and, grasping his stalk tightly, she aimed the head at the ebony succulence beneath her face.

He slid into her with remarkable ease while Sisa licked both his thick length and Micha's pussy alternately. In such an awkward position, he found it difficult to move his lower body adequately but Micha made up for it by thrusting her hips firmly against him. He could feel himself nearing the end, but he didn't want to come yet. He pulled himself quickly out of the hot honeyed sheath in order to pause for a moment and regain his control, but Sisa was having none of it. She grasped his exposed length and immediately forced the head into her mouth. It was too much for him. He came with a long, low moan, his cream jetting into the warm sucking envelope of the lovely blonde's mouth. She swallowed everything that he had to give, apart from a little trickle that slipped from the corner of her mouth, and he watched as it dropped slowly on to Micha's gaping sex-lips.

It had been swift but it had been good. Suetonius extricated himself from his awkward position and struggled to his knees. He looked around and suddenly realised that Catus had gone. Cursing himself for his stupidity, he got to his feet and donned his cloak. He was about to go off in search of his friend when, without warning a group of Iceni guards crashed through the bushes. Two of them grabbed hold of him by the arms while the others brandished their swords menacingly.

'What is this?' he demanded angrily. 'Am I not a guest of your queen?'

One of the soldiers, who was apparently their leader, stepped forward. 'We have been sent by the queen to find her beloved servants,' he said as he leered at the two naked forms on the ground. 'She will not be best pleased to learn that they have been impaled by a mere merchant. Bring him.'

Suetonius knew that struggle was likely to be in vain and he allowed himself to be dragged from the bushes and back into the encampment. The hilt of his knife prodded against his side as he walked and he knew what he had to do.

Eight

Suetonius felt a mounting anger as he was dragged unceremoniously through the jeering crowd of Iceni warriors towards the queen's tent. His fury was directed not at the rabble of battle-weary and exhausted peasants but at himself, for allowing his emotions to cloud his good sense.

Boudicca had lain helpless before him, less than an hour ago. She had been naked and vulnerable, and his knife had been within easy reach. He knew that he should have despatched her to greet her pagan gods there and then, rather than allowing himself to become entranced by her powerful sexuality. Now it was too late. Now it would be he who would be slain.

He became curious as to the fate of his friend. Catus had clearly been intent on killing the queen when he had sneaked away during Suetonius' delightful interlude with the two serving-girls, but there had been no sounds of uproar nor signs of anything amiss in the encampment. He considered that Catus might already be dead. Perhaps his friend had been caught in his attempt and put to the sword for his trouble.

Suetonius was pushed roughly inside the tent and he fell to his knees on to the hard ground. One of the guards immediately pressed the sole of his boot against his neck, forcing his face against the dank, dried mud. He braced himself and waited for the blow of a spear to his back.

'You have gone too far this time, merchant.' He recognised the harsh voice as that of the queen herself. He tried to raise his head but found it impossible. He gasped for breath and his mouth became choked with foul-tasting earth. He coughed and spluttered in an attempt to spit the dirt from between his lips. He felt totally degraded, lying naked on the ground, apparently surrounded by numerous men and women who were clearly mocking him in his shame.

'You had been banished from this place and yet you chose to insult me further,' continued the queen. He opened his eyes. All that he could see was her boots as she stood in front of him but even the sight of them caused his cock to stir beneath him. He remembered her lying naked on the cot, her huge breasts glistening with water as he bathed them and the nipples long and thick, begging to be sucked. He thought of the vision of her shaven pussy and the exquisite taste of her sex-lips and his rod stretched to full erection despite his wretched predicament.

Not for the first time, he cursed his lack of self-control. He knew that, if he were made to stand, the crowd would mock him all the more when they saw his rampant erection. He crushed his lower body hard against the ground in an attempt to force the thing into obedience, but this merely made matters worse. Boudicca crouched down in front of him and gripped his hair painfully, raising his head from the ground as the guard shifted the boot from his neck and pressed it against the small of his back. In this position, he found himself looking straight up her short skirt, the open lips of her pussy clearly visible. He considered that she was holding this provocative stance on purpose, and that she was teasing him unmercifully before finishing him for good.

'Sisa and Micha are very precious to me,' said Boudicca, her tone a little gentler but nevertheless sounding as cruel as before. 'You and your friend will be punished severely for your impertinence.'

His heart leapt at her words. Catus was alive! It now seemed likely that the guards had witnessed his friend's pleasurable assault on the two girls and must have arrested him before he could get to the queen. Despite her threatening tone, he felt better. At least he was not alone.

'Have him stand!' barked Boudicca. His heart sank again. His cock had remained as firm as ever, pressing hard against his stomach. He was dragged to his feet and the crowd gasped as his shame was revealed to their leering eyes. 'What think you of this prize?' said the queen, turning to face a group of women, who were staring at his exposed stalk, their eyes wide with astonishment and delight. She turned back to face him and reached out her hand slowly. He winced with pain as she gripped his cock tightly and dug her fingernails into his iron-hard flesh. She stared into his eyes. There was no sign of lust in her expression, merely cruelty and enjoyment. 'We will have much sport with this magnificent weapon before we are done with you,' she hissed. She turned to the guards. 'Bind him!' she ordered.

His hands were quickly tied behind his back and his ankles were strapped tightly together. The leather thongs bit into his flesh but the pain, for some reason that he could not comprehend, felt good. His stalk remained as stiff as before, rising from his groin like a spear. He looked across at the group of women. They were chattering excitedly and laughing as they continued to gaze at his cock and he began to wonder whether his punishment would be to merely have him thrown to their salacious mercy.

Boudicca walked slowly around him, grinning wickedly. A simple chain vest that did little to hide her curvaceous form covered her upper body. Suetonius attempted to avoid looking at the swell of her breasts as she moved in front of him, but found it virtually impossible. He yearned to grasp hold of them and suckle on the hard teats like a baby, or rub his aching cock between the succulent soft mounds of warm flesh until his release soaked her lovely face.

'You use women like they were your playthings,' she said, her anger clear in her tone. 'No doubt you fuck them and then cast them aside. Is that not so?' She stared directly into his eyes, demanding an answer but he said nothing. 'Perhaps you whip them,' she continued, once more walking around him slowly. He felt her draw a fingernail across his back and he gasped with the pain. 'Perhaps you shackle them and lash their poor skin until you tire of the game, and then you ram that foul thing deep into their bodies to sate your lust, without the slightest thought for their own desires or needs. Well, merchant, now it will be your turn to suffer!' She swung around and faced the guards. 'Turn him and hold him firmly,' she ordered.

Two soldiers gripped his arms and forced him to face the tent wall. As he stood there, Suetonius remembered the delightful agony of the cane as it had cut across his buttocks only a short while before and, despite his fear, he knew that it held no terrors for him. His only concern was that he would ejaculate after the first stroke and, with his libidinous desires momentarily lost as a result of spending, he knew that the pleasure would certainly not be so intense.

'Lilani, take the tawse and show the merchant what we Iceni women think of his kind.' He turned his head and looked over his shoulder to see Boudicca offering a short thong of split leather to one of the women. She was possibly the oldest of the group, a tall, heavily built woman with homely, though not altogether unpleasant, features. The look on the woman's face was anything but pleasant, however. Her eyes shone with cruel delight and her grin broadened as she caressed the tawse lovingly. She moved to stand behind him and he turned his face away and waited for the inevitable.

The pain of the first stroke seared across his bruised buttocks and caused him to yelp loudly. The women laughed derisively at his discomfort and he felt angry that he had appeared so weak. The second stroke caught him full on both cheeks, suggesting that Lilani was well schooled in her task. With the third, the savage ends of the tawse lashed against his upper thighs just below the curve of his backside. He felt thankful that his feet had been bound so closely together. Had they not been, had his legs been only slightly apart, the leather thong would certainly have stung against his balls.

There was a pause. He glanced over his shoulder once more and saw Lilani hand the tawse to another woman. She was much younger, barely out of her teens, and with a delicate litheness of form that reminded him of the delightful Sisa. The girl moved to stand behind him and he waited for the pain, feeling confident that her assault on his tender, hot flesh would be less intense.

He could not have been more wrong.

He gasped as the thong lashed across his bottom, the pain sharp and tearing into his groin like a bolt of lightning. His cock throbbed and a jet of cream shot from the angry purple end to streak across the wall of the tent. One of the women laughed and clapped her hands. It was clear that she had witnessed his involuntary spasm. 'He has come! He has come!' she cried triumphantly.

Boudicca stepped up to him and grasped his raging stalk tightly. She squeezed it until it hurt and the shaft throbbed heavily. A sliver of clear fluid slipped from the end and trickled over her fingers. She smiled and turned to face the others. 'Not so,' she said, 'he merely savours the kiss of the tawse. But take care, sister, I fear that one more stroke will finish him!' She put her fingers to her mouth and licked the juice from them while staring into his hungry eyes suggestively.

There was more derisive laughter as the entire group of women moved over to stand by him. Numerous hands fondled and caressed his stinging buttocks as if to soothe away the pain. He looked around at them all. There was not one among them whom he would not have gladly thrown to the ground and fucked to within an inch of her life, were he not bound and held so helpless. The young girl who had been the last to beat him gazed in wonder at his stiff cock, then reached out gingerly until she circled its girth with her fingers. She stared at it as if she had never seen one before in her life.

'Do you want that, Tamina?' said Boudicca, in a quiet, teasing voice. The young girl nodded slowly and began to move her hand up and down the long shaft, causing the loose skin to move against the hard rod in a gentle, tantalising way. 'You had better stop doing that,' continued the queen, 'or he will be no good for you.' The girl released her grip of his cock and stood back. 'Lie him on the ground!' ordered Boudicca.

As Suetonius was forced on to his back on the rough floor of the tent, the women gathered around him like vultures preparing to feast on the carcass of a dead animal. He knew that he was completely at their mercy, and that they could do absolutely anything to him that took their fancy. The thought both terrified and aroused him in equal measure. Lilani knelt at his side, grasped his cock by the root and raised it vertically. Tamina moved to squat across his lower body, facing him. He looked up at her. Her hair was fair and had been cut short, as was the custom of many of the Iceni women who fought in battle, and the otherwise flawless skin of her face bore a tiny fresh scar. It was evident to him that, despite her youth, she was not one to be trifled with. She raised her skirt and bared her genitals to him. He looked between her legs and saw that the lips of her cunt were already red and engorged as testament to her lust. He glanced back up at her face and smiled, but her expression remained stern and unforgiving.

The girl lowered herself slowly on to the proffered pole, absorbing it into her hot silky sheath in one long and insistent movement, until her wet outer lips pressed hard against his pubic mound. He had expected her to move up and down and fuck herself on him, but she seemed content to remain still with his full length buried deep inside her. She looked into his eyes with a cold unremitting stare which he found to be most disconcerting, but the heat of her inner flesh burned into his aching stalk and he chose to ignore her apparent hatred of him.

He felt her use the muscles of her groin to grip him tightly within her. The sensation caused him to stiffen even more. Her eyes widened considerably and he felt proud. 'He is so large,' she said, in a quiet, almost ethereal tone. 'I have waited so long for one such as this to impale me.' Suetonius attempted to move his hips in order to thrust in and out of her but she slapped her hand against his chest angrily and forced her body hard on to him. 'Be still, merchant!' she hissed. He sensed her squeeze her inner flesh against him again, and then again.

Soon, she was using her pussy-muscles rhythmically, clenching and unclenching them over and over again. He looked down between her legs. Her prominent bud seemed to have a life of its own as it bobbed and swelled in time with her movements. The sight thrilled him and he forgot the stinging pain in his buttocks as he watched in fascination. Evidently, she didn't need a touch of fingers or tongue to the hard little button to arouse her, nor did she want the incessant thrusting of a cock in and out of her soaking depths to satisfy her desires.

She came suddenly and quietly with the merest of moans, her juices flooding from her to soak his groin. Sated, she raised herself quickly and let his hard rod flop on to his stomach. It slapped against his skin and she moved away from him without as much as glancing at his face. The other women turned away from him and began to chatter to each other as if nothing had happened, leaving him lying on the ground, bound and feeling totally degraded. The girl had used him to satisfy her own needs without a thought for his own desires, just as the queen had suggested. She had had no need to experience the feeling of his cock plunging in and out of her in order to enjoy her release and he felt useless and humiliated.

He looked down at his hard aching rod. The thick shaft was gleaming in the torchlight, coated with the juices of Tamina's pleasure and the plum-sized purple head was resting above his navel. As he stared, it seemed to thicken and raise itself from his body slightly. A sudden unexpected surge took control of his lower body and he realised that there was nothing that he could do. The semen spurted from the angry end of his cock and the first jet shot over his shoulder to land on the ground behind him. His stalk jumped like a rearing animal as more and more of his cream soaked his chest and stomach until, at last, the urgency passed and his rod sank as if in compliant acceptance of the situation to lie flaccid against his groin.

Suetonius knew at last that, while he may have been lashed, abused and debased, he had enjoyed every single moment of his exquisite torture. The pain had been great and yet, for some reason that he couldn't begin to understand, the pleasure associated with it far outweighed any discomfort. Most importantly of all, he knew that he wanted more.

The revelries of the victorious Iceni seemed destined to continue throughout the night. Thankfully, Suetonius had had the tight leather bonds removed from his wrists and ankles, but he now found himself shackled to one of the stout tent-posts with his arms stretched high above his head and his feet just touching the ground. His limbs ached from the constricting position and his backside still stung from the flail, but Boudicca had seen to it that he was fed and given some water. It was clear that she didn't intend to kill him, but merely use him for her own pleasure as and when the fancy took her.

The queen had long since gone to join her fellow tribespeople along with the group of women and most of the soldiers who had witnessed his humiliation. A solitary guard remained, snoozing in a corner of the tent. Suetonius tugged at the shackles and the iron bit painfully into his wrists. He relaxed, realising that the effort was futile, and decided that he had no choice but to wait and discover what other strange delights were in store for him. He also knew that he had to escape; he had to find Catus and return to his legion in the hope that the promised reinforcements had arrived, and then lead the Roman forces against the Iceni before they could cause further trouble.

There was a sudden noise coming from directly outside the tent. The guard, awakened from his slumber by the sounds, grasped hold of his spear and struggled to his feet. The tent-flap was brushed aside and Boudicca swept in, tugging a length of chain behind her. Suetonius gasped as he saw that the chain was fixed to an iron collar around his friend Catus' neck, and he was being hauled along on all fours behind her like an animal. 'Greetings, merchant,' laughed the queen cruelly. 'Your friend has served us well, but I fear that he now has no more to give!' She yanked the chain hard and Catus fell forward on to his face at Suetonius' feet. The skin of his lower back and bottom was bruised and striped from a dozen cuts of the lash, and it was clear that he was exhausted.

'Chain him to the other one,' barked the queen. Two soldiers who had followed her into the tent did as she ordered, clasping the chain to the shackles binding Suetonius' wrists. The length of the chain allowed Catus to remain seated on the ground and he slumped forward and rested his head on his knees. Content that he was adequately secured, Boudicca turned and left the tent without a further word, closely followed by her guards.

The remaining soldier checked their shackles and then he, too, left them, no doubt to indulge himself in the noisy bacchanalia outside. Suetonius waited for a few moments in silence. He heard laughter echoing in the night and the occasional female shriek and, for a moment, he felt quite envious. He looked down at his friend, who was giving the impression of being sound asleep.

'Catus,' he whispered, 'Catus, wake up!'

His friend raised his head wearily and looked up at him. His eyes were bleary and his face appeared remarkably drawn. 'What is it?' he said, in a voice that could barely be heard.

'We must escape! We must return to the legion!'

'Tomorrow,' replied Catus as his head fell forward once more.

'What have they done to you?' asked Suetonius anxiously. 'Have you been tortured?'

Catus took a deep breath before he replied. 'Tortured? Possibly. But it was the most delightful torture a man could ever experience.'

'I see that you bear marks of the lash,' said Suetonius.

Catus rubbed his face with his hands. 'That was as nothing,' he replied. 'In fact, I found that I experienced a certain amount of pleasure from being whipped by a woman.'

'Tell me what happened to you!' Suetonius said excitedly, anxious to hear his friend's tale.

'Can't it wait until tomorrow? I am finished.' With that, Catus fell over on to his side and curled up. Suetonius kicked him lightly but he merely groaned quietly and slipped off to sleep.

Dawn came and the sun streamed in through the many gaps in the tent-cloth; a couple of flies appeared to be dancing in the shafts of bright light. Outside, there was complete silence, save for the twittering of birds and the occasional bark of a dog. The Iceni had clearly drunk too much wine and indulged in far too many other hedonistic pleasures during the night.

Because of the awkwardness of his stance, Suetonius had only managed to get a little sleep, but he nevertheless felt quite refreshed, if somewhat stiff. Catus still lay on the ground, snoring loudly. Suetonius kicked him full on the backside, knowing that a blow to such a tender spot would be certain to wake him. His friend groaned as he opened his eyes then stretched his body in an attempt to fight off the veils of slumber. He struggled to a seated position and scratched his chest. 'I've been bitten,' he said as he picked at his skin.

'Never mind that,' growled Suetonius, 'rid me of these shackles. My arms feel like they are dead!'

Catus pulled himself to his feet and began to claw at the primitive bands of iron. He broke open one of the hinges with little difficulty and then wrenched the other apart using brute strength. Suetonius let his arms fall to his sides, grasped each one of his wrists in turn and rubbed them hard in order to bring some feeling back. 'I wish you'd been able to do that last night,' he muttered.

'I barely had the strength to stand,' replied Catus. He fumbled with the clasp that had secured his chain to the ring on the tent-pole, but it had been hammered home too well. 'I need a spear or something to hack it out,' he said.

Suetonius looked around the tent but could see nothing but piles of clothing and the inviting comfort of the cot. 'I'll go outside and find something. The Iceni are all either asleep or dead.' He walked over to leave the tent but, just as he was about to stoop and exit, the flap was thrown aside. Two soldiers pushed their way in and forced him back. He sat on the edge of the cot and glanced across at Catus, who merely shook his head sadly and looked down at the ground in dismay.

190

'You are to come with us,' barked one of the guards, while his colleague forced the chain holding Catus free of its clasp with the blade of his spear.

'Oh, what now?' asked Catus, wearily.

'The queen has need of your services,' replied the guard, with a broad grin.

Catus shook his head and sat next to Suetonius on the cot. 'I couldn't, please, no more,' he complained.

The guards answered by brandishing their spears menacingly and forcing them to stand and move to the doorway. Outside, the two men blinked as their eyes became accustomed to the brightness of the morning sunlight. They were marched quickly through the mêlée of sleeping peasants towards the rear of the encampment, where a smaller tent had been erected. Once there, one of the soldiers slipped inside while the other stood guard, pointing his spear threateningly towards them.

After a few moments, the tent flap was brushed aside and, to their surprise, Risa stepped out. She was naked, her hair was dishevelled and her normally white skin was flushed and bruised. She smiled when she saw her two colleagues. 'The queen awaits within,' she said, in a sultry tone of voice. 'She wishes to witness my final degradation.' Puzzled by her words, Suetonius glanced across at Catus, who merely shrugged.

Risa turned her back on them to re-enter the tent. The men could now see that her pert bottom was criss-crossed with marks of the cane and the cheeks were red and glowing. It was clear that her punishment had been recent. Suetonius felt the touch of the tip of the guard's spear to his back and they followed her into the tent.

Once inside, they found Boudicca sitting on a high-backed chair with Sisa and Micha sitting on the ground on either side of her. Her pose would have been taken as distinctly regal, were it not for the manner of her attire. She was dressed in a tight figure-hugging bodice made of black leather studded with jewels, the ample swell of her breasts clearly outlined under the shiny material. The lower part of her body was naked save for a narrow strip of leather which only just covered the prominent mound between her legs; the shape of her thick sex-lips was easily discernible though the constricting material. The outfit was completed by a pair of black leather boots that covered her legs almost entirely, the tops being less than an inch below her groin. She was sitting with her legs splayed wide apart and held a cane in one hand and a long stump of stiff hide in the other, the shape of which closely resembled an erect penis.

Risa bowed before her and then knelt at her feet. Boudicca tapped her lightly on the shoulder with the tip of the cane and she bent forward and tugged the strip between the queen's legs aside and dutifully began to lick her pussy. Boudicca looked up at Suetonius and Catus, her expression giving no indication of the pleasurable feelings that she had to be experiencing as Risa sucked noisily.

'It seems that all three of you need to learn some manners,' she said. 'I found this one lying with three of my best soldiers, having completely sated them, their cocks limp and useless. Their wives were denied their just pleasures as a result, and had to take solace elsewhere. She has been punished, as you can see from the marks on her skin, but it is not enough.'

'What do you want of us?' asked Suetonius.

'I want you to use her, just as you used my serving-girls, Sisa and Micha. I want you to fuck her until she is unable to stand. I want her jaw to ache from sucking your cocks and I want her loins to be stretched, not only by your magnificent rods but also with this.' She threw the leather phallus to the ground in front of them.

Suetonius bent down and retrieved it. He looked closely at the hard pole. It was slightly longer than his own stalk and considerably thicker. He put the end to his face and breathed in deeply. The scent was strong, a mixture of hide and the delightful aroma of woman. It was quite obvious that it had been used recently.

He looked down at Risa. The queen was clearly goading them into torturing their own colleague, but the sight of the young girl's lithe body and the way that she was nuzzling her face against the queen's pussy was irresistible. 'Whatever your majesty commands,' he said, knowing that, even if they had the will to do so, they would not be able to refuse.

Boudicca pushed Risa gently away from her and brought her thighs together before Suetonius could get a glimpse of the shaven prize between her legs. Risa shuffled over to kneel before the two naked men, her head bowed in total submission. Suetonius felt his cock thickening as he anticipated the joys to come. He looked across at Catus and saw that his cock had already risen to full erection. 'It seems that we have work to do,' he said, with a grin.

Risa reached up and gripped their stalks in her hands. She tugged them, forcing the men to move together and then she opened her mouth wide. She took both of the plum-sized heads into her mouth at the same time and began to lap her tongue around them, while gently rubbing their shafts. Her lips became so remarkably stretched that the corners of her mouth turned white with the effort and her cheeks bulged as the two men attempted to force as much of their cocks into her mouth as they could. The sensation of Catus' flesh pressing against his own once more gave Suetonius a distinctly odd feeling, but the girl's expert ministrations soon allowed him to overcome his discomfort.

He glanced over at the queen and the two serving-girls. They were watching the proceedings intently. It seemed strange to him that he was about to perform before the eyes of the one woman whom, above all, he most wanted to impale. She was quite clearly a person with a strong libido and yet she continually denied him this ultimate pleasure. His desire for her had been obvious when he had bathed her; his cock had never felt so hard and so erect as at that time.

He considered that this was all part of a game that she was playing. It was quite apparent from her attitude that she liked to dominate the men and women who served her and it seemed likely that she would exercise similar forcefulness when it came to matters of the flesh. Perhaps, he thought, if he swallowed his pride and succumbed to her and offered to delight her in any way that she chose, then she might fulfil his dream.

He looked down again at Risa. The sight of the elfin-faced girl accommodating two large cocks in her mouth was one that he found intrinsically appealing. It was as though she had no other purpose in life other than to give pleasure. He stroked her head fondly and she glanced up at him through smiling eyes.

Catus withdrew from her mouth and moved to stand behind her. He bent forward and grasped her hips, then raised her bottom until her legs were straight and slightly parted. Suetonius took the opportunity to slip nearly half of his length into her welcoming mouth and thrilled as she rolled her tongue around the head and sucked gently at the stiff shaft. Catus crouched behind her and began to lick her bottom, concentrating most of his attentions on the cleft between her pert buttocks.

Risa seemed oblivious to his flicking tongue and started to work harder with her mouth. Her oral expertise was magnificent. One moment, she would be sucking heavily on his cock and taking it deep into her throat, and the next, she would let him fall from her mouth and lap hungrily along the full length or over his balls, drawing them into her mouth and tickling them with the tip of her tongue.

'Enough of this!' barked the queen. The shock of her sudden cry startled Suetonius and he almost lost control, very nearly filling Risa's mouth with his seed. Boudicca jumped to her feet and walked over to them. She took the leather phallus from Suetonius and handed it to Catus. 'Fuck her! Fuck her with this!'

Risa let Suetonius' cock slip from her mouth and she looked over her shoulder at the long, thick dildo then turned her face back and resumed her oral homage to his aching rod. The idea of having the thing rammed into her seemingly gave her little cause for concern.

Catus wet the phallus with his spittle and then carefully began to ease it into the girl's pussy. 'Force it in!' shouted Boudicca angrily. 'She is here to be punished!' Catus obeyed immediately, plunging the full length of the pole into her. Risa gave a muffled groan but continued to suckle on Suetonius' cock. He knew from experience that she would experience nothing but pleasure from such an intrusion. She had accommodated both him and Catus in the same hole simultaneously. The singular insertion of the dildo, despite its size, would merely give her feelings of delectation.

Catus rose to his feet and wet two of his fingers with more spit. Suetonius watched expectantly as he eased the fingers into Risa's tiny anus. He could see the end of the phallus jutting from her pussy and it bobbed up and down as Catus worked his fingers in and out of her bottom. Catus spat on to the palm of his other hand and then worked the wetness over his hard cock. His intention was clear. He slipped the fingers from her sphincter and replaced them with his cock. He pushed hard against her, so much so that she fell forwards against Suetonius and engulfed virtually his entire length down her throat. Once his stalk was completely embedded in her backside, Catus reached under himself and Suetonius could see, from the rapid movements of his arm, that he was pleasuring Risa with the dildo while steadily fucking her arse.

'Fuck her! Fuck her!' cried Boudicca, her voice cracking with emotion. 'Ram that rod of yours deep into her! Make her squeal!'

Catus obeyed her command by beginning to hammer his cock in and out of the poor girl's rear and forcing the dildo inside her over and over again with long swift strokes.

The queen seemed content and resumed her seat. Sisa and Micha were leaning forward, avidly observing every detail of Catus' performance. Suetonius meanwhile was more than happy to allow Risa to continue delighting him with her mouth and slippery tongue, at least for the time being.

Catus pulled himself from her after a short while and eased the phallus from the grip of her sex-lips, then deftly inserted it where his cock had just been. Risa purred serenely as the long thick pole was slipped carefully into her. Content that it was firmly trapped in her tight sheath, Catus rammed his stalk into her pussy with such force that she gave out a breathless cry and fell forward on to her hands and knees between Suetonius' legs.

His cock sprang into view and he noticed, with some pride, that both the queen and her servants gazed in awe at its size. Sisa and Micha knew what it felt like to be impaled by it, but the queen could only imagine the sensation of being stretched to the limit. He looked at her face, but her gaze was firmly fixed on his jutting weapon. Surely she couldn't resist the temptation for much longer, he mused.

He decided that he would show her how well he could use the thing. He watched as Catus slammed his groin heavily against Risa's shuddering body over and over again. His friend wouldn't be able to last long, at this rate, and then he would take her and Boudicca would marvel at the way the girl accepted his long, thick cock and would hear her cries of delight as he fucked her into an oblivion of ecstasy.

As he had expected, Catus suddenly uttered an oath and groaned loudly as he filled Risa with his cream, the young girl clawing at her pussy with the fingers of one hand in a vain effort to join him in his release. The couple collapsed on to the ground and fell apart. Catus lay on his back, his wilting cock lying across his stomach and a small trickle of his juice seeping from the end to mingle with his sweat. Risa quickly moved to kneel at his side and she took his soft penis into her mouth and sucked it, as if attempting to make it rise again.

Suetonius could see from the look on her face that, whatever had happened to her during the previous hours, she was desperate for more and that Catus had left her unfulfilled. He moved behind her and knelt down. He gazed lustfully at her upturned bottom. The end of the leather phallus was protruding from her anus and her sex-lips were wide open and inviting. As he watched, a small drop of Catus' semen slipped from her honeyed sheath and hung momentarily from her engorged flesh like a strand of spider's silk. He reached out and massaged the cream into her soft, wet lips. Risa let Catus' flaccid cock fall from her mouth and looked over her shoulder at him, her eyes glazed with passion. She mouthed the words "fuck me", but uttered no sound.

Suetonius gripped his cock by the root and aimed the head at her waiting succulence. He slid in with remarkable ease. Catus had prepared her well for him. Her hot inner flesh gripped him tightly and seemed to undulate against his hard stalk as he held himself deep inside her. He could feel the hardness of the phallus jutting from her bottom pressing against him. He gripped the end of it and began to move it in and out of her arse with a steady, gentle rhythm. Risa rested her face on the ground and thrust her bottom higher. He used the full length of the dildo, withdrawing it from her tight puckered hole and then plunging it deep into her again and again, while fucking her cunt with the same, measured pace.

Boudicca slipped from her seat and knelt beside them. He increased the rapidity of his movements and ensured that she got a good view of his erection each time that he withdrew it from Risa's juicy pussy. Despite the fact that he was fucking a beautiful young girl, he yearned to reach between the queen's legs, tug the leather thong to one side and slip his fingers into her. He felt her fingertips brush against his bottom and he slowed his movements to savour her touch. She stroked his buttocks gently and traced their firm shape with her palm, then pressed a finger hard against his anus. He took a deep breath and gritted his teeth as his cock seemed to swell to even greater proportions within the grip of Risa's lush flesh. He knew that he mustn't come, not now. The queen was going to give herself to him, of that he was certain. The sight of him fucking Risa had been too much for her to resist.

He barely moved his hips against the kneeling girl as he felt Boudicca slip her finger into him. He leant forward and rested his body against Risa's back. He could feel the end of the dildo pressing against his stomach. The girl merely moaned contentedly as he forced the full length of his cock into her and crushed his balls against the cushion of her wet sex-lips. Boudicca moved her finger in and out of his bottom and the tightness of the ring of muscle eased, as he became more accustomed to the delicate intrusion.

After some moments, he felt her remove her finger and then he experienced a slight jab of pain as she inserted two, or possibly three, into his resisting orifice. Her fingers seemed to have been oiled and soon she was able to move them in and out of him easily. He raised his body a little and began to fuck Risa slowly again, taking care not to force Boudicca's fingers from him. The sensation of her prodding and probing fingers was driving him to distraction.

The queen reached round with her free hand and gently pulled the phallus from inside the girl's bottom. He gazed at the little hole, the sphincter now dilated and inviting. It appeared that the queen wanted him to fuck Risa in the arse, but he was content as he was, her fleshy sheath gripping him and undulating against his hard cock in the most pleasing manner.

Boudicca eased her fingers from his backside and he felt strangely empty and unfulfilled. Suddenly, he gasped as he sensed her licking the hole. The Queen of the Iceni was actually licking his bottom! She seemed to be deliberately soaking him with her spittle as she probed and explored his anus with her long tongue. He held himself completely still, his raging erection threatening to explode inside the warmth of Risa's juicy pussy. Boudicca lapped wetly against his sphincter and then prodded and circled her fingers inside him once more.

After a few moments, she eased her fingers from his sheath and appeared to move away from him. Maddened with lust, he gripped Risa's waist tightly and began to slam his length in and out of her at a furious rate, his stomach slapping noisily against her buttocks. Risa gasped rhythmically as he thrust into her, each time using the full length of his magnificent cock. Suddenly, she threw her head back and uttered a long, low groan, followed by an uncontrolled squeal. He felt her inner muscles pulsating against his plunging rod as she came and he rammed his stalk completely into her and held still as her entire body shuddered with the force of her orgasm.

The two of them remained motionless for some moments. Suetonius gripped her waist firmly, keeping her bottom pressed against him and his cock deep inside her hot cunt. He heard Risa sob quietly and he knew that he had done well. The queen would surely not refuse him now. He sensed her move back behind him and waited in excited anticipation for the touch of her tongue or fingers.

Instead, he felt a sharp searing pain in his backside. His first thought was that he had been stabbed with a knife, so severe was the hurt. He looked quickly over his shoulder to see Boudicca kneeling behind him, a near-manic expression on her beautiful face. From his position, he couldn't see what she was doing, but he soon realised the truth. Slowly but assuredly, she eased the huge phallus into his bottom, the oil and her earlier ministrations making the task relatively simple. The pain eased rapidly and the thing touched something inside of him that caused his cock to jump. He had never imagined that he could gain pleasure in such a way, even though Catus had often told him that women crave for such an intrusion once they have been introduced to its carnal delights.

The queen began to use the phallus like a cock, fucking his arse with a steady, gentle movement and using the full length to afford him the greatest sensation. His response was to start moving against Risa once more and she accommodatingly raised her bottom again so that he could plunder the very depths of her soaking pussy with his long cock.

Boudicca pushed the phallus all the way into his backside and then moved back to her seat and retrieved her cane. He knew what to expect and he knew that he wanted it. She returned to stand at his side and he waited for the pain of the first cut excitedly. When it came, he thrust hard into Risa, causing her to gasp loudly. With each subsequent stroke of the cane, he repeated the action, each time feeling the head of his cock ram against the young girl's cervix and thrilling to her cries of joy.

The pain was intense but merely served to heighten his enjoyment. At last, he knew perfect bliss. The feeling of the dildo deep inside his bottom, the sight of Risa's lithe form wriggling under his pumping body and the incessant stinging blows to his backside combined to bring him rapidly to the point of no return. He came with a roar, his cream jetting deep into Risa's tight cunt as the cane cut across his buttocks for the last time.

Exhausted, he eased his wilting length from inside Risa's lovely body and rolled over on to his back. The dildo remained inside him but he had neither the will nor the energy at that moment to remove it. Boudicca stood above him, still clutching the cane. The strip of leather between her legs had been pulled aside exposing the puffy engorged lips of her shaven pussy. It was evident that she had been fingering herself while administering the punishment. She looked at him and grinned cruelly. 'Know this, merchant,' she hissed. 'Disobey or abuse my hospitality again and the punishment will be even worse!'

Suetonius said nothing. He glanced across at Risa, who was still kneeling face down and trying to suppress a grin. It was plain that she knew that it would be unwise to show the queen that she had endured nothing but intense pleasure. Boudicca was plainly happy that she had beaten Suetonius into submission and he was more than willing to let her go on believing it. He reached under himself and eased the phallus from inside his bottom. He examined it closely and marvelled as to how such a huge thing could have slipped into him so readily. Yet again, he had learnt and experienced something new and he wondered what other treats lay in store for him. Thoughts of escape had melted away from his consciousness, at least for the time being.

Boudicca walked slowly down the hillside towards the river in order to bathe herself. The mist of early morning had dissipated and the sun was beating down warmly on her back. Birds were singing in the trees behind her and a gentle breeze was playing through the flowing tresses of her long red hair. It seemed so peaceful, and yet they were just a few short miles from the charred remains of the sacked city of Verulamium.

Reaching the river, she pulled off her smock and

slipped, naked, into the cool water. She glanced back up the hill. A solitary guard stood in the distance, his face turned away to preserve her modesty. She would not be disturbed. No one would dare to invade the queen's privacy when she was at toilet.

She immersed herself to the waist, splashed herself with water and then rubbed her face with the palms of her hands. The stream was flowing quite quickly and the water caressed her pussy as it rushed between her legs. She found the sensation to be quite exhilarating. She touched herself and found the button of her clitoris. Rubbing it gently, she pictured an image of the two merchants and their young charge on the floor of the tent. It had been good to abuse them so, but she nevertheless felt empty, as if it had not been enough.

She thought particularly about the taller and more handsome of the two men, the one whom she had impaled with the leather phallus. She had been sorely tempted to allow him to sink his magnificent weapon into her, but that would have ruined the game. He would have had the upper hand, and she knew that she could never allow such a thing to happen.

Boudicca finished washing herself and clambered back on to the bank. She placed her smock on the grass and sat down on it, then took up a bottle of scented oil that she had brought with her. She poured some of the liquid into the cupped palm of her hand and smoothed it over the front of her body, paying particular attention to her breasts and between her legs. She set the bottle down and, after massaging the oil into her body, she lay back to enjoy the warmth of the sun as it dried her skin. She watched dreamily as the gentle white clouds drifted across the light-blue canvas of the sky and she thought of home. Immediately, she conjured up an image of Arman, the enigmatic leader of the druids. She saw his handsome face and his superb naked body, and remembered with delight the moment when he had impaled her. She wanted him to be with her, here in this perfect paradise. She closed her eyes and began to caress the soft lips of her pussy.

'My queen.' The voice was strong and masculine. Startled, Boudicca snapped her eyes open. He was standing close to her, his tall frame silhouetted against the sun and his hair billowing gently in the breeze. She knew that it was Arman. She knew that he had come for her.

'How did you get here?' she asked lamely as she pulled herself to a sitting position. He knelt at her side and gazed into her eyes. She felt as if her strength were being drained from her under his hypnotic stare.

'I am always with you, my queen,' he whispered. 'I am always at your side, to protect and to care for you.'

His words drifted over her comfortingly. She reached out to touch him, half expecting his image to float away like a reflection on the surface of a pool of water disturbed by ripples. His body was firm to the touch. She ran her fingertips across his chest, feeling his muscular form through his thick cloak. He leant forward and kissed her lightly on the lips. Boudicca slipped her hand under the folds of his cloak and her fingertips found his hard nipple. She squeezed it firmly and then pushed the cloak from his shoulders. He was now as naked as she was, his cock hard and ready for her. She circled the rigid shaft with her fingers and rubbed it slowly up and down.

Arman looked down at her hand. 'I have been watching you bathe yourself,' he said, as if to excuse his lustful display.

'It is beautiful,' she replied as she gazed lovingly at his hard erection. She bent her head and took the end into her mouth. Closing her lips just under the ridge, she circled the soft flesh with her tongue while still gently rubbing the hard shaft with her hand. She felt him stroking her hair. She cupped his balls with her free hand and squeezed them while she engulfed more of his long cock within her mouth. She drew her head back and kissed the tip, then looked up at his face. In the warm sunlight he appeared more handsome than ever. 'Enter me, Arman,' she breathed with a coyness that was alien to her nature. She lay back on the ground and parted her legs, at the same time raising her knees to offer him an unobstructed view of her most intimate treasures. 'Enter me,' she repeated. 'Fill me with your love.'

Arman moved across her with the smoothness of a cat. Boudicca could feel his hard shaft pressing against her stomach and thrilled to the thought that soon it would be inside her. He raised his body slightly and she felt the head of his cock touch the open lips of her pussy. He slid into her with one long stroke and she curled her legs around his waist and pressed her heels against his bottom. He fucked her slowly, possessing none of the urgency of many of her past lovers. When she came, it was a gentle relaxing release, and she sighed with pleasure as her juices flowed and trickled between her buttocks to soak her smock below her body.

He pulled from her, his cock still hard and erect. She raised herself and bent over him, then took it into her mouth again. She tasted the sweetness of her arousal on his stiff flesh. Her fingers touched the bottle, which was lying by her side. Taking his cock from her mouth, she looked up at him and stared deeply into his piercing blue eyes. She knew that the time had come. 'I want you to enter me again,' she whispered, 'but in the other place.'

She gave him the bottle and then lay back once more. She watched as he poured some of the liquid on to his fingers and then she raised her legs and pulled her knees back to rest them against her shoulders, with her breasts crushed between her thighs. Arman put his oiled fingers to her bottom and caressed the little hole, circling the tips against her virgin sphincter and opening it with gentle but insistent prods. He poured more oil, this time directly on to her anus, and then pushed two fingers slowly into her. She found it uncomfortable at first and her muscles seemed to be attempting to force away the intrusion, but she allowed him to persevere until both fingers were clasped deep inside her. She closed her eyes as he circled and probed within her, his movements becoming more and more rapid. The sensation was strange, but oddly arousing.

He took his fingers from her and she opened her eyes to see that he was pouring the last of the oil along the full length of his jutting penis. She began to feel both frightened and curious, wondering how such a thing could be accommodated painlessly. He massaged the liquid around the shaft and over the head, then moved to kneel once more between her legs. She took a deep breath and closed her eyes. She shook inwardly, terrified of the unknown but anxious to experience the ultimate pleasure.

Boudicca jumped as the tip of his cock touched her anus. She sensed the muscle clench automatically and she reached down with both hands and tugged the cheeks of her buttocks apart. The thick head of his rod pressed hard against her. For a moment, she felt that he would be unable to enter her, the little hole feeling as if it was far too tight to allow it. He pushed harder and the ring of muscle suddenly gave way and the head was inside her.

Arman held still for a moment and then eased more of his stiffness into the tight sheath. 'Relax, my darling,' he said. 'You are fighting me.'

Boudicca did her best, struggling to battle against her body's natural instinct to push the other way.

Slowly, more and more of his rod entered her until, at last, his groin pressed against her buttocks. She looked down as he began to gently fuck her. It was a strange sight, to see his cock slipping in and out of her body this way, the fleshy lips of her pussy untouched and open to her gaze. He pumped harder and faster. There was no pain or discomfort. The muscles of her arse had relaxed completely and soon she found that she could barely feel him inside her. The only sensations were at the very opening and deep inside her sheath when he prodded against her inner flesh, sending waves of euphoric pleasure coursing throughout her entire body.

Arman gripped her ankles and pressed her thighs firmly against her breasts, then raised and stiffened his body so that his only contact with the ground was with his toes. He pounded in and out of her, moving ever faster until, suddenly, he pulled himself from her and rubbed his cock furiously. His cream shot across her body, soaking her breasts and face. Boudicca lowered her legs and smoothed the semen over her breasts, then scooped it from her cheeks and licked the warm fluid from her fingertips.

She closed her eyes. She had expected her bottom to ache, following such a violent onslaught but there was no pain whatsoever, just a feeling of emptiness. The sun felt warm on her skin and the breeze cooled her slightly. She opened her eyes to gaze at her lover, but he had gone.

Boudicca sat up quickly and looked all around her, but there was no sign of him. She looked sadly down at the ground. Had it been another dream? She reached between her legs and touched her puckered sphincter. It was oiled and relaxed. She eased her finger inside herself. There was no resistance. She had been fucked there, of that she was certain. Besides this, she had the taste of his semen still on her lips. It had been real enough. She lay back once more and gazed up at the sky. She sensed a slight feeling of anger that she had permitted the druid to subdue and dominate her. In a strange way, she considered that Arman's sudden departure was fitting.

Nine

'You must relate your story,' begged Suetonius as he
and Catus walked slowly along the riverbank. 'You
must tell me what happened to you when you were
captured after leaving me in the company of
Boudicca's serving-girls. You appeared to have been
trampled by a herd of wild horses when you were
dragged back to the tent!'

Catus drew a deep breath. 'I would not have
believed that such pleasure could be derived from
such pain and humiliation,' he began. 'I can well
understand now why so many women offer themselves so willingly to the lash.'

'I think I can understand what you are saying,'
mused Suetonius. 'I, too, have experienced the most
exquisite sensations of extreme arousal in situations
when I would have deemed such a thing to be
impossible. When I saw the stripes of the cane across
your backside, I actually felt envious.'

'The Iceni women are adept in the art of
administering punishment,' continued Catus. 'They
appear to treat such matters with an almost religious
fervour. Have you noticed that they are always
careful never to cut the skin? If they were to do so,
then the pain would be too severe and their victim
would be useless to them. He would be unable to
endure further punishment for days, if not weeks. It

is not to say that they don't demand total submission. I fought against them for some time, determined not to show fear or discomfort while I was being whipped, and my apparent anger only served to encourage them. Only when I begged them to stop, only when I showed weakness, did they relent.'

'So, what happened to you?' asked Suetonius again, his cock already beginning to thicken in anticipation of his friend's ribald tale.

'I was captured within seconds of leaving you and the two girls. I could still hear their groans of pleasure when I was suddenly grabbed by two guards and dragged before the queen. When she heard that I had been seen fucking her two precious servants, she flew into a rage. They obviously mean a great deal to her and she made it clear that she had suffered an unforgivable insult. My cloak was stripped from me and with it went my one means of defence, the knife hidden in the lining.

'I stood there, stark naked, waiting for death. She ordered the guards to go and fetch the girls and I knew that you, too, would be captured. There was nothing that I could do. The queen stared with the utmost contempt at my shrivelled little cock, then pointed in derision at it and laughed. "Look at that!" she cackled to the group of women who sat with her in the tent. "How could such a puny thing satisfy my angels?" The damnable thing seemed to shrink even more. I felt both anger and extreme humiliation in equal measure. "Take him," she barked. "Take him outside and do with him as you will!"

'Three of the women stepped forward. One of them was clutching a bronze collar fixed to a long length of chain. She fixed the collar around my neck and then I was made to kneel on all fours like a dog. I was dragged out of the tent into the open, running on my hands and feet. Men and women crowded around me, laughing and jeering as I was dragged through the encampment.

'Eventually, I was tethered to a tree and made to kneel while resting my upper body on my elbows. There were now at least a dozen women surrounding me and, in this position, my backside was presented to their leering eyes in the most obscene manner. I watched as they cut lengths of twigs and bracken from the surrounding bushes and I realised that I was about to be thrashed. In a strange way, I felt comforted by this, hoping that this would be the full extent of my punishment, but I was nevertheless terrified of the pain that I knew I was about to endure.

'The women formed a circle around me. I glared up at them, determined not to show any fear. The first blow came quickly, and stung my buttocks terribly. More and more blows rained down on me as the women took it in turn to lash my backside. I gritted my teeth and breathed hard. I would not cry out.

'After a few minutes, the hags paused to rest. They just stood there, looking at me, their eyes wild with lust. I began to get the strangest sensation within my loins. Most of the women had bared their breasts and, though I would not have normally considered any of them worthy to grace my bed, I found myself looking at them with increasing arousal. Despite the fact that my arse was stinging incredibly, my cock began to thicken and soon jutted at full erection beneath me.

'One of the women noticed my predicament and clapped her hands gleefully. "See," she shouted, "it has risen, and it is a good one!" The women threw away their flails, crouched beside me and fought with each other to grasp my rod. There were hands all over me in moments. I was pulled over on to my back and one of them dived her head down and took my cock into her mouth. As she sucked the end, another of them lay on her stomach between my outstretched legs and began to lick my balls, while two more of them lay their faces on either side of my stomach and pushed out their tongues to lap against my exposed stalk.

'A fifth woman crouched over my head and sat down hard on to my face so that my mouth was pressed firmly against the soaking lips of her cunt. I sucked the lips, her juices soaking my face and running up my nose, as they seemed to gush from within her. The next moment, someone was sitting on my groin, and my cock was firmly embedded inside the hottest sheath that I have ever encountered. In my prone position, I was barely able to move. All I could do was lie there while whoever it was bounced furiously on me. In truth, she was doing the fucking; I could do nothing.

'I heard her squeal and then she fell from me, only to be quickly replaced by another. She, too, ravaged me, assaulting my poor body with a manic fervour. When she was done with me it seemed that another, and then another replaced her. I couldn't see what was happening; I had no idea who it was that was pleasuring herself by using my body at any given time, as I was still blinded by having the cushion of a soft bottom pressed against my face.

'Eventually, I came. No man alive could have held back for long under such delightful circumstances. When they realised what had happened, the women became angry and I was quickly turned over on to my stomach and beaten again. The pain was less severe but once more had the effect of causing my pego to rise, despite my having spent so recently. I was pulled over on to my back and the game recommenced. I was not allowed to do anything; indeed, when I tried to thrust my hips upward, I was slapped hard on the thighs for my pains. The women used me for what seemed like hours. I lost count of the number of times that they impaled themselves on me or rubbed their wet pussies against my mouth.

'When, at long last, they were sated, I was once more dragged on all fours like an animal through the encampment. I was still hard, but a final swinging blow across my backside caused the semen to jet from me, much to their amusement. My entire body ached tremendously as they hauled me along the ground. When I stumbled, they kicked me until I moved again until, at last, I was thrown into the tent and shackled with you.'

Suetonius squeezed the hard shaft of his cock through his cloak, the thought of twelve or more women using him in such a way filling his mind. 'No wonder that you couldn't summon up the strength to release me,' he said, with a broad grin.

The two men continued to walk slowly, enjoying the warmth of the sun and the peace and tranquillity of the moment. Suddenly, Catus grabbed him firmly by the arm. 'Stay!' he whispered urgently.

'What is it?'

Catus eased forward and crouched behind a bush. Suetonius knelt beside him. 'What is it?' he repeated. 'What have you seen?'

'Over there,' replied his friend with a wave of his hand. Suetonius peered through the foliage and took a deep breath. Only a few yards away from them, standing at the edge of the river, were the unmistakable forms of Micha and Sisa. They were both naked and were bathing each other, their hands roaming sensuously over each other's bodies. 'Did you ever see such a sight?' whispered Catus.

Suetonius had to admit that the image before them was erotic in the extreme. His cock, already aroused by his friend's bawdy tale, rose rapidly to full erection as the two men watched the girls playfully caressing each other. 'They are like goddesses, nymphs who have risen from the waters,' breathed Catus.

Suetonius smirked at his colleague's attempts at poetry. 'They are two beautiful women, and we have fucked them both,' he remarked, crudely. 'Now, come, we must get away from this place. If we are caught again with these two, it will be our necks.'

Catus grasped his arm tightly. 'No, no, stay a little longer,' he whispered. 'Just a few more minutes.'

'It is too dangerous,' hissed Suetonius. 'Come, before we are seen!'

He made to move away but Catus grabbed him again. 'Look! Look!' he said excitedly. Suetonius glanced in the direction of the two naked girls to see that Micha was now fondling Sisa between the legs and the young blonde was stroking Micha's firm ebony buttocks lovingly. He crouched down again, much against his better judgement and moved one of the branches of the bush to one side in order to gain a better view of the proceedings.

Sisa and Micha slipped slowly to the ground, their arms entwined around each other's body. They kissed, the warm and passionate embrace of lovers. Sisa fondled Micha's pert breasts while the Nubian continued to rub her long fingers firmly against Sisa's pussy-lips. Suetonius glanced across at Catus. His friend was openly masturbating; he watched with unblinking eyes as the scene unfolded before them. It was clear that he wasn't going to be shifted from this position until the girls had finished their game.

Suetonius shrugged and looked back at them. Sisa was now lying on her back and Micha was moving across her. Within seconds, she had her head buried between the blonde's legs and her pussy pressed against Sisa's mouth. From their position, the two men could see Sisa licking voraciously at Micha's thickly engorged sex-lips, the Nubian's upturned bottom presenting them with a most appealing and inviting sight. The sounds of the two girls' tongues lapping at each other's pussies filled their ears, as did the occasional gentle feminine moan of pleasure.

Suetonius reached under his cloak and gently rubbed his stiff erection as he remembered taking the two girls in turn while they had held exactly the same pose. He looked again at Catus. His friend was staring, wide-eyed, at the picture as if he had never seen such a sight before and his brow was coated with sweat.

'We must go,' Suetonius whispered.

Catus shook his head. 'Not yet,' he replied. 'Not yet.'

'We have to,' insisted Suetonius. 'We have to return to the legion. If we are caught, all will be lost.'

'Look at the way that the fair one is using her tongue,' drooled his friend, ignoring the warning. 'She is so young, and yet so expert.'

'It is said that women know by instinct how to pleasure those of their own sex,' answered Suetonius as he became resigned to the fact that Catus was going to have to be allowed to witness the act to completion. Besides, the sight of Sisa's tongue flicking rapidly against Micha's prominent bud was having a profound effect on him. He withdrew his cock from under his cloak and rubbed the shaft with increasing urgency as he saw Sisa push two of her fingers inside the other girl's bottom. He heard Catus gasp and feared the worst.

'Just once more,' panted his friend. 'Let us take them, just once more.'

Suetonius released his grip of his hard rod and grabbed Catus by the arm. 'It is too dangerous,' he hissed. 'We will be seen!'

Catus tugged his arm free. 'There are no guards,' he protested. 'Come, friend, we cannot let such an opportunity pass us by!' With that, he pushed himself noisily through the bushes and out into the open. Startled, the girls fell apart and covered their breasts and pussies with their hands. Recognising him, they smiled and let their arms fall to their sides.

'Were you spying on us, merchant?' said Micha coyly.

'We chanced upon your delightful demonstration and couldn't resist the temptation to stay and enjoy the spectacle,' he replied, his voice trembling with arousal.

'We?' questioned Micha. 'Is your handsome friend here also?'

Realising the futility of continued concealment, Suetonius rose to his feet and struggled through the thick bracken until he stood next to his friend, looking down at the prone forms of the two beautiful girls lying naked on the ground before them. He glanced nervously up the hill in the direction of the encampment, but there was no sign of soldiers, just as Catus had promised. He looked back down at the girls. Sisa was sitting with her legs spread wide apart, her sparse pubic hair darkened by Micha's saliva and the juices of her own excitement. Micha was brazenly running her finger up and down between her own puffy sex-lips. She had a broad grin on her face and her eyes were sparkling with excited anticipation.

It was too much for him to resist. Suetonius threw off his cloak in one sweeping movement and Catus immediately followed his example. The women giggled girlishly as they gazed at the two stiff erections presented to them and they moved to kneel before the naked men. Micha took hold of Catus' stalk and gripped it firmly by the root. She bent her face forward and ran the tip of her tongue over the swollen head, then took it into her mouth. Sisa did the same to Suetonius, her lips stretching around the massive girth of his weapon. His stalk throbbed and he knew that she was tasting his juice as she sucked him.

He clutched her head and pushed it back so that his cock sprang from her mouth and then he knelt down, easing her on to her back. Sisa reached down and gripped his tool. She rubbed him a couple of times and then guided the head to her open sex-lips. The heat from her slippery honeypot burnt into his hard flesh as he sank into her. She raised her legs and curled them around his waist, enabling him to force the full length of his cock into her.

He glanced across at the others. Micha was kneeling with her upper body resting on her forearms and her bottom raised high, Catus thrusting heavily in and out of her from behind. Suetonius couldn't tell from his position which of her two delightful holes his friend was plundering, but he had a pretty shrewd idea.

He lay still for a moment with his weight supported by his arms, gazing at the picture of youthful innocence lying beneath him. He felt the sun on his back and could hear the rippling waters of the river. It was a moment to savour. Sisa gripped his buttocks and pressed down on them hard. Her need was clear. Slowly and cautiously, he began to fuck her. She responded by thrusting her hips demandingly. He increased his pace, withdrawing only three or four inches each time before plunging back inside her. He sensed that her silky grip was already drawing the seed from within him and, for once, he gave way to his carnal urges, anxious to sate himself before they were discovered.

He thrashed his groin heavily against her, as the surge within his loins became a climax. He gasped aloud as the first jet of cream spurted deep inside her and he began to hammer his cock in and out of her at a ferocious rate. Sisa squealed with joy and joined him in his release, her fingernails clawing at his back and her heels digging painfully into his backside. He pulled from her and she immediately sat up, grasped his rod and stuffed the end into her mouth to suck and swallow the last of his juices before finally letting it slip from her creamy lips.

Suetonius bent forward and kissed her lightly on the mouth. Her lips tasted salty and her eyes shone. She smiled sweetly at him and then looked over his shoulder. Her expression turned to one of horror. He swung round to see four figures standing behind him, their forms silhouetted against the bright sunlight. He glanced across at Catus. His friend was plainly oblivious to the fact that they were being watched. He was gripping Micha tightly by the waist and was pounding into her from behind like a man possessed.

'Catus!' he hissed, loudly. His friend looked round at him but continued with his violent pumping rhythm, thrusting his thick cock in and out of Micha's shuddering, inviting body. 'Catus! We have company!'

Catus swung round, pulling himself from the girl. She fell forward on to the ground with a gasp of disappointment. The shock caused Catus to ejaculate and streams of his juices shot from his cock in short, sharp bursts.

The newcomers laughed and moved towards them. Catus' eyes opened wide in recognition. 'Well, merchants,' said one of the soldiers, 'it seems that you will never learn!'

'Not merchants,' said another as he moved to stand facing Catus. 'These are not merchants, my friends, these are Romans! This one is Catus Decianus, no less.'

There was a short pause as the other soldiers took in the meaning of their colleague's words. Suetonius glanced at Catus and nodded. In a flash they were off, scurrying along the riverbank, their pace unhindered by clothing. The soldiers gave chase, but the two Romans were soon in the woods. They ran blindly through the bracken, the bushes lashing their bodies and the twigs and stones tearing at the soles of their feet.

Seizing a sudden opportunity, Suetonius dived into a thicket and crawled under the twisted mass of branches and leaves. Catus followed him and collapsed beside him. They lay still, panting in the undergrowth. They heard the soldiers rushing by, beating the bushes with their spears and swords. The two men stifled the desire to breathe, their hearts pounding in their chests.

After some minutes had elapsed, the soldiers returned, clearly having given up the chase. They ambled past the hidden men, grumbling and cursing as they disappeared into the distance.

Suetonius took a long, deep breath. 'We are safe,' he said, 'at least for the moment.'

'They won't return,' answered Catus as he picked some thorns from his feet. 'They will presume we have headed into the hills.'

'The soldiers don't concern me. What do you think will happen when Boudicca hears that, not only did we insult her by fucking her two precious little serving-girls yet again, but she also learns that we are

Romans? We must find our way back to the legion and prepare for battle. We'll need to circle around the Iceni encampment in order to avoid capture but, first we need to find some clothing.'

'If my memory serves me there is a farm not far from here,' said Catus. 'It is owned by one Titus Maximus, a centurion who retired here following the first campaign. I am certain that he will give us shelter and clothing.'

'We have to get word to the legion,' responded Suetonius sharply. 'They will be massacred where they are. We have to order them to march north, to join with the legion at High Cross.'

'We will never get through the Iceni ourselves. Have Maximus deliver your orders. The savages know him and trust him. They will let him pass.'

The two men struggled to their feet and began to trudge through the forest. 'How certain are you that this Titus Maximus will help us?' asked Suetonius.

'He may have settled in this dreary land, but he is still a Roman at heart. You can trust him.'

'I pray that you are right, my friend, otherwise our army will be slaughtered.'

It was close to midday as Suetonius and Catus approached the newly built farmhouse set on a gentle slope near the edge of a rapidly flowing stream. The sun was high and the air barely moved. In the distance, a small flock of long-haired sheep grazed peacefully in a field of lush grass. The scene could not have been more idyllic, but its ambience was completely lost on the two Romans.

'We can't simply walk up to the front door like this,' said Suetonius. 'You may know this Titus Maximus, but he is not going to take too kindly to finding two naked men standing on his porch!'

'What would you advise?' replied Catus impatiently. 'Should we tie garlands of wild flowers about ourselves?'

'Perhaps we'll find something in the barn over there,' Suetonius suggested, indicating an old grey shed close to the main house. 'Come on, and keep low!'

The men moved furtively through the long grass until they were able to slip inside the ramshackle building. A strong stench of animal waste invaded their senses as they closed the door behind them and peered into the relative gloom of the interior. Suetonius searched quickly about the place, anxious to return to savour the fresh air outside. Suddenly, the barn door was flung wide and sunlight streamed in. The two men swung round. A woman in late middle age stood in the doorway, brandishing a long pitchfork.

'Who are you? What are you doing here?' she demanded, in a thick Roman accent. Suetonius stepped forward out of the shadows and the woman's eyes widened as they became fixed on the sight of his long, flaccid penis swinging heavily between his legs.

'Please, mistress, we mean no harm,' he said, holding the palms of his hands forwards in a gesture of geniality. 'We are fugitives, escaping from the clutches of the Iceni. We merely came in here to find something with which to cover ourselves before approaching your home.'

The woman eyed him suspiciously, then looked behind him. 'You, come forward!' she snapped. Catus moved to stand next to his colleague. Her dour expression changed to one of recognition. 'You are Catus Decianus, the procurator! How is it that you are naked?'

Catus smiled and covered his genitals with his

hands. 'Forgive us, mistress,' he said, 'it is a long story. I am sure that your husband Titus Maximus will give us clothing, to hide our embarrassment.'

Still clutching the menacing-looking fork, the woman stepped to one side. 'You had better come into the house,' she said. The two men walked slowly in front of her, heading towards the other building. As they approached the front door, it was opened and a tall heavily built man appeared. He was roughly the same age as the woman with strong tanned features and long silver hair, which cascaded over his bared shoulders. His face broke into a broad grin as Catus walked up to him.

'Catus, my friend,' he bellowed, 'whatever has befallen you?'

Catus shook him warmly by the hand. 'Titus! It has been a long time.'

'Too long, my friend,' said the older man. 'What has happened? Have you been robbed? Come inside, I will find some clothing for you and your fellow traveller.'

The two men entered the house and the woman set the pitchfork against the wall. She beckoned for Suetonius to enter and he noticed that her gaze fell once more to his cock. He sensed the shaft begin to thicken under her stare and he moved quickly inside before it could become noticeable.

Two simple togas were found and Suetonius and Catus gratefully covered their nakedness and settled on a long sofa. Titus was impressed when he learnt that he was in the company of not one but two serving generals in the Roman army, and he listened gravely as they recounted the story of the sacking of Verulamium.

'I do not understand it,' he said, a deep frown on his face. 'The Iceni have always been peaceful people. Why should they rise against the Roman army now?'

'Their queen, Boudicca,' said Suetonius, his voice cracking with emotion. 'It is she who has stirred them up into a frenzy of vengeance.'

'I have heard tales of this woman,' said Titus as he handed them two silver goblets brimming with cool red wine. 'It is said that her appetite for pleasures of the flesh knows no bounds.' The three men laughed raucously while his wife looked on disapprovingly. 'Why,' he continued, 'I have heard that she often takes two or even three men to her bed at one and the same time!'

'Really,' gasped his wife exasperatedly, 'must you go on so?'

Titus shrugged. 'Away with you, woman,' he shouted. 'Fetch our daughters! I would have them meet these fine Roman generals!'

Once she had left the room, Suetonius leant forward and spoke to their host in a whisper. 'It is vital that the legion is warned and ordered to march north. You are known and trusted by the Iceni . . .'

'Say no more, general,' interrupted Titus. 'Write your orders and I will deliver them personally to your men. I have a fast horse; I can be there within a matter of hours!'

The door opened and his wife reappeared, followed by three dark-haired girls in their late teens. Suetonius looked at the girls in astonishment. They were alike in every way, clearly the fruits of a single labour. They were wearing short white smocks that highlighted their deeply tanned complexions and the men could see that their breasts were full and their hips were smoothly curved and inviting. Their big brown eyes shone with youthful innocence and their full mouths were curved in the gentlest of smiles.

'Gentlemen, may I present my daughters,' announced Titus, proudly, 'Penelope, Lavinia and Calea.'

Suetonius and Catus rose to their feet and bowed their heads quickly. The girls responded in like manner and then sat together on a long sofa opposite them.

'I had heard that you had been blessed with triplets,' said Catus as the two men resumed their seat, 'but they have grown so beautiful.'

The girls giggled shyly and stared down at the floor.

'My wife will lead my horse,' said Titus. 'It will look better if I am accompanied. The girls will tend to your needs while we are away. Draft your orders, Suetonius, and we will be off on our journey.'

Suetonius quickly scribbled on a piece of parchment provided by Titus, all the time finding it difficult to stop himself from staring at the three astoundingly lovely girls sitting opposite him. He found that his hand was actually shaking as he penned the orders to his centurions. Catus and the girls' parents made small talk until he had completed his task and then he rolled up the parchment and handed it to Titus.

'I will not fail you,' said the older man as he tucked the orders into his belt. 'Come, woman, we have important work to do!' With that, he marched proudly from the room, closely followed by his obedient spouse. 'See that you behave yourselves,' called Titus from outside, 'and that our guests have everything that they need!'

Suetonius looked at Catus and his friend grinned. 'Would that it could be so,' he hissed.

The two generals washed themselves in icy water brought from the well by two of the triplets while the third busied herself preparing a light midday meal. Suetonius felt good to be rid of the sweat of their chase and the smell of the Iceni camp; being in the company of fellow Romans seemed so civilised after the untidy squalor.

The meal was eaten in silence, the girls serving them dutifully with lean meat, fresh fruit and a seemingly endless supply of fine wine. From his seat at the table, Suetonius found that he was able to capture an occasional glimpse of their shapely firm bodies as they passed between him and the large window set in the far wall. It was plain that they were not wearing undergarments, despite the thinness of the material of their short white smocks.

There was a long silence following the clearing of the table. The three girls sat motionless on their sofa. Suetonius was seated next to Catus opposite them. He eyed them with a kind expression on his face, but his thoughts were anything but benevolent. He could see the dark shapes of their nipples through the sheer material of their smocks and his cock was thickening rapidly. They seemed so near and yet so far.

Catus was regarding the girls with unconcealed lust in his eyes. Rather than appearing uncomfortable under his obvious leer, the three girls merely grinned sweetly at him and their expressions seemed to become more confident. Suddenly, as if to lighten the mood, one of them spoke in a gentle, singing voice that Suetonius found most enchanting. 'You must be very brave, to be generals,' she said.

Suetonius laughed. 'We have earnt our positions, just as your father did before us. Tell me, which one are you?'

'Penelope,' replied the girl, 'but do not trouble yourselves with names. Even our parents have difficulty in telling us apart.'

Suetonius could see the dilemma quite plainly. Their faces and figures were identical, and even their hair had been cropped short in three indistinguishable styles. 'Are you able to tell?' he asked.

The triplets all smirked in unison, as if they were hiding some guilty secret. 'We have devised a way,' said Penelope as she glanced at her sisters conspiratorially. 'A way that is known only to us and – and others who know us well.' She spoke the last few words quickly, as though she were making some sort of confession.

Suetonius was intrigued. 'How?' he asked. 'How can others tell you apart?'

Penelope looked nervously across at her sisters and then stood up. She reached down and grasped the hem of her smock and raised it, pulling it quickly over her head and dropping it on to the floor. Catus coughed and spluttered and Suetonius almost let his goblet of wine fall to the floor. She stood naked before them, her body perfect in every detail, right down to her neatly clipped bush of dark pubic hair.

'I – I don't understand,' said Suetonius, the words straining to come from his dry throat.

Penelope turned to look at the other two girls. 'Show them,' she said, with a grin. 'Show them how they can tell.'

With minimal hesitation, the other two girls got to their feet and quickly removed their dresses. The triplets stood in a row in front of the two men, broad smiles on their lovely faces.

Suetonius could now see the subtle enticing differences between them. Penelope was entirely naked but her sisters each wore a tiny nipple ring. One of the girls had pierced her left breast, the other her right.

'This is Lavinia,' said Penelope, resting her hand on the shoulder of the triplet with the ring in her left nipple.

'And you must be Calea,' interrupted Catus, rising from his seat and walking over to take the third girl's hands in his. He kissed her lightly on the lips. 'I'm sure that my friend and I will remember, from now on.'

Suetonius remained speechless for some moments. The shock of suddenly finding himself confronted by three identically beautiful and deliciously naked women had thrown him completely. He began to wonder if this was how they always treated their male guests when away from the watchful eyes of their doting parents. He found the situation uniquely arousing. He was used to ordering his women to strip or, better still, tearing their clothing from them as they made a pretence of struggle. This was entirely different. The girls were blatantly offering themselves to him and to Catus as if it were the most natural thing to do.

Catus was experiencing no such inhibitions. He was standing with the girls circled around him, his hands raised in the air, as they slowly pulled his toga up to reveal his naked body. His cock was jutting upwards, rampant and ready for anything. Suetonius stood up and looked nervously out of the window. What if Titus Maximus should return unexpectedly?

The worrying thought disappeared from his mind when he turned and saw Lavinia bending over to take Catus' thick erection into her mouth. The sight of her perfect bottom presented in such a way caused his own rod to stretch massively. He tore off his toga and moved to join the fray.

Standing behind the bent form of Lavinia, he rested his cock between the cheeks of her buttocks and watched as her head bobbed up and down while she sucked noisily at his friend's tool. He reached his hand under her groin and his fingers found the lush wetness of her pussy. She was more than ready to take him as, no doubt, were her sisters. He stepped back a little and aimed the head of his stalk at her succulent purse of sex-flesh. He eased a couple of inches inside her and then steadily forced the remaining stiff length within her silky grip. Lavinia raised her head sharply as he filled her, Catus' cock falling from her mouth. She gasped as Suetonius rammed his cock-head against the soft wall of her cervix. He looked at the other two girls, who were watching their sister's delight with intense interest. It seemed distinctly odd to see the features of the woman bent before him mirrored in their own, like something out of a dream.

Calea slipped to his side and he took her in his arms and kissed her passionately on the mouth while gently moving his cock in and out of Lavinia. Calea reached between them and gripped the root of his rod and squeezed it tightly, then cupped his balls while stroking between his buttocks with her other hand. Penelope, meanwhile had taken over from Lavinia by kneeling before Catus and engulfing his shaft within her mouth. After a few seconds, she let him fall from her mouth and turned her back to him. She bent forward and rested her hands on the edge of the sofa. Catus moved against her and Suetonius was able to see every sensuous detail as he slid his thick cock into her welcoming pussy.

Calea moved to kneel behind Suetonius and he suddenly felt the warm wetness of her tongue lapping between his buttocks. The sensation of having one girl lick his bottom while another beauty was accepting his plundering stalk was almost too much for him to bear. He felt a familiar surge building up within his loins and he slowed his movements to a stop, anxious not to come until he had impaled all three of these precious creatures.

Pulling his long stalk from within Lavinia's hot

sheath, he turned to face Calea, who was still kneeling on the floor. She took hold of his shaft and promptly slipped the swollen head into her mouth. She rubbed both of her hands along his full length as she sucked him, her fingers moving the loose skin in a delightfully sensuous manner. He endured this treatment for a while then raised her to her feet and led her over to lie on one of the sofas. He moved his body across her and felt her grip his cock again and guide it into her tightness. He bent his head and took her right nipple into his mouth. Suckling the hard teat, he playfully flicked his tongue around the piercing ring, while beginning to pump into her at a steady measured pace. He gripped her other breast tightly with one hand while supporting his body with his elbow.

He bit her nipple lightly and Calea groaned with pleasure. He sucked hard on her nipple, rasping his teeth against it and she moaned loudly. The young girl's hips moved against him, matching his every thrust. Biting his teeth into the ring, he pulled hard at it, tugging ruthlessly at her nipple. She cried out. At first, he thought that he had hurt her too much but, when he let the ring fall from his mouth and looked at her face, he realised that her cries had not been of pain but of blissful orgasm.

He pounded into her rapidly, determined to sate her completely. Her large breasts bounced and slapped together as he thrust wildly in and out of her luscious cunt. Grasping the firm globes of flesh, he squeezed them tightly and gave her one final lunge, his cock ramming deep into her and causing her to gasp aloud. He pressed his lips against her mouth and Calea wrapped her arms around his neck as their tongues played against each other. They ground their hips together, until she gave a long sigh and relaxed back on the sofa, her arms falling to her sides.

Suetonius eased from her and turned to face the others. Catus was lying on his back with one of the triplets squatting over him as he speared his cock into the open lips of her pussy from beneath. He could see, from the glint of the ring in her left breast, that it was Lavinia who was enjoying the fucking, while Penelope was down on her knees and elbows beside his friend, licking and kissing his chest and stomach.

Suetonius saw his opportunity and moved quickly to squat behind Penelope. He guided his weapon into her, sweat clouding his vision as he forced the head into her. As he did so, he noted a remarkable difference between her and the other two girls. Penelope's grip was far tighter, and he was experiencing great difficulty in entering her, despite the fact that he had seen Catus fuck her only minutes earlier.

Penelope raised her head and looked over her shoulder at him. There were tears in her eyes. 'Please, my lord, it is too big,' she begged.

'It didn't seem to trouble your sisters,' he answered cruelly. He pushed forward as hard as he could and she cried out.

'Please, my lord,' she sobbed, 'not there!'

Puzzled, Suetonius looked down and parted her buttocks with his thumbs. It was then that he realised what had happened. The head and at least three or four inches of his thick cock had plundered the poor girl's bottom without any warning or preparation. He pulled from her immediately. 'I'm sorry,' he blurted, feeling genuine concern. Penelope raised herself and turned to face him, cupping her bottom with the palm of her hand.

'Do not worry, my lord,' she said, in a sweet, angelic voice, 'you are such a size – you must use oil if you wish to take me there.'

'I didn't know . . . I really am sorry.' Suetonius felt his phallus beginning to wilt. Penelope smiled and took hold of it. She rubbed it gently and leant forward to kiss him on the lips. Despite her gentle touch, his cock continued to lose its hardness.

'Oh, my lord,' she purred, 'do not be concerned. I need you to fuck me. I need to feel this monstrous weapon deep inside my aching cunt.'

Her obscenities spurred his desires once more and his rod became thicker and stiffer in her gentle grip. She smiled and lay back on the floor. Raising her legs, she gripped her ankles and offered herself to him. The lips of her pussy were wide open and he could see a trickle of her juices slipping down the cleft between her buttocks. He shuffled forward and knelt between her legs. Carefully, he pressed the head of his cock against the suppliant lips of her pussy and eased it inside her. 'Aah, that's so good,' she mewed, closing her eyes. He pushed further into her until over half of his length was held within her hot flesh. Penelope opened her eyes and gazed at him. 'I want you to fuck my cunt as hard as you can and then, when you are done, I want you to come all over me. I want your hot spunk spraying over my body, soaking the skin and then filling my mouth.'

Hearing such coarseness slipping from the lips of such a beautiful and innocent-looking girl, especially when in the company of her two sisters and his friend, thrilled Suetonius immensely. He gazed into the deep pools of Penelope's soft brown eyes and forced the full length of his cock into her. She gasped and groaned as he crushed his pubic bone against hers.

'Oh, my lord!' she panted, 'such a monstrous weapon. I fear that you will split me in two!'

He ignored her cries, having heard similar outbursts on many previous occasions from other lovers. He began to move at a steady disciplined pace, fucking the young girl with all the finesse of a practised and considerate paramour. Penelope tugged her heels back further until her toes were touching the floor. Suetonius drilled his stiff rod into her, his groin slapping noisily against her bottom. She stared into his eyes with a wild untamed expression, her mouth wide open as she gasped for air. He grinned and rammed himself harder against her, determined to make amends for his earlier blunder.

He heard Catus suddenly moan loudly and then begin to grunt spasmodically and knew that his friend had finally given in to the inevitable. Suetonius looked up and watched as Catus thrust heavily upward while gripping tightly to Lavinia's thighs. For her part, Lavinia was responding beautifully by slapping her bottom down rapidly on him in perfect time with his movements as he came inside her.

'By Nero's arse, that was a good one!' he exclaimed as the girl clambered from him. He knelt beside Penelope and Suetonius, panting heavily, his body coated with sweat. Penelope lowered her legs and curled them around Suetonius' thighs, then reached out and took hold of his wilting phallus and drew it to her. Catus shuffled forward willingly until his soft cock slipped into her mouth and she sucked the last drops of his cream from him.

After a couple of minutes, he could take no more and reluctantly pushed her face away from him. 'We thought that Risa was insatiable,' he said, breathlessly. 'What we have here is three of the same kind!'

Calea crawled over and knelt next to him. She gripped his flaccid sex-flesh and gazed up into his eyes hopefully. Catus pulled her hand from him roughly. 'Enough, girl!' he snapped at her. 'Give me some moments to recover!'

Calea sat back with a disappointed look on her face. She watched as Suetonius pumped back and forth into Penelope and, suddenly, her expression brightened. She moved quickly behind Suetonius and, in an instant, he felt her licking his balls and his anus while he steadily fucked her sister. Lavinia, meanwhile, had positioned herself kneeling with her bottom presented to his face. He licked the copious juices that slipped from her pulsating sex-lips, relishing the taste and their creamy texture.

He could feel Calea prodding her tongue into his anus and he slowed the movements of his hips almost to a stop. Penelope's response was to grip him with her arms and legs and thrust her body rapidly up against him. Suetonius ran the tip of his tongue up between Lavinia's buttocks and pushed it into her tight little hole. The mixture of numerous and incredible sensations tore at his nerve-endings, his cock stretched to the limit within the soft, throbbing grip of Penelope's cunt. 'I'm coming!' he gasped, 'I'm coming!'

His cries acted as a spur to the three girls. Penelope dug her heels into his bottom and rammed her lithe body hard against his, while clawing at his back with her fingernails. Calea drove her long tongue deep into his anus and then moved it rapidly in and out, at the same time squeezing his balls tightly with her hand. Lavinia arched her back and reached behind herself with both hands to tug her buttocks apart, affording him the most perfect view of her intimate treasures as he lapped voraciously at her wonderful bottom.

His release tore at his loins, the first jet of his semen filling Penelope's hot, welcoming sheath as his thick cock throbbed inside her. He gasped and panted, thrusting himself wildly against her, her sisters forgotten for the moment; then, just as Penelope had

233

begged, he pulled from her and rubbed his hard shaft frantically. His cream streaked over her breasts and her face, the whiteness of the fluid highlighted by the dark tan of her complexion. He inched himself forward and Penelope pushed out her tongue. He rested the throbbing head of his cock on the flat of her tongue as the surge of final delight ripped through his lower body until, at last, it was over. Penelope swallowed hard and then took the plum-sized knob into her mouth and sucked him until he had no more to give.

Suetonius fell back, his head resting against the sofa. Catus sat opposite him, gently caressing himself, his cock already beginning to show signs of rising once more. Between them sat the girls, three identical lovelies with bright shining faces and curvaceous bodies coated in a fresh sheen of sweat. He knew that he would have to have them all again; once was certainly not enough with girls as salacious and as demanding as the triplets were. He assured himself that Titus Maximus would be unlikely to return before nightfall, and that would give them plenty of time.

It was Calea who first noticed that Catus' stalk was thickening again. With a little squeal of delight, she suddenly dived her head down on to his lap and sucked the half-hard flesh into her mouth. Penelope slipped from the sofa to kneel between his legs and promptly began to lick his balls, while Lavinia looked hungrily at Suetonius' phallus, which was lying limp but heavily across his thigh. She gazed up into his face, her soft brown eyes seeming to be imploring him to become stiff again.

She circled his soft cock with her long fingers and raised it slightly as if to encourage it to become firm within her grip. A trickle of his juice joined the head to a damp spot of matted hair on his thigh. Lavinia ran the tip of her thumb over the flesh until the head was completely covered with the glinting cream; then she bent down and he felt her engulf it within the warm, wet purse of her mouth. She rubbed his thickening stalk slowly, her tongue fluttering and lapping at his sex-flesh until the tenderness faded and his erection filled out completely.

Lavinia raised her head and stared at the monstrous rod as she gripped the root tightly, making it swell to even greater proportions. She looked up into his eyes and grinned broadly. 'More, please,' she said, coyly leaning her head to one side.

Suetonius was happy to oblige.

Suetonius opened his eyes slowly to be met with the sight of a damp, hairy little pussy just inches from his face. His mouth felt dry and his head throbbed with pain. There was something resting heavily on his groin. Raising his head, he saw that it was one of the triplets, who was lying face down, with her head in his lap. He tried to move her but quickly realised that she still held his flaccid cock within her mouth as she slept. He carefully eased her head back. His cock slipped from her lips and she rolled over on to her back. Noticing the small ring piercing her right nipple, he realised that it had been Calea who had been the last to pleasure herself with his weary body. He struggled to a sitting position. Catus was lying on his back close by, also fast asleep and with another of the girls spread-eagled across his prone body. Whether it was due to the insatiable demands of the triplets or the men's exhaustion following days of libidinous pursuits was difficult to ascertain, but it was plain that he and his friend had quite simply passed into blissful unconsciousness while vainly attempting to sate the rapacious sexual appetites of the three women.

He looked across at the window and snapped into sudden realisation of their situation. It was pitch black outside. He had no idea how long the sun had been down, but he knew that he and the others had to dress before Titus Maximus and his wife returned. The old centurion would not take too kindly to finding his revered generals naked with his three innocent daughters.

He managed to retrieve his toga from the pile of discarded clothing on the floor, slipped it quickly over his body and then knelt beside Catus. He carefully pushed against the naked girl who was lying on top of his friend and she rolled on to her back. He shook Catus by the shoulder roughly. 'Catus!' he hissed, 'Catus! Wake up, you fool!'

Catus opened his eyes and looked at him blearily. 'What – what is it?' he mumbled.

'It is night!' croaked Suetonius. He coughed loudly to clear his throat and one of the girls stirred. 'The devil knows how long we have been asleep! We've got to wake these little vixens and make them presentable before their parents return!'

Realising the enormity of his words, Catus struggled to his feet and kicked the girl who had been lying at his side lightly on the rump. She merely waved her hand dismissively and rolled over on to her front. Catus found his toga and dressed himself while Suetonius attempted to awaken the other two girls. It was useless; they were clearly dead to the world.

Suddenly, they heard the sound of a horse's hooves clattering on the cobbled yard outside. 'They're back!' exclaimed Catus, a look of panic on his face. Suetonius glanced around the room, looking for a way out. The only exit, apart from the front door was the stairway to the upper floor.

'This way!' he barked. Catus followed him without question and the two men hurtled up the rickety, wooden stairs. Two doors faced them on the small landing. Suetonius forced one of them open and they moved quickly into the room, closing the door quietly behind them. He took a deep breath to steady his nerves and glanced around the small bedroom. Apart from three cots laid out in a neat row, there was little in the way of furnishings. Various items of feminine clothing were strewn about the floor, giving him clear indication that this was the triplets' bedroom. There was a single window set in the far wall, but the aperture was far too small for a man to clamber through. He heard the downstairs door slam shut and he realised that they were trapped.

He sat down on one of the cots, his heart thumping and his mind racing. Catus walked over to the window and peered out into the gloom. They heard the sound of raised voices coming from beneath them, the words cutting through the wooden floor like the blades of a thousand swords. 'So! You have been up to your tricks again!' they heard Titus bellow. 'And with my esteemed guests! No doubt they have scurried into the night like rats from a trap. Be off to bed with you! I will deal with you in the morning.'

Catus looked across at Suetonius, a terrified look in his eyes and then, with one uniform movement, the men dived under two of the cots. Moments later, they heard the bedroom door open, followed by the shuffling sounds of numerous bare feet on the wooden floor.

'How many more times must you shame us in this way?' It was the farmer's wife who spoke, her voice shaking with emotion. 'Three times this week, already!' she continued. 'At least the Romans had the courtesy to make themselves scarce after they had used you. To think of the danger your father was in, delivering their message to their legion! Generals or not, he will flay them if he ever catches them. As for you, your hides will be tanned raw by the time he has finished with you.'

The door was slammed shut. Suetonius lay still, barely breathing. He heard Penelope's voice. 'We must get away from here,' she said, tearfully. 'Father warned us after the last time that he would stand it no more.'

'But where will we go?' said another of the triplets.

'I don't know,' sobbed Penelope.

Suetonius was suddenly aware that he was being stared at. He looked fearfully to his side to see the smiling face of one of the girls, the ring glinting in her left nipple telling him that it was Lavinia.

'I think that we may have some help,' she whispered to her sisters, as she beckoned to him to come out of his hiding place. He and Catus pulled themselves from under the cots and stood before the three girls.

'We tried to wake you,' began Suetonius in a whisper. Lavinia put her finger to his lips to silence him.

'Ssh, she hissed, 'our parents are drinking strong wine and will be exhausted from their long journey. Soon, they will be asleep and will not be awakened even if a herd of wild animals roars through the house. For the moment, though, we must be silent.' With that, she raised his toga and pulled it over his head then knelt before him and took his flaccid rod into her mouth. Calea joined her at his feet, and the two girls licked and sucked his stiffening rod while Penelope did the same to Catus. Looking down at the girls, Suetonius knew that they had to take them with them on the long journey to rejoin the legion as it marched to the north. He told himself that he and

Catus would be rescuing the girls from their violent drunkard of a father but, in his heart, he knew that neither he nor his friend could leave such delightful and willing girls behind. He and Catus had much to teach them and he was more than certain that they had much to learn from the girls themselves.

Suetonius woke up with a start. He found himself lying alone on one of the cots. Raising himself to rest on his arms, he looked around the room. Catus was curled up on another of the beds, also alone. The triplets were all lying in deep slumber on the third cot, their arms and legs akimbo and their hair matted with dried sweat. He rose from the cot and walked stiffly over to the door. As he had half-expected, he found it bolted from the other side. He moved over to the window. Drawing back the thin curtain, he blinked with the glare of daylight.

As the cold light of morning filtered into the room, the reality of his situation hit him like a bolt of lightning. The previous hours might have been filled with a thousand delights but he was still a prisoner. He glanced at the bed. The three girls lay naked on the silken sheets in blissful slumber, their angelic expressions belying their true salacious natures. He walked slowly towards them. He knew that he and Catus had to try and make their escape, but not yet . . .

The sound of the bolt being withdrawn from its clasp on the bedroom door interrupted yet another bout of silent but nevertheless enthusiastic lovemaking. Suetonius and Catus flung themselves under two of the cots, while the girls leapt into their own beds and pulled the sheets over their naked bodies.

Their mother's voice rang through the small room.

'Your father has gone to check the traps, to see if we have meat for the table today, but don't be complacent. When he returns, you will be severely punished for the shame that you have brought upon this house. I must go to the well and draw some water. I want the three of you to go to the river and wash yourselves, and be quick about it!'

Suetonius heard her footsteps as she walked back down the stairs. He waited for a moment, then pulled himself from under the bed. 'Now's our chance,' he whispered. 'Do you want to come with us?'

The triplets looked at each other, their eyes wide with excitement, and they nodded in unison. The two men slipped on their togas while the girls dressed and then they gingerly crept down the stairs. There was no sign of the farmer's wife; she had been good to her word and had gone to the well. One of the girls opened the front door and peered outside. She turned back to face the others. 'It's safe,' she breathed. 'Come on!'

Outside, they hurried across the yard, past the barn and out into the fields and freedom. The girls led the way to another field where three horses stood lazily munching tufts of short grass. 'They are old and slow, but they should help us on our way,' said the one that Suetonius thought was Penelope, although he couldn't be certain, as he couldn't see her nipples. It occurred to him that this might present problems for them in the future and he vowed to try to think of another, less intimate, way of telling them apart.

Ten

It was late in the evening by the time that the weary travellers neared the place they called High Cross. The weather had been kind to them during their journey and the horses, although old, had stood up to their arduous task magnificently. Catus had ridden alone and had gone on to join the legions while Suetonius, with Penelope at his back and Lavinia and Calea riding alongside, had made slower progress along the ancient track.

Suetonius drew his mount to a halt as they came close to the edge of the forest. The Roman encampment was less than half a day's ride away but they needed to rest. Soon, the air would be filled with the aroma of a hundred wood-fires and the sounds of fervent activity would echo in their ears but, for now, Suetonius needed to stretch his aching body on the ground.

Penelope hugged him tightly from behind, her exhausted body slumped against him. Calea slipped from her horse and disappeared into the bushes to take a pee while Lavinia leant back and stretched her arms above her head, her large breasts straining against the thin material of her white smock. Suetonius watched her appreciatively.

'Do you think that it will be long before the Iceni army arrives?' said Calea as she returned from the shelter of the thick foliage, brushing some leaves from her dress. 'Perhaps they won't come after all.'

'They will come,' uttered Suetonius gravely, as he carefully dismounted and helped Penelope down from the sweating beast. 'From the little that I have learnt about Boudicca, I know her to be a proud queen. She will wish to take vengeance against the two Roman generals who insulted her.'

Penelope sat with Calea on the remains of a fallen tree half-buried in the undergrowth. 'Do you think the Iceni will defeat the Roman army?' she asked.

'There are three, or possibly four legions at High Cross. It is the Iceni who will be vanquished.' He uttered the words with conviction in his tone, but in his heart he knew that he was not so certain.

Lavinia slipped from her mount and joined her sisters. The three of them sat huddled together as they watched him tethering the horses to the branch of a tree. He turned to face them. They looked so delicate and so vulnerable in the half-light, their dark eyes shining with incongruous innocence. It barely seemed possible to him that, just a few short hours before, the three of them had lain naked with him and Catus, giving their bodies to them in such wanton abandonment.

He sat down on the hard ground and rested his back against an old tree. His thighs ached from gripping on to the back of the horse for so many miles and he was hungry. He decided that they would rest for an hour or so and then they would move on. He looked again at the three girls. They were talking lazily to each other while massaging their stiff limbs, seemingly without a care in the world.

One of them caught his gaze and smiled sweetly at him. 'What are you thinking, my lord?' she said.

'I was merely considering how lucky I am to have found three such beautiful and willing young girls,' he replied. His lame response surprised him. He was not given to such banal compliments, especially where women were concerned.

'Oh, no, my lord,' continued the girl, 'it is we who are the lucky ones! We have found two strong and brave men who will guard and protect us.'

Suetonius smiled. The girls looked at him, their big expressive eyes filled with emotion. For the first time in his life, he felt more than merely lust as he regarded their lovely forms. She was right. He *would* guard and protect them, forever.

The girl who had spoken got to her feet and moved over to stand in front of him. Seated as he was, his face was inches from her stomach and he could easily discern the soft curve of her groin and the tantalising bulge of her pubic mound under the thin material of her dress. She reached down and took hold of his hand and put it to her naked thigh, just below the hem of the short garment. He smoothed his fingertips over her soft, cool skin and then moved his hand up until he touched the moist flesh between her legs. The girl grasped the hem of her smock, quickly pulled it over her head and cast it to the ground. The glint of the ring piercing her left nipple told him that it was Lavinia who was offering herself to him. He eased his fingers deep into her hot pussy. She groaned as his thumb pressed against the hard bud of her clitoris.

He glanced across at the other two girls. They, too, had removed their smocks and were naked, their flawless tanned bodies openly displayed to him. He realised that, despite his tiredness and his aching limbs, he was going to have to fuck them all. He bent his head forward and flicked his tongue over the top of Lavinia's cunt while moving his fingers in and out of her. She responded by stroking the back of his head lovingly and swaying her hips gently.

Penelope and Calea moved over to kneel on either side of him. Within seconds, their hands had slipped under his toga and their fingers were circling his rising erection. He took his fingers from inside Lavinia and pressed his mouth hard against the softness of her lush sex-lips. He found her taste divine, imagining her rubbing herself against the back of her sweating mount as they had ridden through the forest. He put one arm around Calea's bare shoulders and cupped her breast, then pinched her nipple and tugged the tiny ring. Penelope took hold of his other arm and put his hand to her pussy, while the two girls continued to rub his hard shaft slowly. He fingered Penelope's wet softness and she moaned quietly.

His face was becoming soaked with Lavinia's juices. She moved away from him and knelt down. He gazed into her shining eyes and they kissed. He delved his tongue deeply into her mouth and she hugged his neck tightly, then she drew back and licked the wetness from his face. Calea and Penelope were moving their hands up and down his stiff cock with more urgency, and he knew that he would soon be taken past the point of no return. He pushed from the girls and struggled to his feet then wrenched his toga over his head. Now naked, he looked down at the three young girls, who were all gazing in wonderment at his long, thick rod that was jutting from his groin.

Lavinia took the head of his cock into her warm mouth. Penelope and Calea immediately began to lick each side of his stalk, lapping greedily at the bone-hard flesh. The sight of three beautiful women, their faces identical in every way serving him in such a way was almost too much for him to bear.

'Turn yourselves!' he barked suddenly.

The girls pulled back from him, allowing his cock to thrust freely in front of them. They looked at each other in bemusement, clearly unsure as to what he wanted of them.

'I said, turn yourselves,' he repeated, relishing the power that he had over these three delightful maidens. 'Kneel, with your bottoms held proudly before me.'

The triplets turned and knelt on the ground, resting their shoulders on their forearms with their pert little backsides presented to him in the most appealing manner. Suetonius knelt behind them and gazed at the three perfectly formed rears. 'Would you beat us, my lord?' asked Penelope, as she knelt between her two sisters.

'Do you wish me to?' he replied. It seemed distinctly odd to him that he should ask such a question. Normally, he would have slapped their little bums without giving it a moment's thought.

'Yes,' was Penelope's simple reply.

'All of you?' he asked firmly. The other girls nodded and he saw all three of them force their bottoms higher in willing submission. He reached forward and stroked the soft globes in turn, then whacked the palm of his hand against Penelope's backside, making her flesh quiver. She gasped loudly and forced herself back even further in readiness for another slap. He could see the imprint of his fingers on her olive-toned skin. He slapped her again and then again, first on one buttock and then on the other. With each blow, Penelope whimpered softly, but she made no attempt to move away from him.

He turned his attention to Lavinia, giving her three short, sharp slaps, and then he administered similar treatment to Calea. The last girl appeared to enjoy the punishment even more than her sisters did, and he could see that she was fingering her pussy as he spanked her hot little bottom.

Resting, he knelt down and gazed once more at their lightly bruised buttocks. He kissed each one in turn and then lapped his tongue over them, tracing the shape of each sensuous curve. The girls mewed contentedly as he licked their bottoms and each of them groaned with pleasure when the tip of his tongue found their tight sphincters. Their taste was uniformly exquisite. His cock ached painfully and he knew that he had to fuck them.

Raising himself to a kneeling position behind Penelope, he parted her buttocks with his thumbs and pushed the head of his stalk into her hot cunt. Her inner flesh seemed to be sucking him into her as he pushed in deeper and deeper, until his groin became crushed against her bottom. He could feel the heat of her skin against his stomach.

'Oh, my lord,' she cried, 'I don't think that I will ever get used to the size! It is truly a monster!'

'Fuck me! Fuck me!' pleaded Lavinia.

'No, me!' begged Calea, wriggling her body suggestively.

Using both of his hands, Suetonius slapped their bottoms hard. 'Silence!' he snapped, 'you'll get your turn. He slapped them again and they squealed and laughed. He began to thrust his stiff rod in and out of Penelope's tight sheath, her entire body shaking from the force of the intrusion. He spanked the other two girls over and over again simultaneously as he pumped rapidly in and out of Penelope's juicy hole. His cock felt stiffer than it had ever felt before. He couldn't imagine a more perfect situation than this.

He pulled himself from Penelope's tight, wet grip and shuffled to kneel behind Lavinia. She moaned happily as her entered her to the hilt. Penelope moved behind him and he once again enjoyed the sensation of having her tongue lap hungrily between his buttocks as he steadily fucked her sister. Calea inched her body closer to him and he stroked and caressed her bottom before deftly slipping his fingers into her pussy. He almost laughed out loud, so great was his joy. Nothing could be better than this, he thought.

Lavinia started to undulate her inner muscles against his cock, gripping and relaxing her soaking flesh against his stalk rhythmically. He sensed a powerful urge to hammer in and out of her and to fill her with his cream, but he knew that he couldn't disappoint Calea. Reluctantly, he pulled from the lush sheath and pushed Lavinia to one side, then grasped Calea by the waist and tugged her towards him. He was no longer in any mood for gentleness. He rammed the full length of his weapon into her, causing her to cry out with a mixture of pain and delight.

Penelope, meanwhile, had turned over on to her back and managed to wriggle between his thrusting thighs until he felt her tongue lapping against his balls. He slowed his movements in order to savour this new sensation. Not to be outdone, Lavinia also moved behind him and began to lick his bottom. There was no need for him to move. The triple stimulation was more than enough to take him over the edge. With a mighty roar that caused the birds to flee from the sanctuary of the branches above them he came, his semen flooding the sumptuous sheath of Calea's pussy. He felt Penelope bite gently into his sac while, at exactly the same time, Lavinia pushed her long tongue deep into his anus. Time seemed to stand still and his head swam, his cock throbbing heavily as more and more of his juices jetted from him, the climax seemingly endless.

Eventually, it was over. He pulled from Calea's delightful grip and lay back against the tree, exhausted. The triplets casually dressed themselves again and sat opposite him, their faces shining and their eyes sparkling. Suetonius closed his eyes and, within seconds, drifted off into a deep contented sleep.

Boudicca stood alone outside her hastily erected tent and surveyed the scene before her. Her people were gathered in groups, laughing, singing and cavorting on the hillside as if they hadn't a care in the world. Ahead of them, less than a day's march away she knew that the Roman legions were encamped at High Cross, their battalions ordered and disciplined, waiting for her to make the next move.

For the first time in her life, she felt nervous and uncertain. It was true that the Iceni hordes far outnumbered the Roman soldiers, but she knew that they were a rabble of farmers and peasants who were more used to tilling and ploughing the wide fields of the Fens than fighting for their lives. She cursed her stupidity in allowing the two generals to escape her clutches without realising their true identities. She had put their strange accents down to the fact that they were from the West, never imagining for a moment that they were her most hated enemies.

And how they had abused her! They had used and cast aside her lovely serving-girls, not once but twice! One of the men had even had the effrontery to attempt to penetrate her – the queen. She seethed with anger at the memory, picturing Suetonius kneeling between her legs, his long and thick cock jutting from his groin ready to impale her. For a brief moment, she felt an annoying warmth between her legs as she thought of him, and she turned angrily and swept back into her tent.

The sight that met her eyes pleased her greatly. The

prisoner had been brought to her by her guards, one of a group of six Romans who had been careless enough to stray too close to their encampment. Five of them had been left to the tender mercies of the Iceni women but this one, their leader, she had chosen to deal with herself.

Boudicca knew that she held the Roman officer totally within her power. The once proud soldier hung from his shackles, his naked body oiled and ready for the kiss of the lash. The queen smiled cruelly. 'Know this, Roman,' she snarled. 'You will be punished most severely for your impertinence! Soon, you will know the true meaning of pain.' The man stared at her through terrified eyes. His entire body was trembling and his cock was hanging limply between his muscular legs.

The queen grasped it in her hand and looked at it contemptuously. 'Why is it so small and so soft, Roman?' she said, teasingly. 'Do you not find me attractive?' She took her hand away from him and began to unclasp the fastenings of her leather jerkin. The man's eyes widened as her breasts were slowly revealed. She slipped the garment from her body completely and cast it to one side; then she stood before him, proudly displaying her massive globes of flesh to his hungry gaze.

All that she now wore was a pair of thigh-length leather boots and a heavy linked chain drawn tightly about her waist, from which a strip of studded hide stretched between her legs to conceal her moist sex-lips. She smiled inwardly as she noticed the soldier's cock beginning to thicken and rise. She moved close to him until her nipples brushed against his chest and stared meaningfully into his eyes. His stalk hardened completely and she could feel the tip touching her belly. She reached down and circled it with her fingers. 'Ah, that's better, Roman,' she breathed, rubbing him slowly. 'You must show true reverence for the Queen of the Iceni.'

Boudicca released her grip on him and stepped back. The man eyed her suspiciously but his cock stretched firmly upwards, the head thick and purple with his lust. She decided to tease him some more. Pulling aside the leather strip between her legs, she bared her shaven pussy to him and casually caressed her pouting sex-lips with her fingertips. 'Would you like to sink that hard shaft of yours inside this hot little haven?' she purred.

The soldier nodded.

Boudicca moved forward, grasped his cock again and put the tip to her wetness. She rubbed the head up and down between the lips, soaking it with her juices. The tethered soldier attempted to lunge his hips forward in an effort to enter her completely, but she was having none of it. She grinned cruelly and stepped back again, leaving his cock bobbing freely in front of him. She stooped and picked up a whip from the ground behind him and then stood facing him, playing the long leather strands across her fingers. His erection began to wilt.

She spoke slowly as she moved to stand behind him. 'Tomorrow, my people will meet the Romans in battle and many of your brothers will be slaughtered,' she said. 'You are lucky. You will merely suffer pain and humiliation.'

The soldier sneered and spat on the ground. 'Do as you wish, woman,' he growled. His sudden show of courage angered her. She raised the whip and lashed him swiftly across the buttocks. He jumped as the thongs cut across his flesh but didn't utter a sound. She whipped him again, the crack of leather against skin sounding like music to her ears. The Roman officer remained silent, his teeth clenched and his eyes wide open and filled with hatred. She lashed him four more times, each stroke more severe than the one before it. With the final cut, he gasped out loud. Satisfied, Boudicca dropped the whip and moved once more to stand before him. His cock was stiff, his fluids weeping from the tip and slipping down the gnarled length. Her heart softened as she gazed at him and she realised that she no longer had the stomach for the game.

Kneeling before him, she grasped his hard weapon and guided the head into her mouth. She sucked him gently at first, his cock resting on her tongue as she lapped it back and forth, and then she moved forward and engulfed his entire length, taking much of it down her throat. She swallowed heavily over and over again until she sensed his rod throbbing against her tongue and heard him sigh as his release took hold of him.

Only when his cock began to soften did she allow it to slip from the warm, wet purse of her sucking mouth. She stood up and wiped her lips on the back of her hand. The Roman stared bemusedly at her. She felt confused and somewhat awkward, unsure of what to say. Her pleasure had not been in administering the punishment but in accepting the cream of his climax. Retrieving her jerkin from the ground, she quickly donned it and hurried out of the tent.

Boudicca stepped through the mêlée of writhing bodies, her people taking their last chances of pleasure before the battle ahead. She saw Risa, the young girl whom the Romans had brought with them as their prisoner. The queen had taken Risa to her heart and took great delight in seeing the girl enjoy the pleasures of the flesh, something for which she seemed to have an unquenchable thirst. This time, she was squatting over a prone young man with her back to him and with his cock firmly embedded in her bottom, while another of the guards was pumping heavily in and out of her pussy and a third was feeding her mouth with his stiff rod. Boudicca watched them for a moment, the taste of the Roman officer's semen still on her lips, but she decided against joining in. Instead, she found a quiet spot and sat alone in the shade of an old oak tree. The scene before her became ever more orgiastic but her thoughts were far removed from the bacchanalia.

Arman appeared before her as silently as in a dream. His hood was drawn back, his head bared to the sunlight and his blue eyes were filled with warmth. He knelt at her feet and smiled. Boudicca put out her hand and touched his cheek gently with the tips of her fingers. He caught hold of her hand and kissed her fingers lightly. 'Oh, Arman,' she said, 'after all this is done, let us return to the Fens and live together in peace. I've grown tired of war. It all seems so pointless.'

'Do not let your people hear you speak in this way,' he counselled. 'They are fired up for battle. It would not do for them to see their beloved queen losing heart.'

'But I *have* lost my heart, Arman. I have lost it to you.'

Their eyes met and they held the stare for what seemed to her like an age. The sounds around them faded into unreality. They were alone: two lovers in an enchanted land. She bent her head forward and kissed his lips. 'Make love to me, Arman,' she said, her words barely above a whisper. She lay back and unclasped the strip of leather from the chain circling her waist, offering her pussy to his excited gaze. He reached over her and unfastened her jerkin, quickly baring her breasts. He bent his head and suckled each of her hard nipples in turn while his fingers played around the fleshy lips of her cunt. He began to rub harder and she knew that she was coming. She moaned loudly and he bit into her nipple. She bucked her hips against his probing fingers and came with a gasp. It was a gentle but satisfying orgasm and she knew that it would be the first of many.

Arman knelt back and slipped his robe from his shoulders, revealing his naked muscular body to her. His cock stood long and thick, ready to take her. For a moment, she had an overwhelming desire to push him on to his back and straddle herself over him so that she could impale herself on his stiff rod, but she resisted the urge. Instead, she lay back and waited passively for him to do with her as he wished. He was the master now, and she was his slave.

As if sensing her need, Arman moved his body between her legs and she felt the head of his cock touch her sensitive sex-lips. He entered her with one slow movement. She closed her eyes to savour every touch of his thick rod within her hot sheath. She felt completely fulfilled, at one with her lover. He began to move in and out of her, using the full length of his cock with each marvellous stroke. Boudicca raised her legs and pulled her knees back to her shoulders, enabling him to fill her completely. The head prodded against the wall of her cervix, each gentle push sending tremors of pleasure coursing throughout her body.

Arman thrust gently into her over and over again, barely altering his rhythm, as if knowing that this was precisely what she wanted. It seemed so right, to be lying under the firm body of the man she loved, feeling him make love to her gently, without urgency but with true passion. She stroked his hair and then ran her hands down over his strong back until she cupped his buttocks tightly. Arman began to move faster and their groins slapped together noisily. She was coming again. She stiffened the muscles of her thighs as the surge built up inside her and then screamed aloud as the sensations of her climax tore through her. He responded by pounding in and out of her until his expression turned into a grimace and she felt the thumping of his cock deep inside her tender sex-flesh: and she knew that he had joined her in blissful release.

The Queen of the Iceni lay in the arms of her lover, gazing up at the cloudless sky. Her body tingled and the warmth of the gentle breeze caressed her skin. She turned her head and gazed at Arman and knew what she had to do. She would turn her people and lead them back to their homeland, there to return to their farms and live in peace.

Suetonius stood atop the pinnacle and watched grimly as the weary mass of Iceni peasants trooped across the distant hillside. In a way he felt that he had been cheated. There had been a few minor skirmishes with one or two bands of young hotheads who had disobeyed their queen, but otherwise the retreat had been peaceful. Somehow, it had been for the best. The Roman legions had grown considerably in numbers and they were well rested. The Iceni would have been annihilated.

He turned his back on the sombre spectacle and headed back down towards the main encampment. Sounds of revelry filled the air, drunken laughter and girlish squeals of delight echoing in his ears. Normally, such bacchanalia wouldn't have been permitted, but the generals had agreed that their men

254

needed to ease their frustrations. There were many local peasant girls who were only too willing to allow them to do so.

Suetonius stepped inside his tent and unfastened his belt, glad to be rid of the weight of his sword. Catus was lying on one of the cots with Penelope kneeling at his side on the ground sucking his stiff cock. Lavinia and Calea sat close by them, casually sipping wine from silver goblets and watching their sibling with only mild interest. Their naked bodies were coated with an enticing sheen of fresh sweat and their pussy-lips were red and engorged. It was evident that Catus had just fucked all three of them, and yet Suetonius didn't feel any pangs of jealousy or envy, despite his strong affection for the lovely triplets.

They looked up and smiled as he entered. He sat down on another cot and pulled off his boots while the two sisters came over and sat beside him. He allowed them to help him to remove the remainder of his clothing, his cock stiffening as they playfully caressed his body. Soon, he was naked and the two women were stroking his thick erection and the heavy sac below. Four slender hands fondled him delicately, their fingers circling his rod, cupping his balls or probing his anus. He heard Catus groan and watched as Penelope bobbed her head up and down rapidly as she swallowed his friend's seed. The sight delighted him and he realised that, at last, he had found what he was looking for. He and Catus would share the charms of the three sisters for ever. He loved them all, but was fully aware that one man alone could never hope to satisfy their lascivious needs.

Lavinia bent over and took the head of his cock into her warm mouth. Calea knelt at his side and began to lick up and down his long stem while Penelope moved from Catus and squatted in front of him. She looked up at him and grinned, a small trickle of his friend's cream slipping from the corner of her pouting lips. She inched forward and started to lap her tongue around his balls, then sucked one and then the other into her mouth. He watched the girls lovingly; the sight of three identically beautiful young women paying oral homage to his raging erection was one that filled his heart with joy. He glanced across at Catus and grinned. This was how it was going to be, from now on.

He eased himself back to lie on the cot. At first, the girls seemed reluctant to take their mouths and tongues from his genitals but, after a few moments, they stood up and moved around him. Suetonius simply lay there, happy to let them do to him whatever they wished. Penelope clambered over him and squatted over his groin while Lavinia and Calea held his erection vertically, aiming the huge bulbous head at her succulent cunt. She lowered her body slowly and absorbed his length deep inside her silky wet sheath. Lavinia now moved to crouch over his face and he lapped greedily at her pouting sex-lips, while Calea knelt between his legs and he felt her lick his balls. His cock stretched enormously within the lush grip of Penelope's hot pussy and he felt her stiffen her inner muscles as if attempting to suck him in ever deeper.

Thoughts of the Iceni and their ravishing queen, Boudicca, were dismissed from his mind as Penelope began to ride him, thumping her small lithe body up and down on him with wild abandon. He sucked Lavinia's sex-lips into his mouth, rasped his teeth against them and prodded his tongue forward, her juices flowing from her to soak his face. Calea, unmoved by Penelope's pounding body, continued to lick and suck his balls.

It was all too much for him. There was no way that he could hold back under such astoundingly delightful circumstances. With a mighty surge, his semen jetted from him into Penelope's receptive succulence, the young girl hammering herself up and down on him with incredible speed. He heard her squeal of joy as her climax took hold of her, the cries almost immediately followed by a yelp of pleasure as Lavinia joined her in her happy release. He felt a sharp pain as Calea bit into the tender flesh of his scrotum, but the sensation only served to heighten his pleasure as his throbbing cock pumped the last of his cream into Penelope.

Eventually, the girls clambered from him and sat on the ground beside the cot, each one of them gazing up at him through adoring eyes. He laid back his head and stared up at the roof of the tent. A strong breeze had sprung up and the canvas billowed like the waves of the sea. He thought of home and dreamt of the many joys to come when he and Catus returned to Rome with their three beautiful wives. For a moment he remembered Risa, the only other girl to have stolen his heart, and he wondered if she was still safe. He felt a pang of guilt at having left her with the Iceni, but knew in his heart that she would be happier in her own land.

Risa stroked her hot, stinging bottom with her fingertips. The pain had been exquisite, but now she needed something more. She lay submissively on the bed and waited in silence as the guards tore their clothing from their muscular bodies. She felt vulnerable and a little afraid, but the excitement that was building up inside her was becoming almost too much to bear. She had been patient while they had played their games with her. Now it was her turn. She wanted them all, and she wanted them now.

NEW BOOKS

Coming up from Nexus and Black Lace

The Test by Nadine Somers
January 1998   Price £5.99   ISBN: 0352 33320 0
When Rachel starts working for Michael, a high-ranking Government minister, she doesn't realise exactly what kind of job training he has in store for her. She is to be initiated into a mysterious and perverse group of female devotees of discipline; total obedience is expected of new recruits, and bizarre and lewd demands are made of them. Will Rachel pass the test?

Exposing Louisa by Jean Aveline
January 1998   Price £5.99   ISBN: 0352 33321 9
Anton and Magdalena are brother and sister, separated at birth but reunited as teenagers. The forbidden nature of their love for each other only serves to intensify their passion for experimentation – for the darkest of sexual games. Working as dancers, they fall under the spell of the manipulative Sophie and the masterful Dieter, both of whom have secret and perverse plans for the couple. By the author of *Sisters of Severcy*.

There are three Nexus titles published in February

The Submission of Stella by Yolanda Celbridge
February 1999   Price £5.99   ISBN: 0 352 33334 0
Stella Shawn, dominant Headmistress of Kernece College, craves to rediscover the joys of submission. Her friend Morag suggests an instructive leave of absence, and enrols her at High Towers, a finishing school in Devon, whose regime is total submission of women to women. The strict rules and stern discipline at High Towers ensure that even Stella can learn once more how to submit to the lash. By the outher of *The Schooling of Stella*.

Bad Penny by Penny Birch
February 1999   Price £5.99   ISBN: 0 352 33335 9
Penny Birch is a very naughty girl. Not only has she shamelessly revealed her love of the bizarre world of pony-girl carting in *Penny in Harness*, but she has also let us know dark secrets about her best friend in *A Taste of Amber*, and has now, in *Bad Penny*, told us everything we ever wanted to know about her cheeky activities. Fans of Penny's writing will know what to expect from this collection of stories – the uninitiated are in for a treat.

The Image – A Nexus Classic by Jean de Berg
February 1999   Price £5.99   ISBN: 0 352 33350 2
The Image was first published in Paris in 1956, and was suppressed almost immediately. In this piece of classic erotica, the story is simple yet subtle, intriguing and very erotic. The narrator, Jean de Berg, is drawn to the delectable and apparently innocent Anne. But Anne is the sex slave of Claire, an icy beauty whom Jean knew years previously. He becomes involved in the women's games of ritual punishment – but who is seducing whom? This is the first in a series of Nexus Classics – a unique collection devoted to bringing the finest works of erotic fiction to a new audience.

A Feast for the Senses by Martine Marquand
January 1998   Price £5.99   ISBN: 0 352 33310 3
Claira Fairfax leaves her innocent life in Georgian England to
embark on the Grand Tour of Europe. She travels through the deca-
dent cities – from icebound Amsterdam to sultry Constantinople –
undergoing lessons in perverse pleasure from the mysterious and
eccentric Count Anton di Maliban.

The Transformation by Natasha Rostova
January 1998   Price £5.99   ISBN: 0 352 33311 1
Three friends, one location – San Francisco. This book contains three
interlinked and very modern stories which have their links in fairy
tales. There's nothing innocent about Lydia, Molly and Cassie, however, as one summer provides them with revelatory sexual experiences
which transform their lives.

Mixed Doubles by Zoe le Verdier
February 1999   Price £5.99   ISBN: 0 352 33312 X
Natalie takes over the running of an exclusive tennis club in the
wealthy suburbs of Surrey, England. When she poaches tennis coach,
Chris, from a rival sports club, women come flocking to Natalie's
new business. Chris is skilled in more kinds of adult sport than tennis,
though, and the female clients are soon booking up of extra tuition.

Shadowplay by Portia da Costa
February 1999   Price £5.99   ISBN: 0 352 33313 8
Daniel Woodforde-Ranelagh lives a reclusive but privileged existence,
obsessed with mysticism and the paranormal. When the wayward and
sensual Christabel Sutherland walks into his life, they find they have
a lot in common. Despite their numerous responsibilities, they
immerse themselves in a fantasy world where sexual experimentation
takes pride of place.

Nexus

NEXUS BACKLIST

All books are priced £4.99 unless another price is given. If a date is supplied, the book in question will not be available until that month in 1998.

CONTEMPORARY EROTICA

THE ACADEMY	Arabella Knight		
AGONY AUNT	G. C. Scott		
ALLISON'S AWAKENING	Lauren King		
AMAZON SLAVE	Lisette Ashton	£5.99	
THE BLACK GARTER	Lisette Ashton	£5.99	Sept
THE BLACK ROOM	Lisette Ashton		
BOUND TO OBEY	Amanda Ware	£5.99	Dec
BOUND TO SUBMIT	Amanda Ware		
CANDIDA IN PARIS	Virginia Lasalle		
CHAINS OF SHAME	Brigitte Markham	£5.99	July
A CHAMBER OF DELIGHTS	Katrina Young		
DARK DELIGHTS	Maria del Rey	£5.99	Aug
DARLINE DOMINANT	Tania d'Alanis	£5.99	Oct
A DEGREE OF DISCIPLINE	Zoe Templeton		
THE DISCIPLINE OF NURSE RIDING	Yolanda Celbridge	£5.99	Nov
THE DOMINO TATTOO	Cyrian Amberlake		
THE DOMINO QUEEN	Cyrian Amberlake		
EDEN UNVEILED	Maria del Rey		
EDUCATING ELLA	Stephen Ferris		
EMMA'S SECRET DOMINATION	Hilary James		
FAIRGROUND ATTRACTIONS	Lisette Ashton	£5.99	Dec
THE TRAINING OF FALLEN ANGELS	Kendal Grahame		
HEART OF DESIRE	Maria del Rey		

ANCIENT & FANTASY SETTINGS

THE CLOAK OF APHRODITE	Kendal Grahame		
DEMONIA	Kendal Grahame		
THE DUNGEONS OF LIDIR	Aran Ashe		
THE FOREST OF BONDAGE	Aran Ashe		
NYMPHS OF DIONYSUS	Susan Tinoff		
THE WARRIOR QUEEN	Kendal Grahame	£5.99	Dec

EDWARDIAN, VICTORIAN & OLDER EROTICA

ANNIE	Evelyn Culber	£5.99	
ANNIE AND THE COUNTESS	Evelyn Culber	£5.99	
BEATRICE	Anonymous		
THE CORRECTION OF AN ESSEX MAID	Yolanda Celbridge	£5.99	
DEAR FANNY	Michelle Clare		
LYDIA IN THE HAREM	Philippa Masters		
LURE OF THE MANOR	Barbra Baron		
MAN WITH A MAID 3	Anonymous		
MEMOIRS OF A CORNISH GOVERNESS	Yolanda Celbridge		
THE GOVERNESS AT ST AGATHA'S	Yolanda Celbridge		
MISS RATTAN'S LESSON	Yolanda Celbridge	£5.99	Aug
PRIVATE MEMOIRS OF A KENTISH HEADMISTRESS	Yolanda Celbridge		
SISTERS OF SEVERCY	Jean Aveline		

SAMPLERS & COLLECTIONS

EROTICON 3	Various		
EROTICON 4	Various	£5.99	July
THE FIESTA LETTERS	ed. Chris Lloyd		
NEW EROTICA 2	ed. Esme Ombreux		
NEW EROTICA 3	ed. Esme Ombreux		
NEW EROTICA 4	ed. Esme Ombreux	£5.99	Sept

NON-FICTION

Please send me the books I have ticked above.

Name   ....

Address   ....

                    ....

                    ....

                    .... Post code........................

Send to: Cash Sales, Nexus Books, Thames Wharf Studios, Rainville Road, London W6 9HT

Please enclose a cheque or postal order, made payable to **Nexus Books**, to the value of the books you have ordered plus postage and packing costs as follows:

UK and BFPO – £1.00 for the first book, 50p for the second book and 30p for each subsequent book to a maximum of £3.00;

Overseas (including Republic of Ireland) – £2.00 for the first book, £1.00 for the second book and 50p for each subsequent book.

If you would prefer to pay by VISA or ACCESS/MASTER-CARD, please write your card number and expiry date here:

....

Please allow up to 28 days for delivery.

Signature   ....